Praise for Rebecca Goings'
The Wolverine and the Jewel

"Rebecca Goings' talented storytelling spins a remarkable read that depicts a time and place that becomes real with each turn of the page. This story follows The Wolverine and the Rose, and practically leaves the reader breathless from passion that explodes in the pages. I find this precious gem a most recommended read."

~ *Linda L., Fallen Angel Reviews*

"I was very excited when I learned The Wolverine and the Jewel was released. I had truly enjoyed the previous book, The Wolverine and the Rose, and was intrigued as to the direction Rebecca Goings would take this series. I was not disappointed in the least. There was action throughout, further development in the story of Mynos, and we visit with characters from the first book. In her writing, Ms Goings excels at reflecting the passion her characters feel for one another."

~ *Kathy Andrico, GottaWriteNetwork.com*

"The Wolverine and the Jewel is an amazing follow up to The Wolverine and the Rose, with the introduction of a beautiful damsel with an unknown past that is probably best left that way. Yet with its unraveling creates a breathtaking tale of love challenged, lives lost, and a shift in power. Rebecca Goings succeeds in capturing her audience's attention and doesn't let go until its much anticipated conclusion."

~ *UrbanPixie, Literary Nymphs*

"Ms. Goings is a master when it comes to characterization, and this reviewer felt as though she were actually living the lives of the characters. I highly recommend The Wolverine and the Jewel to all who enjoy their fairy tales with a dash of strong spice!"

~ *Regina, Coffeetime Romance*

The Wolverine and
the Jewel

Rebecca Goings

Jennifer,
It was so good to meet
you. Thanks for supporting
local authors!
Believe in your dreams!

Rebecca Goings

A Samhain Publishing, Ltd. publication.

Samhain Publishing, Ltd.
577 Mulberry Street, Suite 1520
Macon, GA 31201
www.samhainpublishing.com

The Wolverine and the Jewel
Copyright © 2008 by Rebecca Goings
Print ISBN: 1-59998-753-8
Digital ISBN: 1-59998-478-4

Editing by Imogen Howson
Cover by Dawn Seewer

First Samhain Publishing, Ltd. electronic publication: May 2007
First Samhain Publishing, Ltd. print publication: March 2008

Dedication

For my children, as proof that dreams really do come true.

Chapter One

Sir Sebastian of Tabrinth smiled at the warm sunshine on his face. He rode his bay stallion on a routine scout about the countryside with his good friend Sir Duncan of Marynville, who trotted not too far behind. Looking across the lush, green fields surrounding Castle Templestone, Sebastian hardly believed they were the same fields Mynos had blackened when Queen Darragh's minions had attacked the castle only three years before. The ancient golden dragon had managed to lay waste to her massive army with his fiery breath alone—a spectacle Sebastian would never soon forget.

Rumor had it land charred by dragon's fire grew vegetation twice as thick as it had been before, but no one alive had ever been a witness to it. Now, Sebastian found himself gazing across lush grasses and young trees swaying in the gentle breeze. Wildflowers bloomed everywhere, lifting their soft perfume into the air, and he groaned inwardly.

It was his rotten luck he'd been stuck on this scouting mission. He'd hoped to slip away and visit the small pond near the castle for a swim. However, before he could make his getaway, Duncan had spotted him. There were duties to attend to. Sighing to himself, he thought he might try to slip away this evening, and perhaps he could bring a pretty little castle maid with him.

Ever since Sir Geoffrey of Emberdale married Lady Arianna of Stollinshire, Sebastian had been the most sought-after Wolverine in the king's court, at least by women. And he had no complaints about that. The king's knights had always been singled out by frisky women, and Sebastian seemed to attract more than most with his blue eyes and dark brown hair, which fell below his ears. It had the annoying habit of falling into his face at the most inopportune moment. He constantly had to snap his head back to keep it in place.

Duncan, on the other hand, was probably the most inexperienced Wolverine at the castle, but not for lack of women's attentions. Duncan was somewhat of a novelty, with his flaming red hair and bright green eyes. If his hair didn't garner attention, his eyes certainly did, as most folk had never seen such an eye color before. Women flocked to him.

Sebastian surmised Duncan could have any lady he wanted if he only smiled more. As it stood now, the man's skin became pasty and he complained of stomach cramps whenever he so much as *approached* a woman.

Feeling sorry for him, Sebastian had taken Duncan under his wing. He'd hoped to make a man out of him one day, yet progress was slow. Sebastian sighed, wondering if Duncan would ever be able to gather his wits when confronted by the fairer sex.

He had seemed horrified that night two weeks ago when a woman at least twice his age had whispered something torrid in his ear. His face had become redder than his hair before he scrambled out of the great hall. Sebastian smiled at the memory, recalling the sensual way the Lady Arlington had laughed delightedly and run after him, piqued by the thrill of the chase. He still didn't know if she'd caught poor Duncan, as the man wouldn't speak of it. Yet he smiled whenever Sebastian brought up the subject.

"I say. What is that?" Duncan's voice yanked Sebastian out of his thoughts.

Sebastian reined in his stallion and looked across the field to where Duncan pointed. A large mound of purple fabric lay a few yards away.

"Let's go have a look, shall we?" Sebastian grinned, thankful something of interest had happened on his watch.

The men trotted over to investigate, only to find a woman lying face down in the grass. Her glorious black hair pooled around her head and blew softly in the gentle breeze. She was wearing a lavender gown, made out of fine silk. It was not the kind of dress one would wear to take a nap in a field of grass.

Frowning, Sebastian dismounted and approached the woman.

"Miss?" The woman didn't answer. "Miss?" he said a little louder. His heart leapt into his throat. *Was* she sleeping? He glanced worriedly at Duncan, who had also dismounted.

Crouching low, Sebastian carefully rolled the lady over to see her face. Duncan jumped back with a start.

"Good God!" he exclaimed. "Who would do such a thing?"

For once in his life, Sebastian was struck speechless. The poor woman had been badly beaten. An angry bruise swelled her left eye shut. A trail of blood oozed from her battered lips, and her nose appeared to be broken. Sebastian imagined there were similar bruises underneath her lovely gown.

"Bring me my water," he said to Duncan, gesturing to his horse. He never took his eyes off the unconscious woman. Carefully, he lifted her to a reclined position, holding her in his lap. Once Duncan handed him his water skin, he uncorked it with his teeth and gently poured a small amount into the woman's mouth.

A groan escaped her and her eyes fluttered as Sebastian patted her cheek to get her to come around.

"Are you an angel?" she whispered, almost inaudibly. "Am I dead?"

"No, sweet lady, you are not dead," Sebastian soothed. "Who did this to you?"

The woman didn't seem to hear him and simply asked for more water. Sebastian gave it to her. A large lavender jewel hung around her neck. It matched her lovely gown, as well as her beautiful lavender eyes.

"What's your name, little jewel?" Sebastian wiped blood from her face with his sleeve.

"Jewel?" she said in confusion. "My name? I... I don't know..."

"Do you know who did this to you?" Sebastian asked again, barely containing the anger simmering below the surface of his emotions.

She shook her head twice before groaning and wincing in pain.

"Take this." Sebastian passed Duncan his water. "Hold onto me, lady, if you can."

"Will she be all right, Seb?" Duncan asked.

"She will be if we can get her to Lady Arianna in time," he replied, lifting her gently off the ground. "Take her for a moment." Duncan nodded as Sebastian mounted his horse. Once he was astride, Duncan lifted the injured woman back up to him.

Sebastian settled the woman sideways across his lap. She was unconscious again, but her head tucked perfectly underneath his chin. He wrapped his arms around her and grabbed his reins.

Gazing at his friend, Sebastian growled, "Look around, lad. Try to find any clue as to who would have done such a heinous thing to a young lady. If you find him, hold him only long enough for me to kill him."

Nudging his horse forward, Sebastian was afraid to go much faster than a brisk walk. He didn't know the extent of the lady's injuries, and anything quicker might do more harm than good.

"Damn!" Sebastian cursed under his breath. He wanted to get to the castle as fast as he could. This slow pace was excruciating.

So many emotions raged inside him, he had to concentrate to keep them all in check. Anger such as he'd never known boiled to the surface, and he had no doubt he would kill the one responsible for the wounds on this dear, beautiful girl. He was certain she was beautiful under those bruises, although at the moment he couldn't see much of anything.

Those lavender eyes had pierced him to the core and he knew he'd want to look into them again. Her long black hair swirled around him, caressing his face in the breeze. It smelled faintly of roses and he lowered his face to smell its sweetness.

She fit snugly in his arms and Sebastian was nearly overcome with the urge to hug her closer, as if he could melt away her aches and pains with his arms alone.

"Are you an angel?" she had asked him, touching his heart without even knowing it. He wanted to protect her and kill the cowardly bastard who would dare take out his rage on a defenseless woman.

She stirred, and somehow she had the strength to lift her head to look at him. She must have sensed he was taking her to safety. "Thank you," she whispered.

Gazing once again into those beautiful lavender eyes, Sebastian smiled. "You're most welcome, my lady Jewel."

Chapter Two

Lady Arianna sat at her dressing table combing the long auburn hair her husband loved so much to run his fingers through. She'd mentioned cutting it once, and he'd practically yelped his rejection of that idea. A smile curved her lips at the memory. Sir Geoffrey of Emberdale was not an overly harsh man, yet he had threatened a swift spanking if she ever had that ridiculous idea again.

She hadn't really been serious about cutting her hair, but she knew how much he loved it and had thought to tease him a little. What she hadn't expected was for him to pounce on her from across the room and lay her across his lap anyway. She had screamed and squirmed, but had been unable to move from her precarious perch. Geoffrey had laughed when she tried biting his leg, but she had soon realized his playful hand never once struck her backside.

"You scoundrel!" She smiled as she stared at the floor a few inches from her face.

Finally, he allowed her to stand, but she stood between his legs, his arms wrapped around her waist. Geoffrey's chin rested on her belly as he looked up at her with a wicked grin.

Gazing at him, she twined her fingers in his golden locks. "It would appear I've found your weakness, milord."

"So you say!" he scoffed loudly. "A Wolverine has no weaknesses."

"Is that so?" Arianna's hands found their way under his shirt to tickle his ribs.

She squealed when Geoffrey scooped her up and threw her on the bed. In a split second he was on top of her, pinning her with his weight.

"You don't fight fair, milady," he said, nuzzling her neck.

"Neither do you," she teased.

That had been the day Arianna knew for sure she was pregnant. After three long years of trying, their dream was becoming a reality. The dragon, Mynos, had warned her that wielding her magic through his powerful Crystal could have some effect on her body. Arianna hadn't thought it would've taken so long to get pregnant, however, and she'd resigned herself to the horrid thought of never becoming a mother.

But that possibility had been pleasantly discarded. Arianna rubbed her swelling belly with a contented smile. They were having a girl, she was sure of it. No one could tell her otherwise. Geoffrey had been the proudest man in the castle when she'd told him he was going to become a father. She'd never seen him beaming so brightly as when they had accepted congratulations from friends and family.

Arianna had two months left in her pregnancy and Geoffrey insisted she stay close to their rooms in the royal apartments. He didn't want her to have any complications, and he had been granted simple guard duty along the castle's outer curtain walls in order to stay close at hand. Even now, Arianna could feel him through their Remembrance bond and she knew he was ridiculously happy. This little girl growing in her belly would have a wonderful father indeed.

A loud banging on her door snapped Arianna out of her reverie. She stood from her dressing table, and raced as fast as she could to open the door. She gasped at the sight on the other side.

Sebastian stood holding a badly beaten woman, his eyes wild with concern.

"Please..." was all he choked out before Arianna understood and ushered them quickly inside. He laid the woman tenderly on the bed and ran his fingers through his hair.

"Who is this, Sebastian?" Arianna took a seat next to the bed.

"I do not know," he answered. "Duncan and I found her in the fields like this. Can you help her?"

"Of course." Arianna took the woman's face in her hands. "Would you like to wait outside?"

"*No!*" he barked, surprising them both with his vehemence. "I mean... I'd rather stay if it's all the same to you, Lady Arianna."

She raised her brow, but gestured to a padded chair next to the fireplace for him to sit. He took it gladly. Without another word, she closed her eyes and concentrated.

"She's been beaten within an inch of her life," Arianna said. "My magic is showing me her nose is broken, as well as three of her ribs. She's lucky one of them didn't puncture a lung."

Sebastian squirmed on his seat as further injuries were confirmed to him. He felt helpless. Yet he knew Arianna would be able to heal the woman fully.

A low hum filled the room as Arianna's hands glowed white. She was a healer, but Sebastian still was unprepared for her casual use of magic and found himself staring as the woman's bruises began to disappear. Her nose straightened itself and she took a long, deep breath.

It had only taken a few moments to heal her. Arianna sat back and smiled to Sebastian.

"Are you done?" he asked.

"Yes, she is healed, Seb."

A few more silent moments passed as Sebastian stared at the woman's newly healed face. She was glorious. And she thought *he* was an angel? He grinned as he thought the same of her.

Arianna patted the woman's face gently until her eyes fluttered open. "Hello, my dear."

"Hello," the woman said weakly. "Where am I?"

"You are at Castle Templestone. Do you know your name?"

The lady closed her eyes as if in deep thought. "*He* called me 'Jewel'. That must be my name."

"Who called you 'Jewel'?"

Opening her eyes, she said simply, "The man did."

Arianna looked questioningly at Sebastian.

"I only called her 'Jewel' because of her necklace. That's not her real name."

"Do you remember anything about yourself?" Arianna asked the woman.

"I...remember drinking water...strong arms...blue eyes..."

Arianna once again glanced at him. "Do you remember anything else *before* meeting Sebastian?"

"Sebastian? Is that his name?" The woman smiled, looking at Arianna. A lump lodged in Sebastian's throat at the sight of it. Merciful God, he'd thought her to be a mere *angel*? No, she was a goddess!

"Yes, dear." Arianna gestured to him sitting in the chair. "He is still here."

Jewel gazed at him and he was pinned by her lovely lavender eyes.

"Sebastian," she sighed through another smile.

"Do you know who did this to you, milady?" He was amazed to find his voice after a few moments of basking in her beauty.

She suddenly looked confused. "I...I can remember nothing...except for you."

For whatever foolish reason, Sebastian grinned at her answer. He was smitten—there was no use denying it.

The lady moved to sit up. "My head aches."

"It is to be expected, Jewel." Arianna helped her up. "You were beaten quite badly. My magic has healed your wounds, but you will be weak for awhile."

"It appears I have much to thank you for." Jewel looked shyly at Sebastian. "Both of you."

"Think nothing of it." Arianna made her way to the bell pull. "I'll call my maid and she can take you to a room to sleep or bathe as you see fit. You'll be welcome here at the castle, Jewel, until we figure out who you are. Perhaps that lovely gem around your neck will give us a clue to your past."

Jewel grasped the necklace as if noticing it for the first time. She took it off and examined it.

"May I?" Arianna asked, holding out her hand.

"Of course." Jewel handed it to her.

Arianna hefted it for a moment. "Hmm, I wonder..." She gazed into the teardrop-shaped gem, biting her lower lip.

"What is it, Arianna?" Sebastian asked, seeing the look of concentration on her face. Was she channeling her magic into it?

Glancing from Sebastian to Jewel, she said, "It would seem this stone is more than it appears. Would you mind if I kept it for awhile?"

Jewel appeared about to object, but Sebastian placed his hand on hers before she spoke. "You can trust Arianna. She is an old friend. Perhaps she and the dragon, Mynos, can figure out who you are."

"If she is your friend, then she is mine," Jewel said quietly.

A soft rap on the door interrupted them.

"Ah, that will be Madeline now." Arianna crossed the room. Even seven months pregnant, she still moved with grace.

A pretty young maid stepped into the room and curtseyed to the group.

"Maddie, I'd like you to escort Jewel to a nice room. And take these with you." Arianna opened her wardrobe and pulled out five lovely dresses. "These don't fit me any longer," she said jovially, patting her large belly. "They can be yours."

Jewel stood from the bed. "Milady, you don't have to..."

"Oh posh!" Arianna laughed, waving her hand. "I know what it's like not to have any clothes save for the ones on your back. Don't think any more of it, my dear."

"Thank you. Very much."

Arianna gave her a small hug and ushered them out the door. "If you're feeling up to it, perhaps you can meet us in the great hall for dinner this evening."

"I'd like that," Jewel said.

"Now go and follow Maddie. She'll make sure you're well taken care of."

As soon as they were out in the hallway, Maddie gestured for them to follow. Sebastian fell in step next to Jewel.

"Are you all right?" he asked, still concerned.

"I feel quite well, actually." Jewel watched the carpet in front of her. "Will you be at dinner tonight?"

"I never miss a good meal, milady," he said, seeing a smile on her face.

After a short silence, she whispered, "I'm afraid." She glanced at him, terror in her eyes.

"You have nothing to be afraid of." Sebastian felt as if someone had punched him in the gut.

"I don't know who I am. I don't know how I got here. I don't know who...who...beat me."

An overwhelming urge to pull her into his arms and comfort her came over him, but he refrained. "Have no worry about that, my lady Jewel," he said, scowling. "If I find out who is responsible, he will not live to see another day."

Jewel's hand took his as they followed the maid to her room. She didn't say a word—and Sebastian didn't pull away.

Chapter Three

Jewel rubbed her hands together as she stood at the entrance of the great hall. Many people were present for the dinner feast, laughing and drinking ale, but the food hadn't yet been served. Bits and pieces of the lords and ladies' gossip were about her, and a few of the bolder guests gave Jewel curious glances.

She scanned the crowd for Sebastian but could not find him. He was the one person she trusted, despite only knowing him a few short hours. He was the only tether thrown to her in a roiling sea of the unknown. Kind, caring, and devastatingly handsome—was that why she was so eager to seek him out? She'd been bewitched by the depths of his blue eyes since the moment she first looked into them. Jewel had been so in shock at their beauty, she'd asked if he was an angel.

She had to support herself on the nearby wall as she remembered his strong embrace. She'd felt so safe, she had never wanted to leave his warmth. She'd even shocked herself when she took his hand in the corridor. Never had she been so bold. Or had she?

Frowning at the floor, Jewel tried to remember something—anything—about herself but to no avail. Would she ever remember? Did she want to remember? Someone had beaten her so severely, both Sebastian and Lady Arianna had refused to tell her the full extent of her injuries. That scared her more than anything else. For all she knew, the culprit could be right here in the castle.

That thought consumed her as she glanced around the room like a cornered animal. A young man made his way toward her. He wore the sword and blue sash of the Wolverines, who she had learned were the knights of the king.

"Good evening, milady," he said melodically. He grasped her hand and kissed it.

"Good evening, sir," she managed to say without sounding too dismayed.

"My name is Ethan, if you please." He grinned, his brown eyes twinkling. "Might I have the pleasure of yours?"

"It's...Jewel."

"Well, well, *Jewel*, you certainly do sparkle tonight."

Jewel fidgeted in the pale yellow satin dress Maddie had chosen. It was glamorous with white silk embroidery along the sleeves and neckline, contrasting richly with her long black hair. She'd thought to wear a more subdued color so as to not attract attention, but Maddie had insisted. The maid had pulled her hair up on either side of her face with ivory combs and let the rest fall freely down her back. It smelled faintly of jasmine after her bath and was still damp to the touch.

"Thank you, sir." She blushed at his compliment.

"Ethan," he corrected with a smile.

"Sir Ethan," she amended, looking at him. He was handsome, with sandy colored hair swept away from his face by a strip of leather tied at the nape of his neck. He had expressive eyes the color of mahogany, which made her feel uncomfortable under his bold scrutiny.

Ethan stood there for a few more moments, holding his ale and talking about the king and the castle, but Jewel was no longer listening. She'd finally noticed Sebastian.

He sat across the hall talking amiably with another woman and laughed heartily at something she said. Jewel felt a pang of jealousy she wasn't the one to hold his rapt attention, however she marveled at simply watching him from afar. He was a man full grown, but he still had a boyish quality about him that appealed to her. She imagined herself pushing away that stray lock of hair which seemed to fall into his eyes of its own accord. She wondered what it would be like to be kissed by him.

Jewel found herself blushing at the thought, making Ethan pause in his narrative.

"Are you all right, my dear?"

"Oh yes, quite," she answered. "Please do continue."

Ethan droned on again and Jewel felt guilty for not paying him any heed. But she simply could not tear her gaze from Sebastian. She wondered if the lady he spoke with meant anything to him. Did he love someone? Was he married? Her heart screamed in protest at the possibility.

Jewel willed Sebastian to glance at her, to turn her way and see her. He scanned the hall every few moments, but never saw her. She supposed it might be because Ethan paced while he spoke to her, somewhat shielding her from Sebastian's view.

Then, like the sun breaking through the clouds, Sebastian finally noticed her and smiled magnificently. Jewel was only slightly aware she'd stopped breathing. He said something to his lady friend and began to cross the length of the hall to her. A strange nervous tension pooled in her belly.

He was dressed the same as Ethan, carrying his sword on his hip and wearing the blue sash identifying him as a Wolverine. His hair was neatly combed, save for that one contemptuous lock, and he was cleanly shaven. Blue breeches fit him snugly, and a white linen shirt was tucked into them.

He was beautiful, he was breathtaking, he was...

"Hello, my lady Jewel," he said, breaking her out of her thoughts. He took her hand, pressing his lips to her fingers.

Her heart raced at the pressure of his mouth on her skin. Sebastian lingered there, as if loathe to let her slip away from him. She had the silly notion of turning her hand in his grasp and let him kiss her palm, her inner wrist, the crook of her elbow...

"I trust you rested well?" His voice washed over her like a caress.

Jewel blinked and swallowed hard, realizing she'd been lost in her thoughts again.

"Yes...yes...I did, th-thank you," she stammered.

"Why, Sebastian, what a nice surprise." Ethan obviously mourned the interruption by the look on his face.

"Yes, nice indeed." Sebastian stared only at Jewel, smiling at her blushing cheeks. "Would you be so kind as to sit next to me at supper?"

"I'd be delighted," she said over Ethan's loud protests. Sebastian held out his arm for her and she took it graciously.

"I expect you can find your own way to the table, Sir Ethan?" Sebastian said, moving Jewel away with him. She glanced over her shoulder only to see Ethan glowering at his back.

ಬಿಡಿಡಿ

Jewel was desperately hungry, but didn't eat much. She was too nervous with so many people staring at her. Quite a few dinner guests had stopped Sebastian on his way to the table to ask about the lovely woman on his arm. With her dilemma revealed, she was confronted by their sympathy, something she wasn't comfortable with.

Now she sat at the table, and she could feel their eyes on her. It didn't help matters that there were so many people at the table they had to squeeze together in order for all to have a seat. It also didn't help that she sat so close to Sebastian, her shoulder and her thigh rubbing against him in a most inappropriate way.

Jewel tried to concentrate on the conversation floating around her. She listened to Sebastian talk with Duncan about what he'd found, or rather hadn't found, in the field where they'd discovered her. There were no tracks of any kind save for their own, and no bent blades of grass to suggest tracks might have been hidden. Duncan had been thorough with his investigation, even going as far as his hometown of Marynville, which wasn't far from the castle, to ask about her. He had even asked a few of the visiting lords and ladies if they knew anything. Jewel could only surmise this was how her story had circulated so quickly.

"Well, my lady Jewel, it seems as if you've fallen from the sky," Sebastian teased.

Jewel gave him a small smile. "I'm not so sure I want to know where I come from. I don't want to go back to the person who...who..."

"Shh," Sebastian whispered in her ear, raising goose bumps on her arms. "I told you before you need not be afraid. If you choose to stay at the castle, every Wolverine in the king's service will honor your decision."

"But what if they find me and drag me away?"

"That will not happen, my lady Jewel." Sebastian's warm breath caressed her neck. "You will be protected here. If they try to take you by force, then we will force *them* to see things *our* way."

Jewel turned her head to look at him. He'd bent closer in order to keep their conversation private. His face was only inches from hers. She had but to sit up straight in order to kiss him. The twinkle in his eyes seemed to dare her to do it—scatter propriety to the wind and kiss him right there at the dinner table. He grinned slightly, as if reading her thoughts.

Before she lost her wits completely and gave in to his silent challenge, Jewel stood and backed away to put a bit of distance between them.

"I'm feeling rather flushed, milord. I would like to go back to my chambers."

Sebastian stood a heartbeat after she'd spoken and took her arm. "Come with me to the gardens instead," he pleaded. "The night air will cool your skin."

She glanced down at his hand and wondered how her skin could ever be cooled in his presence. She should go back to her room. It wasn't prudent to be alone with Sebastian in the gardens. But he seemed to be silently challenging her again to take his offer.

The silence between them stretched on and Jewel's cheeks burned once more. Finally she gave in.

"That sounds wonderful."

Chapter Four

Sebastian led Jewel to the terrace where the perfume of nearby flowers floated on the breeze. The full moon was out, bathing the gardens with its soft white glow. They were completely alone and the silence was soothing compared to the noisy hall they'd left behind.

"Come. Let me show you the grounds." Sebastian led her down the steps into the garden.

Jewel marveled at the flowers, all different colors and scents. Sebastian divulged those he knew—roses, lilacs and lilies, to name a few. Suddenly his face lit up as if he'd remembered something and he tugged her arm excitedly.

"Over here." He walked toward the large fountain in the center of the garden. "You'll love these, but you have to close your eyes."

Jewel giggled and did as she was told while Sebastian positioned her in front of his surprise. His voice drifted from behind her.

"Open your eyes, my lady Jewel."

Beautiful lavender carnations filled her vision. "Oh Sebastian, these are exquisite!" She smelled every one.

"I thought you might like them," he said, obviously pleased with himself. "They match your eyes to perfection."

Jewel glanced at him standing with his hands clasped behind his back. He smiled smugly. She was thankful the shadows hid her hot cheeks from his gaze.

"Do a lot of young lovers come here to pick the flowers?"

Sebastian sighed. "Alas, no. The royal gardener forbids the picking of any flowers without the express permission of the king. Anyone caught doing so could be fined. Depending on the flower, they could be fined heavily."

Jewel gasped.

Sebastian looked back at her with a devilish grin, reminding her of a boy about to do mischief. "But there are those who ignore the punishment and pick them anyway."

Jewel turned away from the lovely lavender flowers and made her way toward the three-tiered gurgling fountain. "We don't need to be courting chastisement, Sebastian. They are perfect right where they are."

"Indeed." Sebastian chuckled and guided her to sit on a marble bench.

After a few moments of silence, Jewel said, "Tell me about yourself, Sebastian, since I have nothing to tell you."

"What do you want to know?"

She thought for a moment. "How old are you?"

"I have seen twenty-four winters. You seem younger."

"Perhaps the years have been kind to me."

Sebastian cocked a brow. "Perhaps."

Jewel noticed his sword and touched the pommel, gazing at the Wolverine expertly engraved into it, crouched and ready to pounce. Sebastian stood and unsheathed his sword to give her a better look. The blade was well polished and reflected the moonlight so well the sword seemed to glow.

"How did you become a Wolverine?" she asked, looking up at him.

Sebastian dug the point of the blade in the dirt and knelt behind it, still holding onto the hilt.

"My grandfather was a Wolverine many years ago and wished for his son to be as well. But my father chose to become a merchant instead and set up his family in a town called Tabrinth along the northern border of Lyndaria. When Grandfather died, I decided as a young boy to walk in his footsteps. I came to Castle Templestone and trained with other young boys right after my fifteenth winter. I learned fast and was knighted after my nineteenth. I was sent on a few missions here and there and trained under Sir Cederick of Breckenwood."

Jewel leaned closer to him. "Did you have any exciting missions?"

He smiled. "Well, my most 'exciting' mission, as you call it, was a few years ago. The king sent Cederick to retrieve a valuable scroll stolen from the castle by the Dark Knights of Darragh. Since Sir Geoffrey was one of the king's best and I was one of Cederick's top students, he chose us to go along with him."

"Sir Geoffrey... He's Lady Arianna's husband?"

"One and the same. It was on this very mission he met Arianna. We succeeded in retrieving the scroll from a band of Dark Knights, but they were hot on our trail. Geoffrey panicked and gave a young girl the scroll for safe keeping."

"The young girl was Arianna?" Jewel asked, enthralled in his story.

"Yes. She was merely a farm girl caught up in our mission, even more so than we had first realized. When Geoffrey told us he'd given the scroll away, Cederick demanded he get it back at any cost. Geoffrey did retrieve the scroll, but failed to notice he'd been followed by the Dark Knights. With Geoffrey being one of the king's best, I have no idea how they managed to elude him, unless they used their magic to shield themselves.

"As soon as he located Arianna's farm, the Dark Knights struck, burning the house and killing her family."

Jewel covered her mouth in shock.

"Geoffrey didn't know what else to do but save her and bring her back to the castle. They fell in love and got married after they killed Queen Darragh."

"They killed a queen?" Jewel asked, bewildered.

"Goodness, I'm getting ahead of myself." That pesky lock of hair fell into his eyes and he snapped his head back in exasperation. He gave Jewel a sheepish grin. She smiled at him and urged him to go on.

"The Dark Knights were the followers of Queen Darragh, a woman obsessed with possessing the Crystal of Mynos, a powerful talisman made by the dragon Mynos."

"Isn't Mynos who you were talking about regarding my necklace?"

"Yes. The jewel on your necklace is similar to Mynos's Crystal. That is probably why Arianna wanted to talk to him since she was the one who wielded the Crystal's power to kill the Queen."

"Lady Arianna?" Jewel exclaimed in disbelief.

Sebastian sighed and pushed the lock away again. "I'm sorry. I'm such a poor storyteller."

"Do go on."

"The scroll Geoffrey gave to Arianna for safekeeping had been inscribed with an ancient elven spell to wake Mynos. He had turned himself to stone to escape the pain of loneliness. He was the last dragon, you see, after a horrid war millennia ago destroyed all of dragonkind."

Jewel gasped. "That's horrendous!"

Sebastian nodded. "We needed the dragon to take us to his Crystal in order to defeat the evil queen. She was brainwashing the villagers in every town her Dark Knights came across, increasing the numbers of her army. We needed to defeat her quickly.

"When Mynos awoke, he contacted Arianna's mind and knew she had elven blood in her veins. Her father had fled the Wolverines after she was born due to his elven heritage, or so it's thought. In fact, Arianna is the grand niece to King Kaas of the elves. Her grandmother was Kendra, the king's own sister. However, what they didn't know was that Arianna's father and Geoffrey's father were best friends so long ago. They had devised a plan for their children to marry, and betrothed them to each other."

"Yet they found each other by accident?"

"It's not quite that simple, my lady Jewel. Isaac knew the ways of magic and ensured Geoffrey and Arianna would meet later in life after he had fled the castle. He enchanted them with a bond known as the Remembrance. It allows them to talk to each other silently and know where the other is at any given moment. I hear it said they were meant to find each other."

Jewel sat silently for a moment. "Arianna didn't know she had an elven heritage?"

"No, her father never told her. But Mynos knew of it and he knew of her potential, and chose her to retrieve his Crystal. It bonded to her so no other could use it. Unfortunately, before she was able to control its power, she accidentally killed one of our Wolverines."

Jewel gaped at him. "No!"

"Yes. That was a terrible day. The castle was being attacked by Darragh's army. Arianna had only used the Crystal in an attempt to help us, but its power was too much for her. The magic lashed out and killed Sir Nathan of Emberdale."

"I can't even imagine..." she whispered.

"King Brennan had sent most of his Wolverines to Breckenwood to fight the Dark Knights the evening before. No one knew Breckenwood was a trap. With the castle's defenses down, Darragh struck and we would have lost the castle that day if it weren't for Mynos."

"What did he do?" Jewel asked, her eyes wide.

"He flew over the fields beyond the castle and destroyed the entire army with his fiery breath alone. To this day I will never forget it." Sebastian sighed, looking at the ground, deep in thought. "It was an amazing spectacle and the whole of Lyndaria knows Castle Templestone is now guarded by a dragon. I seriously doubt such a siege will ever be tried again."

"And Arianna succeeded in killing the queen?"

Sebastian nodded. "The queen kidnapped her out from under our noses. She came right into the castle and spirited her away. However Mynos was able to find her at Darragh's stronghold. But about that time, we realized Queen Darragh wasn't human, but a black dragon named Iruindyll."

"I thought you said Mynos was the last?"

"Everyone else thought so too, but it was revealed Darragh had instigated the very war thousands of years ago which killed all the dragons in her desire to obtain Mynos's Crystal. She had not been killed then, but had been looking for the Crystal ever since."

Jewel let out a breath she hadn't realized she'd been holding and shivered. "That's quite a story."

"Cold?" Sebastian asked.

She nodded.

"Perhaps it is time to take you back to your room." With that, Sebastian stood and sheathed his sword. Offering Jewel his arm, he escorted her back to the terrace.

ꙮ

Early the next morning, Jewel awoke with a start. She sat up in bed wondering what had awoken her. Sunlight poured into the room and she rubbed her eyes, yawning as she stretched. Then she remembered. There had been a knock at the door.

It hadn't been a loud knock, just three light raps. Did she really hear it? Perhaps she had dreamt it. She decided to check just to be sure. Grabbing her robe, Jewel glided to the door and cracked it open.

No one was there. Getting bolder, she opened the door wider to reveal the entire hallway, yet she still saw no one. Smiling to herself, Jewel realized it must have been a dream after all. But before she closed the door, something caught her eye.

There on the floor, right in front of her threshold, was a freshly picked lavender carnation.

Chapter Five

Jewel sat at her dressing table, brushing her hair, humming to herself. The purple flower lay before her, and she was staring at it with a smile on her face when there was a sharp knock at the door. It opened before she could answer.

"Good morning, miss." Maddie walked in, glancing at her. The maid bent to straighten up the blankets on the bed.

"A good morning indeed." Jewel sighed and grinned.

Maddie opened the curtains wide and sunlight poured in. "What has you so happy on this fine day?"

"What do you know of Sir Sebastian?" Jewel asked without directly answering the maid's question.

"Ah, so it's Sebastian who's put that smile upon your pretty face, now is it, milady?"

Jewel's blush betrayed her as she turned back to her table and picked up the brush once again.

"He's devilishly handsome, is he not, lady Jewel?"

Looking at the flower, Jewel grinned again. "He is that."

"Yes, that and more. He's not just *Sir* Sebastian, milady, but *Captain* Sebastian."

"Captain?" Jewel asked, looking at the maid in the mirror.

"Yes, miss. Sebastian is the Captain of the Guard here at Castle Templestone."

Jewel gasped and spun around in her chair, her brush forgotten. "Captain of the Guard?"

Maddie nodded. "He earned a promotion from the king for what he'd done the day Queen Darragh's army attacked the castle."

The maid opened the bureau and chose a lovely deep blue gown for Jewel to wear. "How's this one, miss?"

Jewel waved her hand. "It's fine. What did Sebastian do?"

"Why, he took command when no one else would. He barked orders left and right, telling people what to do and where to attack. It was Sebastian who pulled the men together to fight the army when we were vastly outnumbered here at the castle. He alone gave morale to the men despite their imminent defeat. Even after the dragon Mynos routed the army with only his breath, it was Sebastian who held everyone in check, making sure the injured were taken care of. He was very young, only twenty-one winters at the time, and I do believe he is the youngest man to have been promoted to Captain of the Guard."

"What happened to the previous captain?"

"He was killed at Breckenwood, bless his soul."

Jewel glanced at her flower and picked it up. She smelled it once again for the hundredth time. "I wonder why he didn't tell me."

"Sir Sebastian is many things, my dear, but a braggart he is not. If he wants to win your heart, then he'll do so on his own merit."

Jewel blushed again at the thought of Sebastian trying to win her heart. Surely he wouldn't want a girl who had no idea where she came from? How could he possibly know what kind of life she had led before? Perhaps she was a criminal and deserved the beating she got. Perhaps she was married and her husband had found her dallying with another man.

Jewel gasped and Maddie glanced at her.

"What's the matter, dear?"

"What if I'm married?" Jewel gazed at her, horrified.

Maddie scoffed. "I highly doubt it, milady. Not only do you have no wedding ring, but your hand doesn't bear the mark of one. No, I think you are as pure as the driven snow."

"Is...is...Sebastian..." She couldn't finish her question before she dropped her gaze to the floor.

"I think that flower is your answer, milady," Maddie said with a wink and a smile, urging Jewel to stand and get dressed. "Would you like me to find a vase for you?"

Jewel nodded, another grin forming on her lips.

ಬಂಬಂ

Jewel wandered the outer bailey of the castle studying the daily routines of the Wolverines. Many of them, young and old alike, stopped what they were doing to watch her walk by. A few talked with her, asking politely about her well-being and how she was enjoying her stay at the castle.

She wanted to catch a glimpse of Sebastian as he worked. She scanned the walls and the grounds but didn't see him.

She came upon two Wolverines practicing swordplay, a small crowd gathered around them. Jewel recognized one of the parrying men as Sir Ethan whom she'd met the night before, and the other as Sir Duncan, the man who'd found her along with Sebastian. Both dodged each other with ease, both fighting with shirts off in the warm morning sun. She blushed at the sight, but could not turn away. She was fascinated watching them fight. They seemed as if they were dancing rather than attacking with swords.

Both men were supremely muscled and Jewel found herself admiring their physiques. Would Sebastian look the same with his shirt off? Sighing to herself, she realized she once again wore a silly grin.

At that moment, Sir Ethan spotted her watching their display and decided to become heroic for her benefit. He parried and thrust with vigor, beating Duncan down and proving himself superior with his skills. The fight had gone from friendly swordplay to a win-or-lose match, and Jewel feared it was all because of her.

After long minutes, Duncan's sword was ripped from his hands and he conceded defeat. The crowd cheered at Sir Ethan's success. He crossed the bailey to intercept Jewel. He saluted her with his sword before he sheathed it and bowed before her. "Good morning, Jewel. I'm glad you've come to watch me practice with my sword."

Jewel didn't know what to say. She hadn't come here for him, but she suspected he knew that.

"You fought superbly," she answered with a tight smile.

"Why thank you." He bowed. An uncomfortable silence passed between them. "It's a beautiful day, is it not?"

"Yes, a wonderful day," she agreed, looking up at the white clouds.

"Would you consider riding with me today?" he asked.

She paused before she said, "Why Sir Ethan, that does sound lovely, but—"

"But she's already agreed to go riding with me this morning, isn't that right, my lady Jewel?" said a familiar voice behind her.

Jewel's heart leapt into her throat at the sound and turned to see Sebastian grinning from ear to ear.

Ethan turned to her as if asking if this were true.

Jewel didn't want to call Sebastian a liar, but neither did she want to lie to Ethan. "It must have slipped my mind."

"My apologies, Sir Ethan." Sebastian tucked Jewel's hand under his arm as he began to walk away. "Perhaps another time."

"Perhaps," Ethan said through clenched teeth, his fists balling at his side.

୨୧

"You really shouldn't do that, you know."

"Do what?" Sebastian asked, leading Jewel to the stables.

"Steal me away from Sir Ethan."

Sebastian gave her an incredulous look. "My lady Jewel, in order to steal something from someone, one must first allow that the something in question was first owned by the said someone. Since you are neither Ethan's property nor his wife, what I have done is perfectly acceptable according to the Rules of Courtship."

Jewel smiled at him. "Rules of Courtship?"

Sebastian nodded. "Indeed, madam. He means to court you, and I mean to thwart him. 'Tis a fair game we play."

"I see," Jewel said, nodding. "But do these 'Rules of Courtship' govern the preference of the woman involved?"

"Hmm, I must say I haven't quite read the manual that far."

Jewel was laughing when they entered the stables. He liked the sound of it. She looked stunning in the deep blue dress she wore. He could barely tear his eyes away from her.

Clearing his throat, Sebastian ordered the stable boy to saddle his bay stallion along with a timid dappled-gray mare Lady Arianna liked to ride on occasion.

"I hope I know how to ride," Jewel said under her breath as she eyed the sidesaddle on the mare. Sebastian heard her and attempted to calm her fears.

"Do not fret, my lady Jewel. If you should fall off your mount, I shall do the noble thing and allow you to ride Blaze."

"I'm assuming Blaze is your horse?" She nodded to the stallion with her chin as she patted her mare's neck.

"Of course."

"And am I to also assume you would ride him with me?"

"Naturally," he said with a mischievous grin.

The groom offered to help Jewel into the saddle, but Sebastian interrupted him. "An honorable gentleman helps a lady onto her horse," he said, his voice echoing throughout the stable. The groom shrugged and walked away.

Sebastian stood in front of her and grabbed her waist. He could feel her heat through her dress as he lingered there. He didn't offer her a boost, but gazed into her eyes instead. Jewel placed her hands on his, either as a nervous gesture or to keep them there, he wasn't sure which.

Jewel held his gaze. Holding onto her waist, he could swear she leaned closer to him.

"Bastian?" she whispered.

His eyes widened at the seemingly intimate nickname she'd called him. "Yes?" He pulled her closer to him. Her hips pressed against his.

"Shouldn't you lift me up on my horse?" Her voice trembled.

"Yes, I should," he answered, not making a move. "You called me Bastian." He dropped his head lower.

"Should I not? I'm sorry if..."

"No," he interrupted. "I rather liked it."

Jewel moved her hands slowly up his arms to rest on his shoulders. The woman was so beautiful. He wanted to kiss her in the stables for all to see. And so far, she wasn't stopping him.

"Me too," she breathed.

They stood there for a few moments, neither one of them moving. Jewel curled her arms around his neck, urging his head lower. He felt the whisper of her lips on his.

"You two haven't left yet?" The groom snickered at them, causing them to jump away from each other in embarrassment.

Jewel turned three shades of red and stared at the floor.

Sebastian sighed and turned his head away, pushing the stray lock from his face in frustration.

"He's right, you know," he said to her. "We should get going."

Once again, he grabbed her waist, but this time he succeeded in swinging her onto the mare.

Chapter Six

Sebastian led Jewel through the gates of the castle and into the fields beyond. She rode behind him a ways, embarrassed at her own behavior in the stables a few minutes before. She'd practically begged him to kiss her. She tried pushing it from her mind, but she was still charged from his touch, her heart still racing. After what had happened, she wasn't sure if riding with Sebastian was such a good idea. She would be completely alone with him. Could she trust him? Could she trust herself?

Jewel kept both hands on the reins, not wanting to betray her inner turmoil by her trembling. Why did Sebastian make her feel this way? What was it about him that made her lose any form of self-control?

She was so lost in thought she didn't realize she had no trouble at all riding the mare. She sat straight in the saddle, as if she'd ridden many times before. Sebastian noticed. He dropped back a little to point it out.

"It looks as if you know how to ride," he said with a grin, as if nothing had passed between them in the stables.

"So it does." Jewel kept her eyes averted. She was afraid if she looked at him, she might do something foolish—like jump onto his horse and kiss him like a wanton. Good Lord, she had to get away from him.

Jewel nudged her horse into a trot. Sebastian wasn't about to be so easily left behind. She found him trotting alongside her.

"There's a beautiful pond I go to often a short distance from the castle. Would you like to see it?"

The sooner he showed her his pond, the sooner he would bring her back to the castle. And perhaps she would be able to get away from these inappropriate thoughts.

"I'd love to," she exclaimed, chancing a look at him. That was a mistake. His smile was so knowing, so devilish, so…thrilling, it sent a shock of heat through her limbs. It was as if he were a wolf about to pounce on his prey. She closed her eyes and groaned to herself. Hopefully, he didn't hear that.

Soon they crossed the large field and began weaving their way through the trees on the other side. Sebastian seemed to be following an old trail that twisted and turned at random. Thankfully, the trail was only wide enough to allow one horse to pass at a time, so they rode single file. Jewel trailed him. Anything to get those magnetic blue eyes off her for a few minutes.

They came upon a small clearing with a pond in its center. A bubbling stream entered the pond at one end, and exited on the other, leaving inviting whirls and eddies on the surface of the water. A large boulder sat half submerged in the pond, with grass growing around its base.

Sebastian turned in his saddle, watching Jewel as she gazed at his sanctuary.

"This is where I come when I want to be alone. I can hear my thoughts clearly here." He dismounted while he was talking, and now he stood next to her mare, gazing up at her.

Jewel looked at him, a pang of nervousness washing over her at the thought of his hands on her once again.

He must have sensed her hesitation and tried to give her a reassuring smile. "Do not worry, my lady Jewel," he said. "I won't do anything you don't want me to."

She closed her eyes and bit her lower lip in consternation. It was exactly that—what she wanted him to do—that made her nervous.

Snapping her eyes open, she decided to be bold. "I am not worried, milord," she said before practically jumping down on her own. Sebastian wasn't quite ready for her and almost didn't catch her. But as soon as he did, she pulled out of his reach, walking briskly to the water's edge.

She trembled, looking out at the water, yet not seeing a thing. Taking a deep breath, she succeeded in calming herself somewhat.

"I come here for a swim sometimes as well," Sebastian stated right behind her. Jewel jumped at the nearness of his voice. She hadn't heard him walk over to her.

Again, she retreated, walking along the edge of the pond, trying to keep her distance.

"It is quite lovely," she said, glad there was a soft breeze to cool her face.

Turning to face him, she noticed he was slowly walking toward her, but not looking at her. His hands were behind his back in a most proper fashion as he studied the pebbles along the shoreline, kicking some with his boot.

He reached down, grabbed a flat stone and hurled it out toward the water. It skipped three times on the surface before plunging into the depths.

Jewel smiled at him in wonder. "How did you do that?"

"Come here, I'll show you." He beckoned innocently.

She walked hesitantly to him, ready to flee again if need be. She stopped a few feet away.

"Find a flat stone," he told her as he chose another one.

Looking around, Jewel found one and picked it up.

"Now hold it like this." He showed her how he meant to throw it. She mimicked him. "Now toss it!" He sent another stone skipping along the water.

Jewel tossed it, but it merely plunked into the water.

She placed her hands on her hips and pouted. "What happened?"

Sebastian laughed, picking up another stone, and flipped it to her.

"Try again. You just need practice." Grasping another stone, Sebastian sent that one skipping on the pond.

Jewel held the stone in her hand and threw it, once again hearing the solid *plunk.*

"What am I doing wrong?" she asked.

Sebastian picked up another stone and closed the distance between them. "Let me show you."

Before she could protest, he turned her around, her back pressed into his chest with his arms enfolding her, as he placed the rock into her palm.

"Hold it like this," he whispered into her ear. She shivered at his warm breath. Molding his fingers around hers, he showed her how to hold the rock.

"Then bring your arm back—" he lifted her arm, "—and toss it." With that, he swung her arm to throw the stone and finally it skipped across the pond.

"Did you see that?" she said joyfully. "It skipped. I did it!"

"Yes you did!" He laughed.

In her excitement, she hadn't noticed that Sebastian hadn't released her. However now, with the excitement gone, she was acutely aware of him, his arms tightening around her, his warmth pressing on her back.

Closing her eyes again, she fought against the urge to lay her head against his shoulder, to let him kiss her neck and the sensitive spot behind her ear. She groaned again at the thought and there was no doubt he heard it this time.

"Did you like your flower?" he asked, his breath burning her ear.

Oh God, not now. Not the flower! She remembered with clarity his romantic gesture this morning and began trembling anew.

All she could do was nod.

He chuckled. "I thought you might."

Amazingly, Jewel found her voice. "You shouldn't have done that, Sebastian…"

"Call me Bastian."

She ignored his plea. "Wh-what about the heavy fines?"

"You're worth it."

She turned her head to look at him, but he didn't give her another chance to look away. His lips were on hers in an instant, kissing her softly. Her heart jumped at the contact and she tried to pull away, but Sebastian held her fast. Her lips smoldered under his, making him groan into her mouth and deepen the kiss.

His tongue ran along her lips, urging them to open, yet she was afraid to surrender fully. Was this really happening? Was she dreaming?

No, this tingling sensation wasn't a dream. Wanting to pull him closer wasn't a dream. Wanting to press against the length of his body *definitely* wasn't a dream.

"Jewel, I won't hurt you," he said against her lips, sensing her reluctance. "I will never hurt you."

Remembering her bruises, remembering there was someone out there who had beaten her, and remembering it was Sebastian who had saved her, made her whimper in response to his words. She wanted to be safe, she wanted stability. She wanted reassurance that everything would be all right.

And Sebastian was offering all of it to her now.

Jewel finally surrendered, turning in his embrace without breaking the kiss, her hands finding the sides of his face to hold him there.

Opening her mouth, she let him in, let him explore with his tongue, playing with hers passionately.

She was timid at first, but then matched his ardor, giving and taking. She could smell him, feel him, taste him—at that moment her entire world revolved around him.

Her hands found their way from his face up into his hair, feeling its softness and marveling at it.

Slowly, Sebastian lifted his lips from hers to look deeply into her eyes. He was panting, and she saw the fires of passion burning in his blue depths.

"We cannot... We cannot..." he stammered, resting his forehead on her shoulder.

"Cannot what, Bastian?" She trailed kisses down his cheek and neck.

"Good God, sweet lady, I want to make love to you right here and now, I swear it!"

"You said you wouldn't do anything to me I didn't want you to do," she whispered hotly in his ear. "I don't want you to stop."

Lifting his head again, he looked into her eyes and kissed her hard at her admission. She was soaring with him again, beckoning his tongue in and capturing it with her own. Jewel was surprised at her brazenness as she drew his bottom lip into her mouth. She touched him everywhere at that moment, it seemed, his neck, his chest, his face... And then suddenly, he held her at arm's length.

"We cannot!" he yelped.

Jewel looked at him, confused, her lips swollen and her hair in disarray.

"I don't know if you have someone... I don't know if you love another. You don't know it either," he said forcefully, as if he were fighting himself. "I couldn't live with myself if I took from you what you would never have given me otherwise. I will not take advantage of you."

Jewel reached up and pushed the hair from his eyes as she had wanted to do many times before.

"You are an amazing man, Sebastian," she said. "I admit I've wondered the same thing. I've wondered if there is another man who loves me..."

Sebastian looked away, his hands still on her shoulders.

"But I do know this. I know in my heart of hearts I've never felt about anyone the way I feel about you, Bastian. You are gentle, caring, and so amazingly handsome."

Taking one of his hands from her shoulders, she turned it in hers and kissed his palm as she had wanted him to do to her the night before. She then kissed every one of his fingers.

"My lady Jewel..." he began, but she stopped him with her hand to his lips.

"You are all that I know, all that I remember. I try to think back on my memories and all I see is you, Bastian. Only you."

He grabbed her in a hug so strong, she never wanted him to let go.

"I cannot take the chance there is no one else," he said, sounding tortured.

Jewel hugged him fiercely.

"You will ride back to the castle on Blaze, my lady Jewel," he said. "If I cannot make love to you this day, then I will be as close to you as I possibly can. Will you deny me this selfish request of mine?"

Jewel leaned back and kissed his lips. "I can deny you nothing."

Chapter Seven

Lady Arianna held Jewel's necklace up to the window and marveled at its beauty. It twinkled in the light, seemingly of its own accord, as if it were wrought with many facets. Lavender rainbows danced on the walls as she turned it in the light.

Arianna had channeled her magic into it when Jewel had first handed it to her the day before. It was unnaturally warm, and she had wondered if this gem was anything like Mynos's Crystal. It was altogether possible there were more draconic talismans in Lyndaria. Perhaps Sebastian had just stumbled upon one.

She tried to touch the gem with her magic once again, but was unable to feel the presence she'd felt earlier. It stayed warm to the touch, however, giving Arianna a sense of surety that she hadn't imagined it being there.

She longed to show Mynos the Jewel, yet he was scouring the countryside, searching for evidence of other dragons. It had become a passion of his to try and find any living remnant of his race after he had learned Iruindyll was, in fact, alive after all these years. If *she* could survive, surely others could too. In the three years since Iruindyll's death, Mynos had investigated the ancient lairs and crags that had once housed the proud dragons, but as of yet, he hadn't found a single living one.

In his absence, he left his Crystal with Arianna to guard the castle if need be. Walking over to the small box she kept it in, Arianna decided to pull it out and hold it up to Jewel's necklace to see if she could determine any similarities.

She opened the lid and the Crystal filled the chamber with its white glow.

"Daughter!" Its many tinkling voices echoed in her head.

Smiling, Arianna grasped it and held it in one hand while holding Jewel's necklace in the other. An amazing thing happened. Both gems blazed forth with blinding light, and a sudden wind whipped around the room. An unfamiliar feminine voice called, *"Mynos!"*

It came from the necklace.

"Who are you?" Arianna asked mentally. The hair on the back of her neck stood on end.

"My beloved is alive!" the voice said.

Arianna could not mistake the sense of joy she felt from the Crystal, as if it knew the gem of Jewel's necklace.

"It is her! It is her!" the Crystal shouted triumphantly.

"Who?"

"I must go," the mysterious voice said again. *"I have not the strength to stay long."*

"Wait, you must tell me who you are," Arianna pleaded, but it was too late. The light from the lavender Jewel winked out. The Crystal also diminished, only to hum steadily in her hand. No matter how hard she tried to talk to the Crystal, it would not talk back.

Frustrated, Arianna called to Mynos mentally.

"Mynos," she said wearily, *"I think you should come home. There is something you need to see."*

ജ്ഞാരള

Sebastian held Jewel close, weaving Blaze in and out of the trees at a slow pace. He led the dappled mare behind them and was in no hurry to get to the castle. In fact, he seemed to be taking a longer route back. Jewel surmised they should have returned by now. She didn't think long on it. She knew he was deliberately going slowly, taking a route that would lead to the castle eventually. But not yet.

She'd surprised him by wanting to face him in the saddle, yet he made no objections as she curled her arms around his waist and pressed her cheek to his chest.

Jewel sat astride, not caring that her voluminous skirts hiked about her legs in a most unladylike fashion. In order to sit facing him, she had to rest her legs on top of his and she savored the feeling of it. She sighed contentedly and closed her eyes.

"Are you comfortable?" Sebastian's deep voice rumbled in his chest.

"Yes," she answered. "You?"

"Most definitely."

She smiled at his answer.

They said nothing more as they enjoyed the day, enjoyed the ride, enjoyed each other. She felt so safe with Sebastian, so protected. Jewel found herself wishing there was no one else to go back to, no one waiting for her to come home. She was so comfortable, she eventually dozed in his embrace.

Sebastian finally brought Blaze to a halt and looked down at the woman who clutched him. It brought a smile to his face that she cared so much. Would he be able to let go of her if she left the castle? He decided not to think on such things.

Jewel lifted her head and rubbed her eyes.

"As much as I'd love to continue holding you on my lap, my lady Jewel," he said, "I'm afraid I do not want to shame you upon entering the courtyard of the castle."

Jewel looked at him with confusion on her face. "Shame me?"

Sebastian touched her bare knee and his warm hand instantly got her attention.

"As fine as your legs are," he murmured with a smile, "I couldn't bear the thought of someone other than myself getting a glimpse of them."

Jewel smiled. "You think you're the only one with the right to look at them?"

"No, I do not have the right," he said. "But if you're willing to show them to me, who am I to argue?"

Giggling, Jewel hugged him again. "And what if I'm not ready to let you go yet?"

"Then we'll sit here until you are."

"You might be in for a very long wait, Bastian."

"I'm counting on it."

ഈഐഔ

Jewel did in fact hold onto Sebastian for a long while, until the sun was high in the sky. She reluctantly let go due to her protesting stomach. Sebastian heard it growl and chuckled.

"Hungry?"

"Very."

"Perhaps it is time for us to get back."

With a forlorn sigh, Jewel let go and allowed Sebastian to help her smooth her skirts and mount the grey mare. She felt a pang of loss as they made their way to the castle. She had no idea if she would ever be able to hold Sebastian like that again and it pained her to think of it. There could very well be someone else waiting for her. Would she still love them? Would she be able to go back to her old life and leave Sebastian behind?

Jewel knew a two-day acquaintance with Sebastian could hardly compare with a proper courtship if there was indeed another suitor at large. However she felt drawn to Sebastian's deep blue eyes and the rich, dark hair that always fell into them. When she closed her eyes, she could see only his smile, feel only his warmth, and Jewel began to wonder if she was obsessed with him. Perhaps a healthy bit of distance would do her good.

Her mind made up, Jewel decided not to seek Sebastian out any longer. Instead she would try to make her own friends and perhaps find out more about herself. She wouldn't be able to bear it if she got any closer to this wonderful man only to be taken from him.

She had to admire him, though, for once again she had thrown herself at him near the pond, demanding he continue his seduction, and he'd had enough sense to put a stop to it all. If they continued, she would probably come to regret it. No, she was definitely glad Sebastian had pulled away when he did.

Then why did she still feel this tremendous ache in her heart?

As soon as they dismounted in the stables, Sebastian was waylaid by an animated young Wolverine who began complaining about this and that, rattling off the problems and duties of the day to his Captain.

"Unfortunately, my lady Jewel," Sebastian stated as he turned back to her, "I have neglected my duties for far too long this morning. Apparently, Castle Templestone is falling apart around us."

The poor young boy looked at her sheepishly. He'd sounded desperately relieved to have Sir Sebastian back within the castle walls.

Jewel smiled. "I understand. I'm rather tired myself. I think I'll retire for awhile."

Sebastian gazed at her with a knowing grin. "After that nap you just had?"

Blushing, she turned away from him, trying not to give away her embarrassment to the young Wolverine standing with them.

"I'll be sure to send you up some lunch." Sebastian winked at her and walked away.

After a few steps toward the castle, Jewel noticed Sir Ethan fall into step right beside her.

"Care for an escort?" he asked, offering his arm.

Without wanting to be rude and remembering his previous alarm over losing her twice to Sebastian, she could not refuse him.

"Of course." She politely took his arm.

"Sir Sebastian is truly a scoundrel," he said with mirth, surprising Jewel. He was far from furious.

She shot him a glance. "You aren't mad at him?"

"Whatever for? It only means I'm going to try twice as hard to get your attentions, and perhaps you will remember me instead of Sebastian in your dreams."

Jewel's mouth dropped open at his forwardness. "I'm thinking it isn't Sebastian who is the scoundrel, sir," she said a bit too harshly.

"Do forgive me, milady." Ethan gave her a wounded look.

Ethan was quite handsome and Jewel admired him for that fact. His dark brown eyes shone as he looked at her, hiding nothing about how he felt. Unlike Sebastian who had kissed her with her permission, Jewel had the uncanny feeling Sir Ethan would try to steal her kisses without it.

"My lady, I would like to ask you to sit with me this evening at dinner."

"Well, sir..."

"Ethan," he corrected.

"...I have a rather bad headache at the moment and was contemplating eating dinner in my quarters," she continued as if he hadn't interrupted. She had also just told him a fabrication, one she hoped he would believe. Jewel didn't dislike Sir Ethan, but she didn't want to encourage him either.

"That's even better!" He looked at her with sultry eyes. "It's where we'd end up...eventually."

Jewel stared at him in shocked disbelief. His audacity was almost crude. She was about to tell him so when suddenly the same boy who had accosted Sebastian in the stables came running up to them.

"Sir Ethan! Sir Ethan!"

"What is it, lad?"

"You're needed on the battlements, sir."

"What, now?" he asked, somewhat dismayed.

"I was told you should make haste. You are needed right away!"

Ethan turned back to Jewel. "Duty calls," he said formally, taking her hand and kissing it. "Until we meet again." He turned on his heel and walked away.

Jewel glanced up to the top of the outer stone wall and noticed Sebastian watching her with his arms crossed. She had no doubt he'd saved her again from Sir Ethan. Being Captain of the Guard certainly had its advantages.

She tilted her head in silent thanks just as Sebastian gave her a small nod of satisfaction.

Chapter Eight

Sebastian spent the rest of the day with a smile on his face. It wasn't long after Ethan had sprinted to the top of the battlements that he'd realized what Sebastian had done.

"You are making me look like a fool," Ethan said through clenched teeth.

"Well, that *is* the idea," Sebastian shot back, chuckling.

"Don't think I will be defeated so easily, *Captain*," Ethan said mockingly. "Lady Jewel is an exquisite woman, and I mean to get to know her."

"By all means you can try, Sir Ethan. But if I find you have compromised her in any way, I will challenge you. And I will win."

Ethan knew full well Sebastian's skill with a sword. But he seemed shocked at the sudden threat of a sword fight, as one Wolverine hadn't dueled another in many years. The Wolverine's Challenge, as it was called, was frowned upon by the king, but tolerated. Men were often wounded and sometimes killed, depending on the anger of the opponents. If an opponent died, a panel of judges would deliberate if the death was justified. If so, the victor would go free. If not, he would be tried for murder.

Ethan scoffed with feigned bravado. "You're bluffing, Sir Sebastian," he said, examining the dirt beneath his nails. "You have not the heart to kill me."

"Oh I wouldn't kill you, Sir Ethan." Sebastian grinned fiercely. "I would simply make certain you would never do it again...to *any* young maiden."

Sebastian's eyes trailed down Ethan's large frame and rested at the top of his legs, leaving Ethan no room for doubt about what he meant to do.

Scowling darkly, Sir Ethan stalked away without another word.

"Don't touch her," Sebastian warned again to his retreating back.

A few hours later, Sebastian heard cheers from his men as they glanced at the sky, raising their swords in salute. Looking skyward, Sebastian found what they were cheering at. In the distance he could see the outline of a dragon flying toward the castle.

As Mynos approached, Sebastian marveled at his beauty. The ancient dragon's golden scales glistened in the sun as if they were wet, with a translucence that had a rainbow-like quality. With each beat of his wings, a loud clap of thunder echoed throughout the courtyard and into the fields beyond.

Sebastian wished Jewel were here to see it. Watching Mynos flying in the sky was indeed a sight to behold. He closed his eyes and remembered the first time he'd seen Mynos as he flew out to engage Queen Darragh's army. He remembered the shock he had felt at the sight of a living dragon and the speechlessness that had followed as Mynos's fiery breath was released with a vengeance. Sebastian shuddered at the memory, and found it almost unbelievable that this enormous golden dragon could change his shape at will into that of a mere man. What *couldn't* he do?

The dragon flew low over the courtyard, stirring up quite a wind with his wings. He was headed for his lair beneath Castle

Templestone, located in the side of the cliffs upon which the mighty fortress stood.

Sebastian had no doubt Arianna had called him home. Had she found something regarding Jewel's necklace? He didn't know and the suspense was almost unbearable. He couldn't wait for his work to be done.

ಐಇಐಅ

Geoffrey and Arianna sat together on the sofa facing the fireplace in their chambers, talking softly about their future family. His arms were around her as he cradled her in his lap, her back on his chest as they reclined comfortably. Arianna's stomach swelled underneath Geoffrey's warm hands. She could feel the life inside her kick, as if the baby knew its father was nearby.

"How are you so sure we're having a girl?" Geoffrey massaged her belly, something Arianna had grown to love to relieve the aches and pains of her stretched skin.

"It's a feeling," she told him. "I have dreams about her, holding her, cooing to her..."

Geoffrey was silent as Arianna closed her eyes and sighed in her comfort.

"Do you think she'll want to be a Wolverine like her parents?" he asked inside her head. Despite the fact that Geoffrey and Arianna spoke half of their conversations silently through their Remembrance bond, she still managed to jump at the sound of his voice in her head.

Opening her eyes, Arianna gazed at Quicksilver, her father's sword, hanging proudly over the mantel of the fireplace. She smiled, remembering the day the king had knighted her with Quicksilver, the weapon that had slain the dragon Iruindyll.

Arianna was Lyndaria's one and only female Wolverine, and she knew it was mostly an honorary title she held. If ever her magic was needed for the good of king and country, she had no doubt she would be called upon to do her duty. But as it stood, the king never sent her on any missions and never expected her to make rounds along the castle walls.

"Perhaps she will," Arianna said out loud, snuggling closer to her husband.

Geoffrey's hands still caressed her belly and slowly worked their way upward until Arianna realized where they were headed.

"Sir Geoffrey of Emberdale!" she snapped at him as she pushed his greedy hands away from her breasts. "Behave yourself!"

She turned to look at him and he gave her a grin and kissed her nose.

"Want to try for twins?"

"Oh!" Arianna scoffed, laughing. "I'm afraid we'll have to get creative," she said through her chuckles. "My belly seems to be getting in the way more and more."

A devilish light played in his eyes. "Don't worry, Rose," he said, whispering the intimate nickname he had given her when they'd first met, "I'm sure we can think of something."

At that moment, a loud knock resonated through their chamber.

"It's Mynos," Arianna said in answer to Geoffrey's questioning look.

Untangling himself from the sofa, Geoffrey stood, then opened the door, allowing the dragon, in his human form, into the room.

Mynos stood as tall as Geoffrey, and his golden human hair shimmered with the translucent quality of his dragon scales. His skin also had a golden tone to it, along with his slitted metallic eyes, much like a cat's. With those eyes, no one could mistake him for being completely human.

He gave Arianna a strong hug. A few proprieties were spoken before the dragon asked Arianna why she'd called him back to the castle.

"A girl was found outside the castle walls, lying in the fields," she told him. "The woman was badly beaten and Sebastian brought her to me for healing. She doesn't remember where she came from. The poor dear couldn't even remember her own name. So Sebastian decided to call her 'Jewel' after a large lavender gem she wore around her neck."

Arianna gazed at the dragon and was unnerved by his silent stare. She continued.

"The gem is large, shaped like a teardrop, and very warm to the touch. When she first showed it to me, I felt a presence inside it. I tried to reach through the gem like I do with your Crystal, but the presence wouldn't answer me. When I decided to investigate the gem with your Crystal, a strange thing happened. Both the Crystal and the gem flared to life and...there was a voice."

"A voice?" Mynos appeared stunned.

"Yes, coming from Jewel's necklace. It called your name and said, 'My beloved is alive.' After that, the Crystal shouted, 'It is her!' I tried to contact the voice again, but it said it didn't have the strength to stay long." Arianna squirmed underneath the dragon's scrutiny. "I...I think perhaps this gem is similar to your Crystal, and maybe it will give you the evidence you need to prove it was made by another dragon."

Mynos's voice was soft. "It has no facets, yet glitters like a lavender diamond."

"Yes! How did you know?"

"May I see it?" It wasn't a request, but a demand.

"Of course." Arianna lifted herself off the couch with Geoffrey's help. Opening the case that held both the gem and the Crystal, Arianna grasped the gold chain and held it up for him to see.

Mynos crossed the room, his eyes glittering with unshed tears. "My God," he breathed reverently. "I didn't think it actually survived all these years." The mighty dragon fell to his knees, his voice filled with emotion. "I thought it had been lost. I was wrong. So wrong!"

"Mynos," Arianna asked, concern lacing her voice, "what is it?"

"It's Malnan's Jewel!"

Chapter Nine

The lavender gem hanging from the necklace twinkled in the soft light of the room.

"Mynos, are you sure?" Arianna finally asked, her voice shaking.

"Give it to me," he commanded. Without another word, Arianna placed it in his outstretched hand.

At the moment his hand touched it, the room flashed with a glorious light. A brisk wind suddenly whisked around them as a feminine voice rang out. *"Mynos!"*

The great dragon said nothing, yet Arianna felt his magic. He was channeling into the Jewel.

Geoffrey stood next to Arianna and watched in awe.

The winds swirled near the fireplace and the shape of a woman emerged from the gusts. She was beautiful, of that there was no doubt.

As her form began to solidify, Arianna could see she was wearing a gown of light, a wondrous shimmering gown which illuminated the room. Her hair fell down her back in waves, deep green in color. Her eyes were a lighter shade of green, yet had slits, just as Mynos had. Arianna gasped in amazement. She was seeing the ghostly human form of Malnan as she had appeared millennia ago.

Arianna remembered the stories Mynos had told of his mate Malnan, a beautiful green dragon, who'd traveled to the Isle of Dragons to lay her eggs so long ago. Yet Malnan had been killed in the first war for the Crystal before she'd ever had the chance to give birth to her children. Mynos had spoken of her with such regret and pain that Arianna had never asked about her again.

Still on his knees, Mynos spoke, his voice cracking, "*Malnan.* You're alive!"

The woman shook her head with a look of sorrow on her face. "I am dead, my love." Her voice seemed to echo off the walls.

"I don't understand," he groaned, his shoulders slumping in disappointment.

"I made my Jewel as you taught me," she said lovingly, "but I had yet to enchant it as your Crystal is enchanted. I never had time. When you rallied us all to find the Crystal at any cost, I knew I would die fighting for you. You had forbidden me to go into battle, but I had to follow you, Mynos. I had to make sure you would be all right."

At that, Mynos hung his head. A golden tear fell from his eye, embedding itself deep into the stone the moment it hit the floor.

Reaching down, Malnan's ethereal hand gently lifted his chin. "When the mages spotted me, I knew I would die, but I didn't want to be parted from you, Mynos. Much like your Crystal bonds itself to the one wielding it, I bonded my soul to the Jewel. The moment I fell in battle, my soul was pulled into the Jewel, but I never had the chance to tell you...until now."

"Can...can you be brought back?"

Malnan smiled. "Yes," she said excitedly. "I only need a dragon's egg to breathe my essence into and I can be with you again."

The hope on Mynos's face was dashed as more tears spilled from his eyes, collecting into golden pools on the floor. "I cannot bring you back."

"But the Isle of Dragons?"

"Destroyed. It sank into the sea three years ago."

Malnan stood in sadness, her hand falling to her side. "Then you must release me, Mynos. You must release my soul from the Jewel."

"I cannot," he cried. "I cannot let you go so soon. Not when I've found you again!"

Malnan knelt next to Mynos and took his hands in both of hers. "It will be harder for you if I stay."

"You think I don't live in hell now?" he asked, his face a mask of pain.

Malnan said no more as she looked into his eyes.

"There might be a way," Arianna said.

Both dragons looked at her curiously.

"The island sank, that much is true. But there still might be an egg somewhere underneath the water."

"It would take a lifetime to find one," Mynos lamented.

"Do you have anything better to do?" Arianna shot back, trying to instill his hope once again.

Mynos smiled with sadness in his eyes. "I will do everything in my power to bring you back to my side, Malnan."

"I must go." She swayed back and forth. "Even with your magic, Mynos, I am so tired. I cannot stay."

"Wait!" Arianna yelped, suddenly remembering Jewel and how she had arrived at the castle with the gem around her neck. "Do you know anything about the young lady wearing this necklace?"

"I felt pain and anguish, I felt she was in mortal danger. I knew I had to save her. I brought her to the castle, knowing Mynos might be here, that she might find help."

"Do you know her name?" Arianna asked, hope flaring in her heart.

"No," Malnan answered wearily. "I only awoke to pain and knew I had to save her."

Arianna sighed and glanced at the floor.

"I do know one thing," Malnan said. "Only one word. Evendria. I hope that helps you."

"I hope so too." Arianna smiled.

"Goodbye, my love," Malnan said to Mynos before her form shimmered and disappeared. Mynos still knelt on the floor, and he slowly put Malnan's Jewel around his neck.

"Evendria," Geoffrey said thoughtfully. "I believe that's a city far to the south. King Brennan can write a letter of inquiry to see if Jewel came from there. Sebastian can send a runner."

Arianna nodded her agreement.

"I believe it is time for me to visit the girl." Mynos stood. "Perhaps she will know how she came across this necklace."

Chapter Ten

Jewel finished her dinner in her quarters as she remembered the scenes from the day. She couldn't quite keep a smile off her face. She felt sorry for poor Ethan, but was thankful to Sebastian for saving her time and again from his presence. For whatever reason, she didn't feel as comfortable around him as she did with Sebastian. Perhaps it was because she wasn't attracted to him. He was handsome enough, and maybe she would have taken notice and encouraged his advances—if she hadn't met Sebastian first.

Jewel walked to the bureau and pulled out her robe and nightgown, preparing to settle down for the evening. At that moment, a demanding knock sounded at her door.

Jewel's mind flew to who it could be. Ethan? Sebastian? Maddie? She crossed the room and opened the door, then gasped at the sight on the other side.

The man standing before her didn't look like a man at all. His hair shone like liquid gold and his skin was the same unusual color. And his eyes... His eyes made her step away from the door in shock. Those were not the eyes of a man. They gleamed like pure gold, similar to his hair, yet they reminded her of cat's eyes, with slits for pupils.

He also wore her necklace.

"Who... Who are you?" She panicked and backed away from the door.

Lady Arianna and her husband, Sir Geoffrey, stepped through the entry to comfort her.

"Don't fear, Jewel," Arianna soothed. "This is the dragon Mynos. He is a friend."

"A *dragon*?" she squawked in disbelief. "But...but he's human!"

"I can take many forms, Daughter," he said, strolling into the chamber. Jewel made it a point to keep Arianna and Geoffrey between them.

"Why is he wearing my necklace?"

"I was about to ask you the same question, my dear." Mynos sat casually on her bed and gave her a friendly smile.

Jewel stared at him, stupefied. "What are you talking about?"

"Jewel," Arianna began, "the gem in the necklace you were wearing was made by a dragon named Malnan many centuries ago."

"What?"

"It is much like this Crystal," Arianna explained as she held out the glittering talisman. "This is called the Crystal of Mynos."

Jewel's eyes flashed to the dragon. "You made this?" she asked in wonder.

Mynos smiled at her. "Yes."

She turned her gaze back to Arianna. "This is what you used to defeat Queen Darragh?"

Arianna nodded. "I see Sebastian has been telling you a few things. Would you like to touch it?"

Jewel shied away from Arianna's outstretched hand. "I... I..." she stammered.

"Do not worry. It won't hurt you."

Reaching out her hand, Jewel touched the Crystal tentatively. It was ice cold and strange voices whispered in her head. She couldn't make out what they were saying, but she shivered.

Suddenly, as she held the Crystal, a vision slammed into her head without mercy. Fist after fist smashed into her face until she fell from the force of it. Lying prone on the floor, still clutching the Crystal, she could see her stomach being kicked over and over by a booted foot and willed herself to make it stop.

"No," she choked out. "*No!*" She finally screamed.

๛๛๛

Screams rang through the corridor as Sebastian strode to Jewel's chambers. He recognized her voice and sprinted the rest of the way, his heart in his throat. He'd meant to visit with her for a short while after his duties, and was shocked to hear her shrieking as he approached her open door. She wept on the floor at Arianna's feet. Without a thought, he ran to her, dropping to his knees as he swept her into his arms.

"What is going on here?" he demanded of the three who looked on in stunned silence.

Jewel crawled into Sebastian's lap like a frightened child as he sat on the floor with her. She tried to pull herself as close to him as she could. Clutching his shoulders almost painfully, she buried her face in his neck as tears poured from her eyes in broken sobs.

"I...I think the Crystal gave her a vision," Arianna whispered through her own shock.

"I saw it, Bastian!" Jewel cried. "I saw it happening! I saw...the fists, I saw the boots, and I saw... I saw..."

"Shh," he whispered in her ear, smoothing her hair. "You are safe with me, my lady Jewel."

"Don't leave me," she pleaded. "Please don't let me go."

"Not a chance."

Glaring at Arianna over Jewel's head Sebastian asked icily, "She *touched* the Crystal?"

Arianna nodded, her eyes wide. Geoffrey gazed back at Sebastian with a warning glance as he placed his hands protectively on his wife's shoulders.

"I...I thought perhaps the Crystal could make her remember something of her past, or tell us who she is," Arianna explained.

Sebastian's face softened as he looked at Geoffrey.

Jewel's sobs quieted, but she still hugged Sebastian fiercely, keeping her face hidden in his neck.

"Jewel?" Arianna asked. "Did you see a face?"

"No." Her voice was muffled. She moved her face away from Sebastian's neck. "I just saw fists...and boots."

Arianna gave Sebastian an apologetic look. The anger in his heart melted into worry.

"I am sorry, Jewel," Arianna said. "I thought you might see clues to who you are. I never dreamed you would relive... I am sorry."

Jewel was barely aware that Sebastian slowly rocked her back and forth in his arms. She was still trembling, but her grip on him loosened somewhat.

The deep voice of the dragon rumbled in the silence. "The necklace you were wearing, Daughter, has the soul of Malnan inside of it. She is the one who saved you from your beating. She brought you to the castle through her magic, knowing you would find sanctuary here."

"My...my necklace saved me?" she asked, raising her head to look at the dragon.

"Malnan saved you," Mynos corrected. "She is my mate."

Jewel's eyes were swimming with unshed tears. "I don't understand."

"I don't think any of us do," Arianna said, shaking her head. "Have you ever heard of Evendria?"

Closing her eyes, Jewel concentrated on the word, trying to find anything in her mind that might be familiar with it. But all she saw were the fists, the boots, and the pain. The horrible pain.

Crying out again as the vision once more bubbled to the surface, she clutched Sebastian with renewed vigor, making him hold her tighter.

"All I see..." she said brokenly, "are the fists...and the pain."

"I think we should let her rest this evening." Mynos stood and made his way to the door. "She has been through enough already." Arianna and Geoffrey followed him out.

"Good night, Jewel. Sleep well," Arianna said, a pang of sorrow in her voice. She silently shut the door, leaving Sebastian and Jewel alone in the room.

Jewel had no idea how long Sebastian sat there on the floor holding her. She was so warm and comfortable, she didn't want to leave his shelter. When she finally tried to pull away,

Sebastian stopped her and held her tighter, somehow knowing she was only leaving his embrace for his sake.

"Bastian, I—"

"I will hold you, my lady Jewel, until I am satisfied you are all right," he said in a tone she didn't dare argue with.

She relented and sat on his lap, on the floor of her room, holding him close. Giving in to exhaustion, Jewel sighed and closed her eyes, tucking her head underneath Sebastian's chin. It wasn't long before sleep overtook her.

Chapter Eleven

Opening her eyes, Jewel found she was in bed. *How did I get here?* The last thing she remembered was Sebastian holding her, his warmth surrounding her and his gentle voice telling her everything was going to be all right. At some point in the night, he must have laid her in the bed and tucked her in.

Looking across the room, Jewel noticed with surprise that her blue dress from the day before was hanging across the back of an overstuffed chair by the fireplace. She didn't remember taking it off. Rather, she didn't remember *Sebastian* taking it off. He must have, because she lay in the bed with nothing more than her silk chemise covering her.

A blush suddenly stole up her cheeks at the thought of Sebastian undressing her for bed. Rolling over, she half expected to see him lying next to her, but what she *did* see brought a warm glow to her heart and fresh tears to her eyes.

Lying on her pillow was another lavender carnation.

Jewel lifted it lovingly off the pillow and brought it to her face. Its intoxicating fragrance filled her with an overwhelming urge to find Sebastian and melt in his arms.

Jumping out of bed, Jewel placed the bloom in the vase with the first flower. Smiling at them both, she knew she was in love with Sebastian. It hadn't taken long, but there was no point in denying it. He was all her heart longed for, all she knew of herself. She knew he would stand by her no matter what she had to face, last night had proven that. Even the thought that he'd seen her barely clothed didn't embarrass her. She wanted to share everything with him.

Choosing an ivory gown, she dressed quickly, weaving her hair into a single braid down her back. Gazing at the purple carnations, Jewel grabbed one of them and tucked it behind her right ear. She looked at her reflection in the mirror and noticed the flower did indeed match her eyes to perfection—as Sebastian had said. She had no doubt he would know she cared for him by wearing his gift in public.

Satisfied, Jewel left the quiet room to find her angel.

ဆာဆာ

Jewel didn't know what she was going to say when she found Sebastian. But inspiration struck, and she knew what she wanted only at that very moment. She wanted to give to Sebastian the tenderness and the joy he had given her. This time she wouldn't take no for an answer.

It wasn't hard to find him. Sir Sebastian of Tabrinth, the Captain of the Guard, was hard at work in the bailey of the castle, barking orders and reading reports from his men. He stood with his dark head bent over the papers spread upon a wooden table on the far side of the courtyard, and she remembered him holding her well into the night. She also recalled his fiery kisses and his lazy smiles. Jewel stopped in her tracks and admired him as he worked, unaware she was watching him.

Her heart raced as she once again walked purposefully toward him. She was halfway to him when he turned and saw her. He noticed almost immediately that she was wearing his

flower and the smile he gave her was nothing short of magnificent. Jewel's heart skipped a beat and she almost faltered, but she found the strength in her weak limbs to keep walking toward him.

She was almost upon him when he started to say, "My lady Jewel—" but that was as far as he got. Jewel strode determinedly up to him, cupped his face in her hands and kissed his lips fervently. He was startled at first and even let out a small but futile protest before his arms finally curled around her in acceptance. Jewel vaguely heard a few hoots and hollers from the men around them, but she focused all her attention on him. Her kiss was full of promise, full of things to come.

When she finally pulled back, she could see the passion in his eyes lingering just underneath the surface. Jewel traced his lips with her fingers. "Meet me at the pond in an hour, Bastian."

He seemed as if he was going to argue with her, but she covered his mouth with hers once again. "Say yes," she breathed in his ear as she rose up on her toes. He didn't answer her right away, but closed his eyes and trembled.

Getting bolder, she kissed his cheek, blazing a trail down to his neck. "If you prefer," she said through her kisses, "I'll make love to you right here on this table in front of everyone."

He gasped in response and she smiled.

"Why are you doing this?" he asked in an agonized voice.

"Isn't it obvious why?" She kissed his neck and the underside of his jaw.

"Jewel..." he began, but she once again stopped him with her mouth.

"Say yes, Bastian," she murmured against his lips. "Please don't make me beg."

Sebastian raised his head from hers. "Yes," he finally croaked.

Giving him one more dizzying kiss, Jewel said, "One hour. I'll be waiting for you."

With that, she wiggled from his arms and walked away from him, leaving Sebastian to watch her in awe with his mouth wide open.

ಬಿ೫೦೦೩

As Jewel rode to the pond, she began to have second thoughts. Was she being too bold? Was she doing the right thing? Nervously, she gripped the reins of the dappled mare and wondered what Sebastian must think of her.

And she had thought taking his hand in the hallway had been bold? This was practically screaming for the man to make love to her! But she couldn't stop now; she wanted it too much—wanted him too much.

Jewel found herself not caring at all about her former life. Sebastian had been apprehensive there might be another man waiting for her. She was sure she wasn't married, so where did that leave her? Perhaps with a suitor? If that were the case, then why couldn't she spend time with Sebastian? What made him different than any other suitor who would be competing for her attentions?

She supposed the vision of her beating had been the deciding factor, proving to her she didn't *want* to return to her other life. Jewel refused to believe she might simply have been beaten by thieves looking for coin. She had still been in possession of the gold necklace when she'd been found, but of course Mynos had told her she'd been saved before she was beaten to death.

It all meant nothing, of course, as Jewel didn't plan to return, regardless of what anyone found out about her. Sebastian had said every Wolverine at the castle would honor her decision.

She was staying with him.

Jewel entered the clearing and dismounted. Her hands shook as she tied up her horse and unbuttoned her dress. If Sebastian did come, which she was sure he would, she didn't want to give him a chance to argue. She laid the gown and her silk chemise across the large boulder so he wouldn't be able to miss them when he arrived.

Slipping into the water, Jewel gasped at the delicious feeling of it against her bare skin—cool, but not too cold. Unbraiding her hair, she washed it as best she could with no soap. Taking a deep breath, she shivered in the water and waited.

Chapter Twelve

Sebastian was late. He couldn't believe how hard it was to get out of the courtyard within an hour. Men seemed to come from everywhere needing his opinion, his instruction, his signature... By the time he was able to break away, he kicked Blaze into a gallop, sure Jewel would no longer be waiting. The powerful stallion galloped through the main gates of the castle as if the devil himself were on his tail.

Still in a state of shock, Sebastian was unable to remember much of the morning after Jewel had come to him. A woman had never talked so brazenly to him. And it wasn't just any woman—it was Jewel, the woman who plagued his dreams at night. He would move heaven and earth if she only asked.

After riding his horse like a madman, he forced the animal to a slower gait, weaving through the trees on the path to the pond. He wanted to call out Jewel's name just to make sure she answered him. She might no longer be there.

But as he broke through the trees, he saw her, totally oblivious to him, swimming lazily through the water. His eyes widened at her gown draped across the boulder and once again his mouth hung open. Her bare shoulders peeked out of the water with each stroke she took, and he dared not look away as he quietly dismounted.

She was a nymph, a water sprite, unaware of her unearthly beauty.

For several long moments, Sebastian merely watched her on the shore until his horse snorted, getting her attention. Jewel spotted him and gave a startled cry.

Relief poured through her at that moment. She was beginning to believe he wouldn't come, that she'd made herself a fool by kissing him in front of the entire Wolverine Order.

The pond wasn't so deep that she couldn't stand on the bottom, so she planted her feet and crossed her bare arms in front of her in a pose of mock anger.

"You're late."

"I'm sorry," he answered. "I sometimes wonder how the castle manages to continue standing. I tried like hell to get here as fast as I could."

After a few silent moments of staring at each other, Jewel said, "Come here, Bastian."

"In the water?"

She nodded, looking at him through wet eyelashes.

"But I've still got my clothes on," he protested.

She gestured to the boulder. "Put them next to mine." He was blushing. She smiled.

"Shouldn't we talk first?" he asked.

"About?"

"About who—or what—may be waiting for you."

"I'm not married, Bastian, I am sure of that. If I have a suitor, what makes you any different than him?"

Sebastian didn't answer. She knew it was his fear of the unknown holding him back.

"Come here." She beckoned again.

"But..."

"Bastian, if you don't come here right now, I'm going to come get you, and your clothing will be hopelessly soaked."

He didn't move at first. Jewel heaved a sigh and began to walk forward.

"Wait!" he snapped. With quick jerky movements, he unstrapped his sword from his waist and laid it against the boulder. He leaned against the rock to remove his boots.

Jewel watched him as he yanked his shirt from his breeches, lifting it effortlessly over his head. *My God*, she thought. He was breathtaking. She had wondered what he would look like bare-chested. What she saw amazed her. Dark hair covered his chest and made its way down his flat belly. His muscles bunched and played underneath his skin and she yearned to put her hands on them. He was perfection personified. She would never tire of looking at him. When he finally took off his breeches, Jewel turned the other way when she heard them fall to the ground.

"*Now* you're shy?" he teased before jumping into the water, making a large splash. He was completely underneath the surface and Jewel couldn't find him. Something brushed her leg and she cried out in both fright and glee. She realized Sebastian's hands were on her calves.

As they worked their way up, so did his mouth, kissing her bare belly below the water line. It tickled and she tried to pull away, but his strong hands stopped her.

His head finally broke the water as he stood, kissing her bare flesh the whole way. Jewel shivered, but not from the cold water. As he pulled away from her, his wet hair was plastered on his face. He snapped his head back in that familiar way, sending beads of water showering down on her. She giggled and flinched.

Sebastian grinned, a boyish grin that reached straight to her heart. While he gazed at her, his hands never stopped their exploration as he touched her in places she was sure no man had ever done before. Jewel held onto his arms, for support more than anything. Having this gorgeous man in front of her was almost more than her knees could take.

Deciding to be bold once again, Jewel glided her hands over his arms and down his chest, touching him as she had dreamed about doing only moments ago. He closed his eyes, seeming to savor the feeling of her fingers on his skin.

"I must confess," he said abruptly, making her jump at the sound of his voice, "you've been invading my thoughts ever since I found you."

Jewel slid her hands up and down his large frame, feeling him shudder at her touch. "And I must confess," she whispered, leaning in closer to him to lick drops of water from his shoulders, "that you've been invading my thoughts ever since you found me."

His arms tightened around her as he lowered his head and sucked the moisture off her shoulder as well. Sebastian's mouth was hot on her skin and his teeth raked across her rapidly beating pulse.

"You taste good..." he moaned into her neck.

"Bastian," she said hoarsely, "I...I don't know what to do. Show me what to do."

Lifting his face to hers, he gave her a tender kiss and said, "Put your legs around me."

She looked at him in confusion but he held her close. "Trust me."

With his help, she locked her legs around his waist. He waded through the water until her back was against the large boulder. When he was sure she was secure, he leaned closer, pressing his entire body length flush with hers, molding himself to her as he took her mouth with a sudden, surprising passion.

She answered him back with her own desire, teasing him with her tongue.

"Good God, you are so beautiful," he murmured as his mouth moved to her ear.

Jewel chuckled, sliding her fingers into his unruly wet hair. "It seems we think alike, you and I." She relished the feeling of his body moving erotically against hers.

He growled at her words as he unwound her hands from his hair, lacing his fingers with hers. He pressed them back against the boulder on either side of her head. The simple gesture of having both her hands entwined with his seemed, at that moment, the most intimate and natural thing to do.

"Are you ready?" he panted.

"More than you know."

"It might hurt."

"I don't care." Jewel kissed him thoroughly, urging him to continue.

A swift pain shuddered through her as Sebastian joined his body with hers. His mouth caught her cry of pain and he didn't move as he kissed her again and again, as if apologizing for it. But the pain was soon ebbing and Jewel began to marvel at the feel of him filling her so completely.

Sebastian lifted his head, a stunning smile of triumph on his face. "You are a virgin!"

Jewel found his statement amusing, and she gave him a small chuckle. "You thought I wouldn't be?"

"I allowed for the possibility," he admitted.

"Then why are you so happy?"

"Because it means you are *mine* and mine alone, my lady Jewel."

That statement was so possessive, Jewel almost melted in his arms. Never again would he call her *my lady* and not mean exactly that.

He moved again, making Jewel gasp and bite her lip. Ever so slowly, he showed her just how a man loves a woman. He let go of her hands and resumed his exploration of her body as he moved against her. Jewel's hands flew all over him, urging him, pushing him, trying to get him to move faster. But he kept his slow pace, building up the tension inside her.

She couldn't stand it any longer, crying his name and tossing back her head. The world fell away all around her as the culmination of her passion took her to heights she couldn't even fathom. Sebastian seemed to be waiting for her. The moment she clutched him closer and called his name, she felt him shudder and call hers right back.

Both panted for long moments, Jewel's head leaning back against the rock, Sebastian's head nestled between her breasts. She didn't want to break the intimate contact they had.

"That was... That was..." Jewel breathed, trying to find the right words.

"Amazing?" he finished for her.

"More like earth-shattering, but amazing will do," she teased as he grinned at her.

A few moments of silence passed before Sebastian looked up at the sky. "It's a beautifully warm day," he said. "Whenever I come here to swim by myself, I dry myself on the boulder in the sun and watch the clouds float by."

Jewel closed her eyes at the thought. "Sounds delightful."

Sebastian pulled away, making her groan in protest. "Come on!" He grasped her hand and began tugging her from the pond.

"I'll be cold!" she squawked, trying to pull away from him.

He returned to her, a devilish gleam in his eye. "No you won't."

She had to smile at him, loving his playful nature, and let him lead her out of the water. The instant the air hit her wet skin, she shivered from head to toe.

But as he laid her on the boulder—its surface already warmed by the sun—he lay down on top of her and all thoughts of being cold vanished. His elbows rested on either side of her head as he settled between her legs.

Jewel pulled his head down to hers and teased his lips with her teeth. "Make love to me again, Bastian."

Sebastian grinned and ran his tongue along her neck, and lower still, to explore with his mouth where his hands had once been.

"Your wish is my command, my lady Jewel."

Chapter Thirteen

"I sent a runner to Evendria this morning," Sebastian said, stroking the damp, dark hair spread out upon his chest.

Jewel didn't answer immediately, but continued her soft caress along his arm. She lay holding him tenderly, the fires of passion significantly sated for the time being. Giving his chest one soft kiss, she lifted her head to look at him.

"I'm not going back."

"Jewel..."

"No," she said, sitting up. "I don't care what life I had before, I'm not leaving the castle." *I'm not leaving you*, she wanted to say.

Sebastian cupped her cheek. "You don't know the circumstances surrounding your beating. You could have family who are worried sick!"

"I know," she conceded. "I'm just so afraid of what I'm going to find."

Pulling her back down once again, Sebastian kissed her cheek. "I will be with you every step of the way, my lady Jewel. Whoever harmed you will be made to meet justice, mark my words. But not before I give him a taste of what you felt."

Jewel glanced up at him and noticed the hardened lines of his face as his grip tightened. She kissed his chest again, immediately bringing him out of his anger. He watched what she was doing with a gleam in his eye.

"When do you have to go back?" she purred, kissing a trail down his belly.

He smiled wickedly at her and answered, "Whenever you're through with me."

"Then, my lord Bastian," she teased, "we will stay here for the rest of our lives. I will never tire of you."

Sebastian chuckled and lifted her to fully straddle him. Jewel gasped as he found her warmth easily. She gazed down at his face with a grin.

"Nor I of you," he confessed. Gazing into her eyes, he began to love her once again.

ഇ⊱⊰ൽ

It was late afternoon before Jewel and Sebastian made their way back to the castle. Sir Geoffrey greeted them at the castle gates, still on duty after a long day. He gave Sebastian a stern look as they dismounted, crossing his arms over his chest.

"Where have you been?"

Sebastian threw a knowing glance to Jewel who blushed and turned away. "Having fun." He grinned.

"Indeed," Geoffrey said sourly, looking from Jewel back to Sebastian. "While you were gone, I had to cover for you and I swear I didn't get a moment's peace!"

"Why do you think I left?" Sebastian laughed, crossing his own arms and returning Geoffrey's annoyed look.

"A simple thank you would suffice," Geoffrey grumbled, tapping the ground with an impatient foot.

To Sebastian's surprise, Jewel stood on her toes to kiss Geoffrey on the cheek. "Thank you, Sir Geoffrey."

At that moment, Geoffrey laughed so hard a few passing Wolverines turned their heads to see what was so funny.

"Ah, it was worth it just for that!" he said happily.

Jewel chanced a glance at Sebastian who smiled at her and winked as well. "Indeed."

"Giving away free kisses today?" a familiar voice said from behind them. Ethan walked up, looking only at Jewel. He bowed low. "If that is true, milady, I'm all yours."

Jewel had to laugh at the murderous glare Sebastian gave him as Ethan pushed his way past him to grab her hand. Ethan lifted her hand to his lips, but before he kissed it, he suddenly yanked her forward, making Jewel fall against him before she could stop herself. She felt his lips on hers for only a moment before he was pulled roughly away from her.

The sound of a solid punch echoed through the courtyard as Ethan fell hard on his back, gingerly rubbing his jaw. Sebastian stood over him. "If you value your life, Sir Ethan, you will never do that again."

Ethan looked up at him and back to Jewel, a slow grin spreading on his face. "I had to try."

"Apologize to the lady," Sebastian growled.

"I am sorry, milady," Ethan said through his grin, spreading his hands wide. "If you would be so kind as to help me up?"

Jewel moved to offer her hand, but Sebastian held her gently back. "Pick yourself up, Sir Ethan. Jewel has better things to do."

Ethan's bark of laughter followed them as Sebastian grabbed her hand and led her toward the castle.

"Does he do that on purpose?" Jewel asked.

Sebastian scowled darkly. "Ethan finds joy in testing my limits, my lady Jewel."

"Is that why he kissed me?"

"He kissed you to see if I would allow it. He thinks to have a little sport chasing after you at my expense. Best if you keep your door locked from now on."

Jewel sighed dramatically. In a small voice, she said, "He won't think to look for me in *your* chambers."

Sebastian stopped in mid-step at her comment, then laughed out loud. "No, I suppose he wouldn't."

ༀ⁊ༀ⁊

Geoffrey was finishing his duties for the day when he felt a twinge of pain through his Remembrance bond. His thoughts immediately flew to Arianna.

"Are you all right?" he thought to her.

It was a moment before his wife answered through her pain. *"No,"* came her labored reply.

"What's wrong?" He briskly left the courtyard.

"Geoffrey," she gasped in his head. *"It's the baby. Oh God, Geoffrey, something's wrong with the baby!"*

Without another word, he broke into a run.

Chapter Fourteen

Sebastian and Jewel were halfway up the grand staircase when Geoffrey ran past them, taking the stairs three at a time.

"Sebastian, get the dragon!" he yelled at them before he disappeared down the hallway.

It only took a moment to register those words before Sebastian turned to run back down the stairs. He didn't get very far before Mynos himself sprinted through the hall and up the steps after Geoffrey.

"What is going on?" Sebastian exclaimed as Mynos passed them without a glance.

"It's Arianna. Her baby is in trouble!"

Jewel gave Sebastian a shocked glance before they both ran up the stairs after the dragon.

They heard Arianna screaming down the hall before they reached her room in the royal apartments. Her door was open wide.

Sebastian saw the scene before Jewel and tried to hold her back, but she caught a glimpse of it regardless.

Arianna was in bed, the blanket covering her as if she had been napping, yet the fine quilt was covered in blood. Arianna shrieked and Jewel had to force down her own screams as she turned away.

"Oh God. Oh God!" Geoffrey cried as he cradled his wife's head. "Can you help her, Mynos? Can you save our baby?" Tears sprang in his eyes as he pleaded with the dragon, his voice tortured.

Mynos closed his eyes and concentrated for a moment before he shook his head sadly. "I cannot stop it, Sir Geoffrey," he whispered. "Your daughter will be stillborn."

Arianna wailed at his words and looked wildly at her husband.

"I tried to stop it, Geoffrey. I tried. I felt her leaving me, and I tried to follow her, but the pain began. I couldn't concentrate with the pain... Now I can't find her, Geoffrey. I can't find her!"

They cried together as Arianna braced for another painful contraction. Mynos came to the side of the bed and calmed her with his magic.

Sebastian strode into the room, tugging frantically on the bell-pull to bring help. Jewel stood in the doorway, tears falling unchecked down her cheeks.

"I couldn't save her..." Arianna continued to moan as Geoffrey held her close.

"Don't worry, Rose, we'll get through this," he breathed, stroking her hair, his own cheeks wet as he drew a ragged breath.

"Geoffrey..." she cried brokenly. "I'm so sorry. I'm so sorry I couldn't save our daughter."

"Shh." He kissed her temple, unshed tears shimmering in his eyes. "You did all you could."

A few moments later, two maids rushed into the room and gasped at the sight. They stood in shock before Sebastian put his command to good use.

"You there, get some rags, clean linens, and new clothing for Lady Arianna! And you, get some hot water and summon the midwife. Now!"

The maids flew from the room without another word. Geoffrey gazed at his friend and gave him a look of thanks through his tears.

Once the midwife arrived, she shooed everyone out, except Geoffrey and the dragon.

"Will she be all right?" Jewel asked in a small voice as they stood in the hall, staring at the closed door.

Sebastian drew her into his embrace. "I hope so."

Taking her hand, he led her quietly back down the hall. A wave of sympathy washed over Jewel. She could only imagine what it must feel like to lose the baby you've been waiting for. Without a word, Sebastian finally stopped and opened a door for her to walk through.

It was evening now, the soft light of dusk just barely peeking through the window as he lit a few candles from the glowing embers of the fireplace. Sebastian must have taken her to his chamber.

When he finished lighting the candles, he turned to look at her. "Are you hungry?"

Despite the fact she hadn't eaten all day, the thought of food turned her stomach. She couldn't bear the thought of eating now—not when Sir Geoffrey and Lady Arianna had just lost their child. She shook her head in answer, afraid that if she answered him aloud, she'd cry once more.

Jewel lay on Sebastian's bed and gazed at the ceiling as the shadows from the room danced in the candlelight. The bed dipped and she knew Sebastian reclined next to her. She rolled into his warmth for comfort.

The silence stretched for long moments as they held each other.

"Bastian?"

"Yes, my lady Jewel?" he replied, kissing the top of her head.

"What did Arianna mean when she said she tried to follow her daughter?"

Sebastian drew a deep breath as if getting ready to tell a long story. Instead, he simply murmured, "She tried to follow her into death's domain to bring her back."

"But that's not possible!" Jewel gasped.

"She's done it before. She brought Geoffrey himself back from the brink of death through the power of the Crystal of Mynos, a feat no other mage has ever done."

"Geoffrey *died*?" Jewel's heart stopped.

"Yes. A Dark Knight of Darragh had given him a mortal wound through his belly and he fell the day they defeated the queen. Arianna was determined to bring him back or die trying, and she succeeded in finding him within the shadows of death. He still bears the mark of the Crystal where it was laid on his chest. I can only assume this is what she meant by those words. She had tried to do the same with her daughter, but was unable to find her spirit to bring her back."

"How horrible!"

It seemed forever that they lay together before Sebastian sat up and unbuckled his sword. He also kicked off his boots and helped Jewel take off her shoes. She pulled the blanket from underneath her and they both crawled into the linens.

Jewel smiled, snuggling closer to him, content just to sleep. His protective arm curled around her and within moments, she was dreaming.

She saw his eyes first, deep-set and blacker than night, gazing at her with a look of hatred combined with lust. His cruel, smiling mouth was next, his hideous laughter echoing around her. A thick shock of curly brown hair topped his head until finally, she saw his complete face.

"Do you honestly think you can defy me, girl? I have your father's blessing to do as I please. It is not wise to talk to me so."

"I hate the very ground you walk upon! I will die before I become your wife," she screamed back.

His foot suddenly slammed into her belly as she lay prone on the floor. She couldn't take a breath to save her life.

"You speak the truth then," he said cruelly. "For you will die right here if you deny me much longer."

He kicked her again and again, and she heard her ribs crack with the force. She tried to scream.

Jewel felt herself being shaken roughly. "Wake up. Wake up, my lady Jewel!"

With a cry, Jewel opened her eyes to see Sebastian above her, grasping her shoulders. Her heart thundered and her eyes were wet with tears. She couldn't catch her breath as she gazed at him in horror.

Sebastian lowered himself until his face was inches from her. "What is it?" His breath caressed her cheek.

"I saw... I saw his face, Bastian," she cried. She trembled violently.

Sebastian didn't need to ask whom she was talking about. He calmed her by kissing her cheeks, her forehead, and her eyes. "You are safe," he whispered before kissing her lips.

Jewel hugged him until her breathing returned to normal.

"Do you remember anything else?" he asked.

"He was kicking me. I heard my ribs... I heard them." She began to cry again, but Sebastian stroked her face, calming her once more. "I think he was trying to force me...to marry him."

Sebastian tensed at that admission. "Are you certain?"

Jewel bit her lower lip and nodded.

"Then we must make sure it will never happen." Such vehemence filled his voice, Jewel felt a touch of fear once again.

Sebastian sighed as he put his forehead on hers. "Perhaps sending a runner to Evendria wasn't such a good idea."

"What are we going to do, Bastian?"

"I don't know, sweetheart," he said affectionately. "But I *do* know that bastard will not take you away from me."

Their eyes locked and Jewel found herself in shock at such a possessive statement. Before she could say another word, his mouth was on hers, passionate and tender. She was lost in his kiss, answering his tongue with her own, trying to pull him closer to her.

She had no idea how her gown ended up on the floor or where Sebastian's tunic had gone, but she didn't care. He was loving her, soothing her fears and telling her without words she belonged to him.

"Don't let me go, Bastian," she pleaded into his ear, her breath catching. He leaned up to look at her with his beautiful blue eyes, entering her slowly, watching her all the while as he moved slow and steady against her.

"Never," he whispered. "Never, my lady Jewel."

Chapter Fifteen

As the days passed, Jewel became more and more apprehensive. The runner was expected to return from Evendria at any time. More often than not, she paced in her chambers, the door locked at Sebastian's insistence. Neither one truly believed Ethan would force himself on her, but it was a chance Sebastian wasn't willing to take.

"I've known him for years," he told her one morning when they had awoken in his chambers. "He loves women and I doubt he will ever hurt you. But Ethan is a prankster, and it's best if we avoid him at all costs."

"A prankster?" Jewel smiled.

"To the extreme," Sebastian answered, a twinkle in his eye. "It wouldn't be beyond him to stroll into your chambers without knocking, especially if he knew you had just ordered a bath."

Jewel gasped, then laughed at the thought. "He wouldn't!"

"He would." Sebastian chuckled along with her. "Sir Ethan is a good man and an even better Wolverine. But he has no tact, and he absolutely does not know when to quit."

"Then I'll be sure to bolt my door and brace it even further with my wardrobe."

Sebastian laughed at the thought of his lovely Jewel trying in vain to push the heavy wardrobe in front of the door.

"Now let's not be too hasty," he said through his grin. "How am I supposed to get in?"

"I have a window, don't I?" she asked flippantly, as if Sebastian were daft for not thinking of it. He stared at her in disbelief before laughing anew, delighted at Jewel's wit.

The days that followed, however, were sorrowful. Geoffrey and Arianna buried their daughter in the cemetery behind the castle near the grave of Geoffrey's own father. The midwife insisted Arianna stay in bed for at least two weeks, but Arianna had demanded to be present when her daughter was laid to rest.

Geoffrey held Arianna cradled in his arms the entire time.

Sebastian watched as Arianna gave the Crystal back to the dragon, practically throwing it at him to be rid of it. Mynos had once told her the Crystal's strong power was what kept her from getting pregnant all these years. Arianna claimed it was the Crystal's power that also made her lose her precious little girl.

She vowed then and there never to touch it again.

ဆဝၵ

Jewel's nightmares continued. Each night she had a similar dream, but each dream was slightly different. More and more of the man's face came into focus. She remembered feeling dread, knowing something wasn't right. She was scared of the man, of that she was sure. She had been scared of him even before he laid a hand on her.

One night, she dreamt of her necklace, of the beautiful lavender Jewel flaring to life and a strange tingling sensation, even as the horrid man continued to kick her unmercifully. For a moment, she felt weightless as a loud buzzing filled her head.

Could she be remembering the moment when Malnan had saved her?

And then, *grass.* She remembered grass of all things. As she thought of her dream while pacing her room, grass suddenly made sense. Sebastian and Duncan had found her on the fields surrounding the castle. Malnan had told Mynos she'd brought her to the castle to help her. Could Malnan have magically transported her somehow? She must have.

A single loud knock suddenly sounded on her door, followed by three soft raps, the knock they had decided on when Sebastian wanted to visit her. Smiling, Jewel pulled the bolt and opened the door for him, flying into his arms before he walked over the threshold.

"Where have you been, Bastian?" she cried, scolding him while she rained kisses on his face. "I thought you were going to visit me this morning."

Holding her loosely, he said, "I'm sorry, my lady Jewel. I couldn't break away, even for a few minutes."

Taking a step back, Jewel saw the tense look on his face and the stiffness of his body. "What's wrong?"

"The runner has returned."

It had been a week since Sebastian sent the runner to Evendria. Jewel knew this day would come, but she had hoped it never would. The past week had been wonderful with Sebastian. He wasn't able to spend much time with her during the day, but the nights were hers alone. She wished she could live like that forever.

"What has he said?" she asked. She stumbled back into the room.

"He says..." Sebastian began, but his voice cracked, making Jewel's breath hitch in her throat. "He says you resemble the betrothed of a man named Lord Merric of Westchester. A woman who disappeared mysteriously on her wedding day."

Tears sprang in her own eyes as he spoke, almost confirming her own bad dreams.

"There's more." He led Jewel to sit down.

As soon as she sat, he knelt before her, both her hands in his. He closed his eyes and sighed before he continued, squeezing Jewel's hands, frightening her all the more.

"What, Bastian? What is it?" A tear fell down her cheek.

"Lord Merric has decided to come to the castle to see for himself if you are indeed his betrothed. If so, he intends to take you back to Evendria as his bride."

Jewel gasped and gazed at Sebastian with such fear and sorrow, it broke his heart. She squeezed her eyes shut making more drops fall from her black lashes.

"It's him, Bastian, it has to be," she moaned through her sobs. "I cannot go with him!"

"Jewel, I want you to be sure it's him. I've brought the runner with me to talk to you. He's waiting in the hall. He can describe to you this Lord Merric to see if he fits the man in your memories."

Sebastian moved to stand, but noticed Jewel trembling violently. Taking her face in his hands, he kissed her to calm her, something he'd learned seemed to soothe her every time.

Jewel still trembled, but her breathing no longer came in ragged gasps. "Send him in," she whispered.

The runner was young, younger than Jewel would have supposed. He seemed to have barely seen eighteen winters as he shuffled into the room. He was still grimy from the road, the dirt and sweat caked on him from hard riding.

"My lady." He bowed as he stopped in front of her chair.

"This is Devon," Sebastian explained.

"Hello, Devon." Jewel took a deep breath before she continued. "Can you tell me anything about the man you spoke with in Evendria?"

"Oh yes, milady," he said. "He was perhaps thirty, and tall, with brown curly hair. His eyes were very dark, almost black if you looked hard enough. He didn't have a beard, but he seemed downright happy to hear about you."

Jewel stared in shock as the runner described the man in her dreams. The runner continued. "You fit the exact description he gave me of his betrothed, who disappeared on the day of her wedding. He said he was very heartbroken to hear of his lady suddenly vanishing with no one knowing where she had gone. He had assumed she'd been kidnapped, as running away wasn't an option for her."

"He said she was willing?" Sebastian cut in.

"Most willing, Sir," Devon said with a smile. "Lord Merric made it sound as if they were inseparable lovebirds."

"What about the scar?" Jewel asked softly without looking up from her lap.

"The scar?" Sebastian asked, confused.

"Yes. I had another dream last night. I saw a scar on his face, next to his left eye. It was small, but deep, and shaped like a..."

"Crescent moon," Devon finished for her.

Jewel's face turned into a mask of horror.

"Oh God, it's him!" she yelped as she shot to her feet. Running to the chamber pot, Jewel dropped to her knees and retched out the contents of her stomach.

Chapter Sixteen

Sebastian didn't know what to do. It tore him apart to see Jewel like this, so lethargic and unresponsive. He'd dismissed the runner a few hours ago, yet Jewel merely sat on the floor, staring into the crackling fire without saying a word. He had tried to hold her, kiss her, talk to her, but nothing seemed to work.

He settled for sitting behind her with his arms wrapped around her, content to be there for as long as it took before she'd talk to him of her own accord. Resting his cheek on her shoulder, he was so comfortable holding her, that he almost nodded off before an idea struck him. His unexpected movement as he jerked finally got Jewel's attention.

"Sebastian?" She was hesitant, as if recognizing he was with her for the first time.

"Are you all right?"

Her chin trembled as she shook her head. "I'm terrified," she whispered, trying to press closer to his warmth.

"I think I might know a way to protect you from Lord Merric." He cupped her cheek in his hand. "Permanently."

A light of hope sprang into her eyes at his words. "What, Bastian?"

He swallowed hard before he said it, only just realizing that he, too, trembled. "You can marry me." He looked away from her, too embarrassed to meet her eyes.

"Are you serious?" she asked in a quiet voice.

"I told you he wouldn't take you from me, my lady Jewel." His eyes met hers once again.

Jewel saw a fierce determination in his face as his arms pulled her closer to him. She stared, amazed at what he'd said and taken in by his beauty once more. His blue eyes were dark, looking intensely at her. Did he know what she was thinking? As always, that dark brown lock of hair was in his face but he didn't seem to care. Jewel smoothed his hair back, then slid her hand down his cheek to feel his day-old stubble scratch her palm.

"You would do that for me?" she asked in wonder. He wanted to marry her. But why? Was it only to save her from Lord Merric? Was it possible he might love her as well?

"Jewel," he said, "you were tortured by a man almost to the point of death. No woman deserves such a husband. If I can save you from a life of hell, I will do everything in my power to do just that."

Glancing away from him, Jewel hid her disappointment. There was no declaration of love, no confession of any deeper feelings other than his protection. Did she think there would be? He had been interested in her, indeed there was that. And making love to him had been the most wonderful thing she'd ever experienced. Certainly marriage to Sir Sebastian of Tabrinth would be most pleasant. But would she be able to have a marriage of convenience? She would love him, but would he ever love her? It was Jewel who had enticed him to make love to her in the first place, practically begging him to do so. It seemed as if he'd been most willing, but how soon would you tire of the deed if you did not love your partner?

"He is still coming to Castle Templestone, Bastian," she reminded him. "He is traveling here to collect me. If he beat me for not wanting to marry him, then what will he do when he finds I've married another?"

"He will never touch you again, my lady Jewel." Sebastian combed her hair with his fingers. "As my wife, you will not only be protected by me, but you will have all the swords of King Brennan's Wolverines behind you as the Lady Jewel of Tabrinth, wife of the Captain of the Guard. You have *nothing* to fear."

Jewel's eyes filled with unshed tears. She wanted to tell him so badly that she loved him, but hesitated. She couldn't bear it if he said nothing in return. But he was offering her the rest of his life—as his wife. Jewel knew she would never be able to live without him.

Leaning into his embrace, she kissed his lips. It was a chaste, but passionate kiss as Jewel framed his face in her hands, trying desperately to tell him without words how she felt. She looked into his eyes once again.

I love you, Sebastian! she shouted in her head, hoping he'd be able to see it in her eyes.

"Yes, Bastian. Yes, I will marry you." She stroked his face with her thumbs. He had no time to answer before she kissed him again. She didn't want him to change his mind.

Without a word, Sebastian turned her in his lap so her legs straddled his on the floor. Slipping his mouth from hers, he blazed a hot trail to her ear. "It must be tomorrow. We cannot wait."

"Tomorrow?" Jewel groaned with disappointment, nipping playfully at his neck. "Is there not a vicar living in the castle? What's to stop us from marrying tonight?"

Sebastian stopped his kisses to gaze at her in amazement.

"Wouldn't it be wonderful—" she purred, pulling him back to her mouth, "—to make love...as husband and wife?"

While she talked, she touched him everywhere, making him growl in response to her words.

"What do you say?" she muttered against his lips.

Sebastian gently eased her away only to give her a brilliant smile. Clutching her hand, he shot up from the floor and walked briskly out of the room, dragging Jewel along behind him.

Chapter Seventeen

Jewel giggled like a child as she tried in vain to keep up with Sebastian's long strides. He tugged her behind him as they followed the sleepy vicar into the dimly lit chapel. He'd seemed shocked and amazed at Sebastian's request for a wedding this late at night, and had even admonished him to come back in the morning. But Sebastian had stuck his foot in the door before the vicar had a chance to close it in his face and insisted, though none too politely.

The vicar tried to stall him, claiming the need for witnesses, but Sebastian had already found Duncan and Ethan drinking together in the great hall only minutes before. Both men simply gaped at Sebastian when he'd told them his purpose, until Ethan found his tongue.

"*What?*" he yelled in disbelief. "You cannot marry Jewel now. I haven't yet stolen her away from you!" His words were slurred and Jewel had to laugh at the incredulous look on his face.

"Sir Ethan," she implored, taking his hand in hers, "you are a most honorable man, and indeed you may have succeeded in your quest had I not been instructed to lock you out of my room." To this she heard a loud scoff from Sebastian behind her. "But I ask of you now to stand with us as we marry, something that must be done tonight. *Please*, Sir Ethan?"

He looked at her with bleary eyes and winked. "Sebastian has won you according to the Rules of Courtship, sweetheart," he said with humor. "I wouldn't dream of denying you my presence at your wedding, and perhaps I can voice my protests to the vicar."

"No, Ethan, you will forever hold your peace," Sebastian glared at him, seeming to dare him to say more.

Ethan chuckled as he stood. "Shall we?"

As they walked down the aisle, all the while listening to the vicar's grumbling about being out of bed so late at night, Jewel saw Sebastian's hands trembling. He was nervous. Was he having second thoughts? Or was he simply kicking himself for choosing Ethan as a witness? Amazingly, however, Ethan behaved himself. He even seemed happy.

When they bowed at the altar, the vicar said a few prayers and asked them to recite their vows. Before they knew it, he was pronouncing them husband and wife, his words echoing loudly through the empty chapel as he blessed their union.

"You may kiss your bride," the old man said.

Jewel turned to Sebastian, curling her arms around him, giving him a shy smile. Sebastian laughed and scooped her off the ground making her yelp in surprise. Holding her in his arms, he kissed her heartily, drawing a shocked gasp from the vicar.

Both Duncan and Ethan were hooting and clapping him on the back just as Sebastian turned to walk back down the aisle—Jewel still in his arms. Her face flamed at his eagerness to leave the chapel.

"Put me down!" She giggled in his ear as he wandered the halls of the castle, appalling some of the servants on his way.

"And deny you being carried over the threshold, my lady wife?" He gave her his boyish grin that made Jewel's breath catch in her throat.

"Then you'd best hurry, my lord husband." She leaned closer to taste his neck with her mouth. "For I'm eager to get to our marriage bed."

"You keep kissing me like that, and I'll merely find some dark corner to ravage you." He was teasing, yet he increased his pace as he leapt up the grand staircase.

"You think I care where we are?" she whispered, leaning up to suck on his earlobe.

"My God, lady, have a care!" he yelped, bringing a grin to her lips.

"You don't regret marrying me, do you Bastian?" she asked innocently, opening the front of his tunic to caress his bare chest.

"What I regret, *wife*, is that my room is so damned far away from the stairs."

Jewel laughed at his consternation, fully aware of what she was doing to him. When he finally kicked his door open, Jewel had managed to open his tunic all the way and slide it off his shoulders. He only had to put her down for it to slide off his arms completely.

The door slammed behind them as Sebastian crossed quickly to the bed, dropping Jewel on it none too gently. He hesitated only long enough for his tunic to fall to the floor before he pounced on her, claiming her mouth with his fierce passion.

"You will pay for that sweet torture." He tugged her dress up and over her head in one swift movement.

"Promise?" she asked playfully, yanking at the ties to his breeches.

"Most definitely." He gave her a devilish grin, claiming her mouth once again.

৪৩৪০৫৪

The first streaks of dawn tinted the sky before Sebastian and Jewel finally slept. When Jewel awoke a few hours later, sunlight streamed through Sebastian's window. *Goodness, it must be near midday!*

Sebastian lay sleeping soundly, one arm above his head on the pillows, the other curling around Jewel as he held her close. Her legs were tangled with his and she had no intention of pulling away. Lying with him intimately was almost as pleasant as making love with him.

Lightly, so as not to wake him, Jewel kissed his broad chest and rubbed her cheek against him. He was her husband. She still couldn't believe it. However, her reverie was short lived as a loud banging came from the door.

A muffled voice shouted from the other side, "Sir Sebastian!"

Jewel groaned when Sebastian sat up scratching his head sleepily. "Go away!" he yelled back.

The banging continued.

With a growl, Sebastian gave Jewel a quick kiss before he scrambled out of bed to carelessly pull on his breeches. Sebastian ripped the door open with such force, the poor boy on the other side jumped back a few feet.

"What is it, man?" Sebastian barked in annoyance.

Jewel recognized the boy as the same one who had called Sebastian to the battlements after their first ride to the pond. He looked up and saw her in the bed and his eyes widened with shock.

"Out with it, Briand! And stop ogling my wife!"

The poor boy's eyes widened even more and his mouth worked silently, as if he couldn't find the words to speak.

Finally, Briand found the words he was trying to say. "It's…it's Lord Merric, sir! He has arrived!"

Sebastian heard a gasp from the bed.

"You are sure it is him?" he asked the boy in a softer tone.

Briand nodded. "He is currently holding an audience with the king. I was instructed to find Jewel and bring her to him."

"It's 'Lady Jewel' now, Briand," Sebastian corrected, "and she will not be seeing him."

"But sir…"

"Tell the king she is now *my* wife and *my* responsibility. I do not want her to see Lord Merric, therefore, she will not. I have every right to deny him."

"Sir, Lord Merric is most impatient to meet Jewel…*Lady* Jewel, to find out if she is his betrothed."

"It matters not," Sebastian retorted. "She is no longer his concern." In a gentler voice he said, "Go, Briand, and tell the king what I have said. I will be down shortly to meet Lord Merric myself." The boy nodded hesitantly before he ran down the hall. Sebastian closed the door and turned to Jewel who looked like a frightened rabbit clutching the bed sheets under her chin.

"You will stay here." He grabbed his shirt off the floor and shrugged it over his shoulders. "I want you to lock the door and do not answer it unless I give you our secret knock. Is that understood?"

She nodded furiously as she scooted against the wall, her lavender eyes wide with fear. Sebastian sat on the bed in front of her and cupped her cheek in his hand. "He will not hurt you."

"Please be careful, Bastian," she pleaded, flinging herself into his arms. "I couldn't bear it if anything happened to you."

Sebastian kissed her cheek before easing back to gaze into her eyes. "You think his fists are any match for Fleetfire?"

"Fleetfire?" Jewel asked, confused.

Sebastian stood and unsheathed his sword. It began to glow a pale white at the mention of its name. A slight hum sounded in the air as she looked at the weapon.

"It's glowing!"

Sebastian smiled. "The swords of the Wolverines were enchanted by the Crystal of Mynos ages ago. Each sword has a name and each is handed down through the families. Fleetfire was my grandfather's sword, and someday, it will belong to our son."

Their eyes locked as he said the last, and Sebastian saw Jewel's eyes brimming with unshed tears. He'd shocked her with his declaration, and he'd shocked himself. He'd never even considered the possibility of children with Jewel until that very moment.

Sheathing his sword, Sebastian strapped it on his waist and hugged her once again. "I will be back soon. Lock the door." Crossing the room, he opened the door and stepped out into the hall.

Jewel wasted no time, as he heard the bolt slide into place before he turned away.

Chapter Eighteen

King Brennan hated his throne room. It was a huge, ornate room filled with brightly colored tapestries and gaudily gilded thrones on a raised dais, for both himself and his wife, Queen Lily. While his ancestors had been expected to hold their audiences with visiting lords and ladies in the throne room, King Brennan had decided long ago to do away with that tradition. It was too big for his needs—he usually had to shout to the men of his court, for no one dared to assume they could climb the steps of the dais and approach the king.

He was the king of Lyndaria, ruler of the Four Realms and sovereign of Castle Templestone, ally to the ancient dragon Mynos and leader of the Order of the Wolverine; however King Brennan saw himself as merely an ordinary man.

And as an ordinary man, he had demanded in years past to receive his court in his study, a large room with huge windows looking out upon the ocean. He loved watching the waves crashing at the bottom of the cliffs upon which Castle Templestone had been built. His desk was massive, usually overflowing with documents and contracts, which were miraculously kept track of by his overworked steward.

Books filled the shelves that lined every wall, and chairs were everywhere to ensure that even a large party could sit comfortably. In one of those large overstuffed chairs, across from his desk, sat a man whom the king had only just met.

He seemed to be an amiable man, a smooth talker who laughed easily and answered the king's every question. His name was Lord Merric of Westchester, and he was charming indeed. However, his smile now appeared forced. Sir Briand of Breckenwood had just informed Brennan that Jewel would not be receiving Lord Merric due to her late night nuptials to the Captain of the Guard.

King Brennan finally broke the silence. "I did not hear you right, boy. Tell me again why Jewel will not be receiving Lord Merric?"

At that moment, Sebastian entered the room and bowed deeply to his king. "The Lady Jewel of Tabrinth," he announced proudly, "is resting and will not be receiving visitors this morning. She was kept awake rather late into the night, I fear. We didn't go to sleep nigh until dawn."

All eyes were on Sebastian at his audacious words, making Briand sigh with obvious relief. The king dismissed the boy with a wave of his hand. Briand jumped to obey, closing the doors of the study softly behind him.

King Brennan stared at Sebastian for a moment as the man sitting in the chair rose ever so slowly, his face red with unspoken anger.

Sebastian's first glance at Lord Merric confirmed this was indeed the man Jewel had seen in her dreams. Dark curly hair swirled around his head, yet was neatly combed. His eyes were dark coals as he glared at Sebastian. A small white scar near his left eye did indeed resemble a crescent moon. That was all the confirmation Sebastian needed. He glared back at the man, daring him silently to do something, anything, that would make Sebastian draw his sword.

"Sir Sebastian, is it true then? Did you wed Jewel last night?"

"Yes, Your Majesty," he said, never taking his eyes off Lord Merric.

King Brennan sighed. "Sebastian, you know if she was betrothed before she arrived, I can have your marriage annulled and give her back to her proper fiancé."

"You cannot annul the marriage, Your Majesty," Sebastian said with a sly grin. "It has already been consummated. Many times, in fact."

Lord Merric bellowed a foul oath and took a step forward, but composed himself when Sebastian's hand flew to the hilt of his sword.

"Gentlemen, please!" King Brennan held up his hands. "There will be no fighting in my study."

Sebastian removed his hand from the sword hilt, but his body was still tense. He desperately wanted to throw himself at Lord Merric and give him a taste of what Jewel had felt at his mercy.

"You do not even know if Jewel is your betrothed, Lord Merric," Brennan told him. "Until I know the truth of it myself, Sebastian has not overstepped his bounds. If it is proven that he has, the matter will be corrected."

Sebastian looked sharply at the king. "*Corrected?* There is nothing to correct. Jewel is *my* wife and she will stay that way."

King Brennan gave him a haughty glare. "Lord Merric has produced a betrothal contract between himself and his intended's father. It is legal and binding, Sebastian. If Jewel is the woman Lord Merric seeks and you have married her illegally, then restitution must be made, as well as punishment for both you and your lady. Lord Merric has every right to challenge you to the death to win her back."

Sebastian let out a bark of laughter. "He can try."

Merric's eyes widened at the insult and his face grew even redder with rage. But Sebastian couldn't resist one more jab. "Who knows if he'll even be able to fight me? When I fight, it's against men, not defenseless women."

"Consider yourself challenged, you pompous, arrogant..." Lord Merric began.

"*Enough!*" Brennan shouted. "There will be no challenge unless Jewel's identity can be verified. Sebastian, summon your wife."

"I will not! Jewel has had dreams of this man, of his fists and his boots being the ones that beat her. She even described his scar. I have no doubt Jewel is in fact the betrothed of Lord Merric. What I did, I did to save her from him. She will *not* go back to him, Your Majesty, not while I yet live."

King Brennan stood agape at Sebastian. "Sir Sebastian, you try my patience. I expect you to speak freely as my Captain of the Guard. However, I also expect my orders to be obeyed without question. Summon your wife."

Sebastian bowed stiffly to the king and said through gritted teeth, "At once, Sire. But as her husband, I must insist Lord Merric keep his distance regardless of her identity."

The king gave his nod of acquiescence. "Agreed."

Sebastian turned on his heel, leaving the king to deal with the seething lord.

ৠৡৣ

"How dare he talk to me in that way. I demand he be punished!" Lord Merric yelled.

"If he has married your betrothed, he will be, Lord Merric. Until we determine that, you will have to deal with his manner. If Jewel is not your intended, Sebastian will be reprimanded for his behavior."

Merric stood staring at the doors that had slammed shut behind Sebastian. His hands balled into fists. He had no doubt this "Jewel" was his betrothed, for Sebastian's words confirmed it. He knew as well as she did Merric was responsible for her beating, but it didn't matter. He decided then and there to kill the arrogant bastard and reclaim what was his. He had gone easy on her the last time he beat her into submission before she miraculously disappeared from in front of him.

She would not be so lucky the second time around.

Chapter Nineteen

Jewel's heart was in her throat as Sebastian opened the doors to the king's study. She had dressed and braided her hair before Sebastian returned for her, and paced back and forth nervously in his room until she heard his knock at the door. As soon as she opened it, however, the look on his face told her she was to follow him with no objections.

Sebastian seethed with rage. "The king demands your presence, my lady Jewel." He held out his arm to her. "Your identity must be confirmed once and for all."

She knew what this meant. She would meet the man in her nightmares. Jewel clutched Sebastian's arm with a vengeance.

"He will not get near you," he said as he strode through the halls. "Not unless he wants his face rearranged."

Jewel would have chuckled at that remark if she hadn't felt like a lamb being led to the slaughter.

"Stay close to me." He stopped before the study doors. "Remember," he whispered, stroking her worried face, "no matter what happens in there, you will still be my wife."

Jewel pressed her face into his hand and nodded, not trusting herself to speak.

Sebastian turned and opened the doors.

King Brennan looked up from his desk, where he'd been rummaging through piles of paperwork. Lord Merric stood behind him, gazing out the windows to the ocean far below. He turned at the sound of the opening doors and smiled wickedly upon seeing Jewel for the first time.

Sebastian took her hand, pulling her even closer to him.

"My wife, Your Majesty," Sebastian announced when no one spoke.

Lord Merric strode around the desk and stopped a few feet away. Jewel squeezed Sebastian's hand. "It's him!"

"Lady Isabella of Evendria," Merric exclaimed, holding his arms wide as if expecting her to fall into them. "I have found you, my love."

Jewel took a step back and shook her head. "My name is Lady Jewel of Tabrinth."

"No, sweet lady," Merric cooed. "You are my Isabella."

"Isabella might have been my name once, Lord Merric, but it is my name no longer. I am Jewel now, and I belong to Sir Sebastian, my husband."

"Are you Lord Merric's betrothed, Jewel?" the king asked as he stood from his chair.

"I suppose I was, Your Majesty," she answered. "However, he is also the same man who beat me unmercifully for refusing to marry him."

"Your father gave you to me to do with as I pleased. You needed to be persuaded to walk down the aisle, but you conveniently disappeared before we were wed. I know not how you did it, but it's obvious to me you were being satisfied elsewhere." Lord Merric gave Sebastian a damning glare. "I did not beat you, Isabella. I persuaded you, that much is true, but I promised you wealth and trinkets. You were most willing."

Jewel gasped. "You lie! Anyone can attest to the fact I was beaten when Sebastian brought me to the castle."

"Perhaps it was your *lover* who beat you, Isabella. You cannot remember your own name and yet you accuse me of this beating?"

Sebastian released Jewel's hand only long enough to draw his sword, pointing it at Lord Merric. "Confess, you damned liar!"

King Brennan pounded his desk with his fist. "Sir Sebastian, drop your sword."

Lord Merric looked shocked for a split second before he smiled smugly and crossed his arms in front of him. Sebastian still held his sword high.

"Sir Sebastian!" the king bellowed once again.

"Confess, you son of a bitch, or I will run you through right here and now." Sebastian was beyond reasoning and everyone in the room knew it. Jewel tugged at his sword arm, whispering in his ear that now was not the time to kill Merric. King Brennan strode to the double doors and roared down the hall for reinforcements. Lord Merric actually seemed worried as the point of Sebastian's blade drew blood on his neck.

The voice of Jewel broke through his anger and Sebastian finally pulled his sword away from Merric's neck just as four Wolverines ran into the study.

"This is an outrage, Sir Sebastian." King Brennan instructed two of the Wolverines to hold his arms. "Never in my life has one of my men so openly defied me!"

Sebastian ripped his gaze away from Lord Merric to glare at the king. "This man *beat* my wife. I have every right to seek restitution from him."

"Not...in...my...study!" King Brennan's face glowed red. "You have no proof of it. He says he didn't do it. Jewel has no memory of it other than her dreams. No one else is a witness to it. You cannot condemn a man on a dream!"

Sebastian jerked free of the Wolverines holding him. "What is to be my punishment for marrying Jewel, Your Majesty?"

"You will not inherit Jewel's lands in Evendria. Those were handed over to Lord Merric upon signing of the betrothal contract with her father and thus will remain his. This is to also be Jewel's punishment." Jewel nodded to the king when he glanced at her. "Your estates in Tabrinth will also be given over to Lord Merric as payment for this outrageous personal attack upon him."

Sebastian's eyes were glassy and his look darkened, but he said nothing.

"As for your deliberate disobedience to my commands, I hereby strip you of your title as Captain of the Guard." Jewel gasped as the king's words began to sink in.

"Furthermore, until such a time as your accusations can be verified against Lord Merric, you will also be stripped of your title as a Wolverine. If Lord Merric is indeed guilty of beating Jewel and you can prove it, you will be reinstated as one of my knights. If your accusations are proven to be false, then you will be stripped of your title permanently, and no one in your family will be able to reclaim it. Do I make myself clear, Sebastian?"

Jewel felt as if the ground had been pulled out from underneath her. Looking at Sebastian as he nodded to his king, she knew he felt the same. She couldn't stop the tears falling from her eyes and noticed Sebastian had a few of his own as well.

Lord Merric glanced at the king in obvious triumph. "And their marriage will be dissolved, Your Majesty?"

King Brennan turned to Lord Merric and shook his head. "No. Their marriage has been consummated and is therefore legal. You will have to be satisfied with the lands you were awarded, Lord Merric. Jewel will remain Sebastian's wife."

Merric turned his murderous eyes upon Sebastian. Before he stormed out the room, he stopped in front of them, whispering under his breath, "Mark my words, *Wolverine,* I will have Isabella. No matter where you go or what you do, I will find you. I will take your *wife* from you and make you watch as I rape her!"

Sebastian tried to jump on him, but the strong arms of his own men were upon him once again, holding him back. Lord Merric bowed to Jewel and walked out the doors with a look of satisfaction on his face.

Chapter Twenty

Arianna sat straight up in her bed with a gasp. Was it just a dream? No, it was too real to be a dream. She had heard the screams, she had seen the blood—Jewel's blood. Trembling, Arianna looked around the darkened chamber for Geoffrey, but remembered he had been summoned by King Brennan a few hours ago. She sat on the bed for a few moments trying to calm her breathing, then realized there was a low hum in the air.

On the wall above the fireplace, her father's sword, Quicksilver, was glowing a soft white, illuminating the room. Quicksilver hadn't blazed to life since it had slain the dragon Iruindyll three years before. Seeing it glow now made Arianna rub her eyes. Yet still it glowed, as if waiting for her to pull it from the wall.

Swinging her feet off the bed, Arianna stood and walked slowly to the sword, wondering if her dream had anything to do with it suddenly flaring back to life after all these years of silence.

"Quicksilver?" She didn't expect an answer. The sword blazed in its brackets on the wall, chasing the shadows from the room with its glow.

"Daughter!" its ethereal voice suddenly whispered in her head. *"There is danger!"*

Arianna's eyes widened. "What danger?"

"You have dreamt what is to come, Daughter. Sebastian and Jewel must flee!"

Arianna's hand flew to her mouth. The scene of Jewel's bloody dress ripped open and hanging from her body returned to her. She remembered from her dream a man slapping Jewel senseless while he had his way with her. He seemed to take pleasure in her pain as he drove into her again and again. All the while a bound and gagged Sebastian fought desperately, yet futilely, to free himself from the bed he was tied to, watching in horror as the man raped her.

It was all Arianna could do to keep the bile from rising into her throat as she lifted her eyes to the glowing sword once again.

"What has happened, Quicksilver?"

"Sebastian is no longer a Wolverine."

"What?"

"He has been stripped of both his knighthood and his sword, Fleetfire. Your own husband, Sir Geoffrey, has now been promoted to Captain of the Guard by the king, despite Geoffrey's loud protests. Every sword in the castle now knows what has happened."

"Why would King Brennan do such a thing?" Arianna asked in sorrow.

"Sebastian married Jewel before her betrothed, Lord Merric of Evendria, could claim her."

"He *married* her? Sebastian?" Arianna remembered the many ladies Sebastian had dallied with in the past. What would make him consider marriage? Even if he felt he had to save Jewel from her fiancé, why would he not simply appoint himself as her champion instead of her husband?

"What else do you know of my dream?" she asked.

"*You have seen what will come to pass should Sebastian and Jewel remain at the castle.*"

"At the hands of Lord Merric?"

"*Yes.*"

Arianna thought for a moment. "He may no longer be a Wolverine, but he did make a promise to Jewel that every Wolverine at Castle Templestone would support her. I know well the importance of a promise." She recalled Geoffrey's own promise to protect her so long ago, regardless of the risk to himself. "I will make sure Sebastian's promise is upheld." With that, Arianna pulled down her father's sword and found its sheath hidden under the bed.

She did no more than yank on her robe before strapping Quicksilver to her waist, striding out her chamber door like a true knight of the king.

૏ૐ૑૒

Arianna's eyes widened when Sebastian's door opened. Geoffrey and Mynos were already in Sebastian's chambers.

"Rose?" Geoffrey asked, ushering her into the room. "Are you all right?"

Glancing from Jewel's stricken face to Sebastian standing dejectedly, gazing into the cold hearth, she said, "I had a premonition."

Mynos nodded as if expecting no less. "As did Malnan, Daughter." He palmed Malnan's Jewel around his neck.

"I dreamed Lord Merric... I saw him..." Arianna couldn't finish when Jewel looked at her curiously. All she could see was Jewel's bloody face and her torn dress as Merric raped her. "You must leave Castle Templestone. Both of you."

"What did you see?" Geoffrey asked.

Tears sprang into Arianna's eyes. "I saw him beating and raping Jewel. I saw Sebastian tied down, unable to help, yet made to watch it all. I saw it! And Quicksilver has convinced me that what I've seen will come to pass if they stay here."

Geoffrey glanced down at her father's sword before he said, "Quicksilver spoke to you?"

"Yes. I didn't believe it myself at first, but it was glowing as it did once before. And it told me it was the future I saw in my dream."

"I will kill him before he lays one hand on my wife," Sebastian growled.

Arianna shook her head. "That's not how it's going to happen, Sebastian. Please listen to me!"

Mynos crossed the room to stand in front of Sebastian. "You cannot kill Lord Merric." Sebastian's eyes flared wide with anger, shooting daggers at the ancient dragon. "You are no longer a Wolverine, no longer a lord yourself. If you kill Lord Merric now, you will be tried as a commoner, imprisoned and executed. Is that how you want to leave Jewel? As your widow?"

Emotions raged across Sebastian's face as he stared hard at his wife. "No!" came his strangled cry. Immediately Jewel flew to him and hugged him. He hugged her back as if he could become one with her, his face tucked into her neck.

"I'm sorry, my lady Jewel," he cried. "I have failed you. I have nothing to offer you. I cannot even avenge you."

Jewel's heart broke for him. "Think you I care whether you are Captain of the Guard or a lowly commoner, Bastian? You have not failed me. You have given me yourself, the most wonderful gift I have ever received."

Taking in a ragged breath, he kissed her entire face, hovering over her lips before he whispered to her alone, "Don't leave me, Jewel. Please don't ever leave me."

Jewel smiled at him and rested her forehead upon his. "Never, my lord husband."

Suddenly, Malnan's Jewel flared to life. Just as before, a brisk wind flew through the room and the form of a woman could be seen shimmering into existence.

"I have seen this same vision," Malnan said as her form solidified, her voice echoing as if from far away. "But Lord Merric won't be satisfied with simply raping Jewel. He will kill Sebastian and marry her himself, beating and raping her until she is nothing but a broken shell of the woman she once was. This cannot happen."

"It will not happen," Sebastian snapped, pulling Jewel even closer. She squeezed his hand in an effort to calm him.

"Then Arianna has spoken true," Malnan said. "You must leave Castle Templestone."

"And go where?" he asked. "We have nothing, nowhere to go!"

"You can stay at my estates in Emberdale," Geoffrey offered.

"No," Jewel said, drawing the attention of everyone in the room. She took a deep breath and continued. "We must go to Evendria. I know Lord Merric beat me. We must prove it. Surely my family is there. Someone must know the truth."

"She is right," Arianna said. "If you want to reclaim your knighthood, Sebastian, you must prove Lord Merric did, in fact, beat her."

Sebastian's eyes lit up. "If we can prove it, then no one will question my challenge against him. As a husband and a

Wolverine, I will have every right to kill him for the honor of my wife."

"Mynos," Malnan said softly, "You must allow me to go with them."

The dragon looked at Malnan in bewilderment, then understanding. "Of course, my love. But I will diligently be looking for a way for you to return to me in flesh."

"Why must Malnan come with us?" Jewel asked, confused.

"The way will be dangerous, Daughter," Malnan answered. "Lord Merric will not sit idly by and let you simply leave. No, he will come looking for you, of that I have no doubt. I must protect you on your journey."

"How can I protect myself or my wife without a weapon?" Sebastian asked in frustration. "King Brennan ordered Fleetfire back to the armory. Do you know how long that sword has been in my family?"

Arianna quietly unstrapped Quicksilver and held it out to Sebastian with both hands.

"You promised Jewel she would have the support of every Wolverine at Castle Templestone," she told him. "That includes me. The king may have forbidden you to wield Fleetfire, Seb, so in its stead, I give to you Quicksilver, the sword of my father, Sir Isaac of Winterborne."

Sebastian's eyes went wide. "I cannot accept that," he whispered reverently. "It is the weapon that slew Iruindyll!"

Arianna nodded with a smile. "I expect it back, Seb."

Sebastian's hands shook as he accepted the sword. Without a word, he hugged Arianna in silent thanks.

"There are always advantages of being Captain of the Guard, as I'm sure you know, Seb." Geoffrey winked at him. "It will be days before anyone even knows you are missing. I'm sure some of the men will want to come up with stories as to why you haven't been seen. They are all still loyal to you."

Sebastian's eyes misted with tears as he grinned at his old friend. "Thank you."

"You must leave at once," Mynos told them. "We can waste no more time with Lord Merric here at the castle."

"Indeed," Geoffrey concurred.

Both Geoffrey and Mynos raced around the room and filled Sebastian's saddlebags with clothing. Mynos then lifted the lavender gem and placed the chain around Jewel's neck. "Take care of her well."

The ethereal form of Malnan smiled. "I will, my love," she said, giving the dragon's words a double meaning. Then, as suddenly as she had come, the form of Malnan shimmered and winked out, the lavender gem once again going dark.

Jewel was thankful for the cover of night when she and Sebastian were ushered unseen into the stables. There, waiting with Blaze saddled and ready to go, was Ethan, a large smile upon his face.

"I figured you might like your horse to go with you."

"How did you—?" Sebastian asked, but Mynos interrupted him.

"I knew you had to leave once Malnan told me what she had seen, Son. Ethan was more than eager to help you with your departure."

"I'm sure he was," Sebastian said dryly.

Ethan laughed at that. "Unfortunately, you are taking my treasure with you." He embraced Jewel, making her blush.

Sebastian stepped in when his hug lasted longer than a few moments. "She's *my* treasure, Sir Ethan, and don't you forget it." They looked at one another, both of them suddenly bursting forth with peals of laughter as they hugged, slapping each other on the back. Jewel shook her head. She would never understand them.

"Take care, old friend," Ethan said as he turned away, seeming to pretend there was something in his eye.

With the saddlebags secure, Sebastian gave Jewel a boost and wasted no time in swinging up behind her. Sebastian nudged Blaze into a trot. Once in the courtyard, she noticed both Duncan and Briand as they silently opened the castle gates for his passing. They grinned as they waved goodbye, making Jewel's breath catch in her throat. His men truly did love him.

Once the gates were opened, Sebastian kicked his horse into a gallop, leaving Castle Templestone behind.

Chapter Twenty-One

Sebastian eased Blaze into a slow trot once they entered the cover of trees. He wasn't following any sort of trail that Jewel could see, but she trusted him to know where he was going. They didn't stop until dawn, when they found a small brook to water the horse.

Jewel walked down to the water as Sebastian set up a rudimentary camp by laying their bedrolls under a low hanging tree. She was exhausted and wanted to clean up a bit. Splashing the cool water on her face and arms felt good, but she still shivered in spite of it.

Now they had stopped to rest, her thoughts began to fester in her mind. Sebastian had lost it all: his title, his rank, his home in Tabrinth—all because of her. And if they couldn't find proof of Lord Merric's beating, then it would become permanent. Even if they had a son together, he would never be able to become a Wolverine himself, no matter how much he might want to. And what would she tell her son? That he couldn't be a Wolverine because his father had married the wrong woman?

What had she done to Sebastian? She'd ruined his life. She loved him with her entire being, yet she'd ruined him. How could he ever love her now? He would always blame her, always know in the back of his mind that she had done this to him.

Jewel sat on the ground, pulling her knees up to her face and wrapping her arms around her legs. Tears fell and she couldn't stop them. She was crying for Sebastian, because she hated herself for what she had done. What if she hadn't begged him to make love to her? What if she simply hadn't been so obvious with her attraction to him? Would everything be different?

She tried not to make a noise, but she supposed her shaking shoulders gave her away. Sebastian knelt beside her, lifting her face to look at him.

Red puffy eyes and wet cheeks greeted him and it ripped at his heart. He said nothing, but wiped the tears from her face.

"How can you touch me after what I did to you?" Jewel asked in a shaky voice.

That shocked him. "What are you talking about, my lady Jewel?"

"This!" She gestured to her surroundings. "Think you would be here if it weren't for me?" Jewel shot to her feet and walked a few steps away, turning her back on him. "If I hadn't teased you, and encouraged you, and begged you to—to—"

"Jewel—"

"—to make love to me." She sobbed.

"Jewel," he repeated, placing his hands on her shoulders. "It is not your fault."

She shrugged him off and took a few more steps away, yet turned to face him. "How can you say that? Because you married me, you are cast out of your own castle, wandering the countryside like some sort of vagabond, taking care of a woman who doesn't even know who she is…"

"My *wife*," he said firmly, following her. "You are my wife and I will do all I can to see to your safety. Neither one of us could have predicted what would happen did I marry you. But know this. Knowing what I know now, I would marry you regardless. Being a Wolverine was my past. You, Jewel, *you* are my future."

Jewel buried her face in her hands and cried.

"You told me you didn't care whether I am Captain of the Guard or lowly commoner. Did you mean it?" he asked.

She dropped to her knees. "Of course I meant it, Bastian," she wailed through her tears. "But I cannot forgive myself for ruining your life!"

Sebastian knelt right in front of her. "You did not ruin my life." He pulled her hands away from her face. She gazed dejectedly at the ground. "Look at me."

Slowly, Jewel's eyes met his and more tears spilled as he gazed at her.

"You did not ruin my life," he soothed. "Ever since I met you you've been in my thoughts and bewitched my dreams. I cannot stop thinking about you when I'm not with you. You've crawled inside of me, my lady Jewel." Tears began forming in his own eyes as his voice wavered. "You've crawled inside of me and captured my heart. I am such a lucky man to have found you..." Sebastian couldn't go on. He drew her close to embrace her.

His words were sinking in as she clutched him, and her heart burst with love. Had he just said—without saying—that he loved her?

"I love you, too, Sir Sebastian of Tabrinth," she whispered in his ear. "No matter what happens to us, you will always be my Wolverine, my heart, my soul, my strength—" She didn't get any further.

Sebastian groaned and twisted his hand in her hair. Yanking her head back, he kissed her roughly, but Jewel didn't care. Her own hands found their way into his hair and tried to pull him even closer. His tongue darted into her mouth and she answered him back in kind, kissing him as voraciously as he kissed her.

Jewel was barely aware he'd picked her up and was walking back toward the bedrolls. She realized what he had done as he laid her down on the soft blankets.

"You will never blame yourself for this again, my lady wife," he murmured, his breath scorching her neck. "You could have prevented none of it, for I would have married you no matter the cost. Is that clear to you?"

Jewel barely heard him as she concentrated only on his hand bunching her skirts over her legs. He was seemingly impatient, unwilling to completely undress to make love to her, yet his fingers suddenly stilled as he repeated, "Is that clear?"

Jewel's eyes snapped open. "Yes! Yes, Bastian. Oh, please don't stop..."

He chuckled, continuing his erotic caress. Jewel pressed her body against his and drew his head down to kiss him as the waves of ecstasy engulfed her, making her rip her lips away from him to gasp, only to kiss him wildly once again.

"Bastian, now. Please? Don't make me wait any longer." She whimpered against his lips.

He needed no more encouraging. No sooner was he fully sheathed than Jewel felt his own release. However, he plunged a few more times. Jewel grabbed his hips to hold him steady, reveling in the sensation of another delicious wave of ecstasy.

She smiled, stroking his hair, lightly kissing his cheek as his head rested on her shoulder. Sebastian lowered his entire weight on her, but she didn't care. He felt wonderful, pressed fully against her, still inside, making her moan as he moved to sit up.

In a frantic gesture, she pulled him back on top of her. "I did not give you leave to go, Sir Sebastian," she whispered playfully in his ear.

He smiled and kissed her softly. "I am sorry, Madame. Next time, I'll be sure to ask first." His blue eyes twinkled, and once again, Jewel lost her breath just looking at him.

"You are so beautiful." She pushed away the dark brown hair from his face.

Grinning, Sebastian repeated the same words she'd told him once before, "We think alike, you and I." After a few moments of lying contentedly on top of her, he asked, "May I get up now?"

Jewel sighed. "If you must."

As he lifted himself from her, he deliberately pressed their hips together even closer, grinning as Jewel closed her eyes and gasped.

"Ah, I do so love it when you do that, my lady wife," he said before he withdrew. Sebastian made quick work of pulling her dress back down and re-tying his breeches before he pulled the blankets up and over them.

"Let's try to get some sleep, shall we?" he asked with a yawn.

Jewel nodded and closed her eyes, asleep even before Sebastian curled his arm around her.

Chapter Twenty-Two

Sebastian barely got any sleep. When he did, his dreams chilled him to the bone. Jewel was screaming for him and he was unable to help her, unable to fight the bonds holding him down. One dream was so vivid, he jerked himself awake and frantically glanced around until he realized Jewel was curled against him, sighing in her sleep.

With a shaking hand, he tugged her closer to place a relieved kiss on her forehead before dropping his head back on the bedroll. The dreams scared him more than anything in his life.

Rolling toward her, Sebastian slipped his arm under his head as he watched her sleep. She loved him. He was still reeling from her confession as he tucked a few of her unruly hairs behind her ear. Of course he'd all but admitted he loved her as well and she'd understood what he had been trying to say. Never before had he felt such a strong love for another person. He had to protect her from Lord Merric, he *had* to. There was no other choice. If anything happened to her, it would destroy him.

The horror from his dreams was still fresh, and he felt helpless against it. He could only imagine they were the same images Arianna and Malnan had spoken of. Sebastian shuddered. If Malnan hadn't saved Jewel from her beating when she did, Jewel would have been married to that monster, Lord Merric of Westchester.

What had he called her? Isabella. Her name. Finally, he knew her name. But she had renounced it. She was Jewel now and that is what he would call her.

Leaning over her, Sebastian lightly brushed his lips against her ear so as not to wake her. "I love you." As he pulled back, her eyes were open. She had heard him.

Jewel was silent for long moments, making Sebastian blush in spite of himself. He looked away, embarrassed at what he'd just confessed. But Jewel placed her hand on his cheek and pulled his gaze back to hers.

"I wondered if you truly did," she whispered.

"Did you doubt it?"

Jewel nodded. "Maddie told me of all the...women...you've had and I thought perhaps I was just..."

"Just what?"

"Just one of them."

"If you thought that, why did you encourage me?"

"Because I was in love with you, Bastian. I knew I loved you the day I found the carnation outside my door. Maddie tried to tell me you were striving to win my heart, but I guess I wanted...well, I wanted you to forget all the others."

"Jewel," he said gently, "the others were forgotten the moment I first looked into your beautiful eyes."

"Truly?" she asked, a hint of disbelief in her voice.

"Truly," he assured her with a kiss. "There no other woman I'd rather be my wife. There no one else, only you, sweet lady. Only you do I want to make love to for the rest of my life and wake up next to every morning."

Jewel gave him a smile that stopped his heart. Throwing her arms around his neck, she tucked her head on his shoulder and held him.

"Bastian?" she asked after long moments of silence.

He contentedly combed her glossy black hair with his fingers. "Hmm?"

"I love you, too."

’’’

It was well past midday when Sebastian rolled up the blankets and handed Jewel some dried beef to chew on. He saddled his horse and covered any trace of their camp.

"Why did we only bring one horse?" Jewel asked, watching him lift the saddle onto his stallion's back.

"I can think of many pleasant reasons." He stole a sly look at her over his shoulder, making her blush furiously. He laughed at her reaction before he continued. "Blaze is much faster than your timid gray. We can cover more ground this way. Not to mention I like the feel of your backside in my lap."

"Bastian!" she squeaked, blushing all the more.

"Well it's true!" He tossed back a grin as he cinched the girth strap.

At that moment, Malnan's Jewel suddenly flared to life. *"You must flee!"* Malnan's ethereal voice rang out unexpectedly. *"Hurry! You have been followed!"*

Looking down at the necklace, Jewel saw an image forming inside the lavender gem of five men riding hard through the forest, making her gasp in horror. The faint sound of galloping horses approached in the distance.

"Bastian," she exclaimed again, realizing Sebastian had wasted no time in mounting his horse. Before she knew it, Blaze charged toward her and in one swift movement, Sebastian reached down and scooped her up into the saddle.

"Hold on!" he yelled into her ear. He gave Blaze his head and galloped recklessly toward the King's Mountains.

Jewel shut her eyes and clutched handfuls of the stallion's mane, concentrating for all she was worth to stay on the horse's back. She'd never ridden so hard before and she was bounced and jostled most painfully.

Sebastian noticed her discomfort and curled an arm around her while he leaned over in the saddle, holding her close to the horse's powerful body. It made her feel more secure. Jewel relaxed somewhat.

But then her stomach flopped violently when Sebastian yanked Blaze hard to the right, galloping in a different direction. Jewel let out a scream of surprise, which made Sebastian hold her even tighter, almost squeezing the breath out of her.

"I've got you!" he hollered in her ear again. It was all Jewel could do to nod in response.

Blaze seemed to enjoy his run as he broke through the trees and into a large meadow. More forest was on the far side, but at that moment, they were out in the open. Sebastian turned his horse sharply again, this time to the left, to bound back within the cover of the trees.

After what seemed an eternity of galloping, Sebastian began slowing his horse. When Blaze loped serenely, once again headed toward the mountains, Sebastian spoke to Malnan. "Are they still behind us?"

The gem twinkled for a few seconds before the dragon responded. "No. You have lost them for the time being."

Jewel felt the tension in Sebastian's body ease at her words. "It seems Lord Merric has second-guessed us," he said, slowing Blaze to a walk. The horse sighed, apparently not used to galloping hard with extra weight to carry. "We cannot afford to stop, my lady Jewel." Sebastian jumped off Blaze's back. "But my horse needs a reprieve. Stay where you are and I will walk with him."

Nodding again, Jewel held onto the pommel of the saddle and bit her lip. How had Merric found them? She trembled at the thought, clutching Blaze nervously, jumping at shadows.

She didn't feel much better when Sebastian finally stopped hours later. He had walked his horse the entire way, telling her he didn't want Blaze exhausted if they had to make another mad getaway. The sun had set hours ago and night darkened the sky when Sebastian dropped heavily on the bedroll next to her. He had just finished bedding his horse down for the night and seemed to be deep in thought.

"What's wrong, Bastian?" she asked warily, becoming attuned to his moods.

He shook his head as he flung an arm over his eyes. "I'm just so tired, my lady Jewel." He sighed. "Didn't get much sleep when we stopped last."

"How did Merric find us?"

"I do not know," he answered after a long silence. "Either he guessed we would flee, or someone informed him of it."

"Do you think he...do you think he'll...find us again?"

Sebastian rolled over to bring her closer to him. "I will not lie to you." He looked deeply into her eyes. "They might. It wouldn't be hard to track us." He cursed when her eyes widened in terror. "Listen to me, sweetheart," he said soothingly, "if they find us again, I will fight every last one of them to keep them away from you. They will have to kill me first before they lay one hand on you."

"But there are five of them, Bastian. How can you possibly fight them all?"

Sebastian flashed her his boyish grin. "A Wolverine I may no longer be, my lady Jewel, but I still know my way around a sword. I've fought more than that and lived to tell about it."

"When have you fought so many?" Jewel whispered, in awe of his skill.

"At Queen Darragh's fortress. When Arianna slew the dragon Iruindyll, the queen's Dark Knights swarmed the Wolverines Mynos had taken with him. I was there that day, surrounded by seven or eight Dark Knights, each intent on killing me, each only succeeding in getting killed themselves. I earned my sword that day," he said with a faraway look in his eyes.

Jewel touched his face. His skin was exceptionally hot. It worried her.

"Bastian, do you feel all right?" She sat up, gazing at him.

"I am fine, my lady Jewel," he said wearily. "It is nothing a few hours of sleep with you cannot cure." He urged her back down to lie on his chest and sighed. Within moments, he was fast asleep.

Chapter Twenty-Three

Sebastian was shivering. The sky was just barely brightening with the first streaks of dawn when Jewel was awoken by his chattering teeth. Opening her eyes, she realized he was tucked as close as could be to her, his blanket clutched tightly under his chin. Jewel felt his skin and gasped at the raging heat that met her fingertips.

"Bastian?" She shook his shoulders in an effort to wake him.

He groaned as he opened his eyes, taking a few moments to focus on her in the dim twilight.

"You're sick!"

"I...am not. I'm...just fine," he stuttered.

"You are not!" Jewel protested.

"Come h—here and w—warm me u—up."

"You are already burning with fever, Bastian."

"But I'm ssso c-c—old..."

Jewel sighed, trying to tamp down her fear. How was she supposed to take care of him out in the wilderness? And how were they supposed to continue on their journey if he couldn't travel?

"Bastian, I don't think you're well enough to travel today."

"Nonsense!" he barked, throwing off his blanket. "I...I will be...all right...I just need...to get moving is all."

Sebastian shivered even more after he threw off the blanket. Before he moved to saddle his horse, he bent over to grab the blanket once again to wrap around his shoulders.

"Aren't you...c-cold?" he asked her.

"There is a slight chill in the air, but I'm not cold," she answered.

Sebastian turned away, stumbling to his horse. After a few tries, Jewel had to help him lift the saddle and cinch it onto Blaze.

"Are you sure you can travel?" Uncertainty swirled within her.

"We must travel whether I can or not." His tone left no room for argument. "We are being...tracked, and if we do not m-m-move, they will f-f-ind our camp by the end of the d-day."

Jewel hurried to pack the bedrolls after his words, not wanting to be found by their pursuers while Sebastian was ill. "Can you mount your horse?"

Sebastian still held the blanket around him as he gave Jewel a boost up. "I'll need...your help," he confessed. Holding out a hand for him, Jewel tugged with all her might when Sebastian placed his foot in the stirrup and attempted to mount the stallion. Finally after three tries, he was astride, holding the reins loosely as he urged his horse into a slow walk.

Jewel's arm hurt at the straining she'd done to help him astride, but she was more worried about Sebastian as he spread the blanket around his shoulders once again. He held her closely, as if feeding off her warmth and she noticed all too well the heat in his skin.

The King's Mountains weren't far away. If they could get there before the sun set, they might be able to hide in the foothills.

Jewel took the reins from him and he wrapped both arms around her. Sebastian rested his cheek against her back and closed his eyes, trying to remember when he'd ever felt so bad. His stomach was queasy and he was so very tired. He hoped he would be able to stay astride Blaze for the remainder of the day, because if he fell off, he didn't think he'd have the strength to climb back on.

Damn, why'd he have to get sick now?

୫୬ଠଓଷ

The day crawled. Jewel didn't dare push the horse any faster than an easy walk. Sebastian had fallen asleep behind her. He still hugged her tight, and she held onto his hands with one of her own to keep him a little more secure. If he began to fall, she wouldn't be able to stop him.

He had woken up several times during the day grumbling about having to see to his duties upon the castle walls and securing new armor for a few of his men. He had even called out to Briand once. Jewel was worried.

Each time he had asked about his duties, she'd made up some story off the top of her head to appease him. He wouldn't last much longer.

Fortunately, even at their slow pace, they managed to make it to the foothills by evening. Jewel wound their way up into the hills before the sun touched the horizon. In the light of the fading day, she spied a large cave on the side of a hill, mostly covered with bushes and rock debris. It seemed to be the perfect hiding place.

Jewel guided Blaze around the rocks and trees toward the cave and breathed a sigh of relief when she realized it was indeed big enough to house the horse as well. The cave reached well beyond the entrance, but not too far back. She could still see the rear wall. It didn't seem to be inhabited by any wildlife.

Jewel reined Blaze to a halt just inside the cave mouth and wondered how she was going to get Sebastian off the horse. She decided to try and wake him.

"Bastian?" She poked him in the ribs none too gently.

Raising his head, Sebastian mumbled, "If you value your life, Sir Ethan, you will never do that again."

"It's me, Bastian. You have to get off the horse."

"Jewel?" he said in confusion.

Turning in the saddle, she managed to place a soft kiss on his dry lips. "I need your help to get you off Blaze."

"Are we going to the pond, my lady Jewel?" he asked, a knowing grin upon his face.

Jewel bit her lip to keep from crying in frustration. How did you talk to someone who wasn't making any sense?

"Yes, my lord husband," she decided to say. "We are here but we need to dismount."

"Jump down and I will catch you," he said, burying his face into her back once more.

"I think I will be doing all the catching, Bastian." Jewel sighed as she peeled his arms from around her waist. "Can you stay astride?"

He didn't answer. He was nodding off to sleep again.

"Sebastian!" She smacked his cheek, making his head snap up in surprise. "I need you to stay awake."

"Yes of course, Your Majesty." His eyes were unfocused on her face.

Rebecca Goings

She decided right then and there she had to take her chances—jump off the horse and pray to God she could catch him as he fell. Swinging her leg over the saddle, Jewel pushed off and jumped. However, Blaze sidestepped as she landed making Sebastian sway precariously on his back.

"No!" she cried out, rushing over to cushion his fall. Jewel had no strength to stop his momentum as he slid off the horse; she only hoped she didn't hurt herself in the process.

Suddenly she was flat on her back with Sebastian on top of her, moaning. She had twisted her ankle and it was dreadfully hard to draw a breath. Tears of frustration stung her eyes as she pushed on Sebastian to roll him over. She was able to stand, but couldn't put her entire weight on her foot.

Wincing, Jewel covered her husband with the blanket he'd draped across himself earlier in the day and hobbled over to Blaze. It was perhaps the hardest thing she'd ever had to do, unsaddle a horse and rub him down with no help at all, all the while trying to hold her entire weight on one foot. The saddle was unbelievably heavy and she thought she would fall again once she had it in her arms, but by some miracle, she was able to keep her balance. She could do no more than drop it on the ground next to the horse, making Blaze neigh and toss his head in surprise.

After she was finished, Jewel tried to get Sebastian to drink some water from the water skin, but most of it dribbled down his chin instead of his throat.

"Please, Bastian. Please drink this," she begged, but there was no response. His skin was still burning hot, and Jewel didn't know what else to do. Wetting a cloth, she rubbed his skin down and took off the blanket, hoping the water would chill him enough to bring down his temperature. Leaning back

142

against the wall, she sighed and decided to eat a chunk of cheese from the saddlebags.

She noticed three strange rocks in the far corner of the cave. They were large and perfectly round, as if deliberately shaped that way. After she finished eating, she decided to investigate further. Standing next to them, Jewel was shocked to find they were as tall as her waist. The rocks were clustered together, just barely touching.

"What do you make of this, Malnan?" Jewel asked her necklace, lightly touching one of the stones.

Without warning, a wind whipped throughout the cave, stirring up quite a bit of dust. Malnan's Jewel was glowing brightly—so bright Jewel had to shield her eyes from it.

"It is not possible," Malnan's ethereal voice gasped with excitement.

"What is not possible?" Jewel yelled over the din of the wind.

"Where are we?" the dragon demanded.

"I do not know. We are in a cave somewhere in the King's Mountains."

"It is not possible!" Malnan repeated, but Jewel detected a hint of joy and elation in her voice.

"Malnan, what are these stones?"

"Eggs, Daughter. We have found dragon eggs!"

Jewel gasped in surprise. At that moment, the bright pulsing light in Malnan's Jewel suddenly flew from the necklace and into one of the stones, making the stone illuminate from the inside and glow of its own accord.

"Malnan?" Jewel asked in a small voice, watching in awe as the light pulsed like a heartbeat inside the large, round egg.

"Soon, Daughter," Malnan's voice sang in triumph. *"Soon I will be with you again."*

Chapter Twenty-Four

Jewel sat watching the pulsing light of the dragon egg well into the night. A low hum reverberated within the cave, getting louder and softer as the light brightened and receded, over and over again. Sebastian tossed and turned restlessly, yet never awoke, making Jewel grip his hand in both of hers, her worry overwhelming.

She was exhausted, yet refused to sleep, not knowing if Sebastian would take a turn for the worse. Inhaling a deep breath, Jewel felt compelled to sing softly, somehow knowing words to a tune she had no memory of.

"Sleep and dream of me, sweet Prince, sleep and dream of me," she sang, *"through pain, through death, through dark of night, sleep and dream of me..."* Jewel faltered, the melody of the song haunting as it echoed off the walls of the cave. What had made her think of that tune? A hazy memory came to her of a woman singing that song to her. Was she remembering her mother?

"Come and hold me in your arms, sleep and dream of me. Make me yours anon, sweet Prince, sleep and dream of me."

The more she sang, the more she could remember about the woman who had once sung this song to her—long black hair and a kind smile. It frustrated her she couldn't think of more—she gave herself a headache just trying to recall her.

With a sad sigh, Jewel placed a lingering kiss on Sebastian's warm lips. "Sleep and dream of me."

Laying her head on his chest, she yawned, lulled by his steady heartbeats. Despite her best efforts to stay awake, Jewel closed her eyes and sleep conquered her.

ಇಾಙಿಯ

Jewel awoke to daylight pouring into the cave. Sebastian still lay oblivious to the world, sweating profusely. Jewel didn't know if sweating was a good thing or a bad thing, but she decided to rub him down with a damp cloth regardless. The egg in the back of the cave still pulsed with light, yet the beating had gotten faster.

"Malnan?" she said, half expecting a reply. None came.

Blaze looked at her curiously, stomping a foot and tossing his head. Jewel knew what he wanted. He was hungry, just as she was, and there was no soft grass in the cave.

Jewel stood and walked to the horse, hugging him. She must have looked like a fool, her arms flung wide around the horse's neck, but at the moment, he was her only solace.

"What am I going to do, Blaze?" The horse rested his head on her shoulder. She glanced at the dragon egg and hoped Malnan would emerge soon. It was rumored dragons lived to be thousands of years old. If that was true, how long would they lie dormant inside their eggs? She prayed it wouldn't be long.

They couldn't travel with Sebastian as sick as he was, and Jewel didn't want to leave Malnan behind. Her best hope was to stay hidden in the cave, and pray their pursuers wouldn't find them. But right now, Blaze was hungry and Jewel had to feed him.

"I'll be back soon, Bastian." She smoothed a hair from her husband's wet brow. Her heart leapt when he stirred, his eyes fluttering. He was getting better. He had to be. But his eyes closed and he was still once more. With her head low, she quietly led the horse out the mouth of the cave.

Jewel became more and more apprehensive as the search for grass took her farther away from safety. Only rocks and brush cluttered the terrain and she found herself out of sight of the cave entrance. Finally, after a long search, she located a small patch of grass and Blaze munched happily. Sitting on a large rock, she watched the horse eat, not knowing how long she should let him graze.

After a few moments, Blaze lifted his head and sniffed the air, his ears perking forward and back. He gazed behind Jewel, then neighed, ears pinned back, and bolted in the other direction.

"Blaze!" She began to run futilely after the horse. She didn't get far.

Arms of steel circled her waist and yanked her against a rock-hard chest. "Where you goin', sweetheart?" The man's foul breath choked her. Jewel panicked. Screaming at the top of her lungs, she flailed about wildly, striking him a few times, making her attacker grunt in pain. His arms tightened, squeezing the air out of her. He clamped a hand on her mouth before she could scream again.

"Where's your man?" he asked cruelly. Jewel couldn't see the man, but she shook her head frantically. "No worries, milady. Lord Merric will be happy enough we found you. Jorvis, go find the Wolverine and kill him."

Jewel's eyes widened when she saw another man walk around the first. He was older, with dark stubble on his face and a few teeth missing.

"How am I supposed to kill a *Wolverine*, Max?"

"I'm sure you can think of somethin', Jorvis," Max said, his arms tightening around Jewel. "He's just a man after all. Besides, he's not a Wolverine anymore."

"Doesn't matter and you know it! He didn't lose his knowledge with a sword along with his title."

"Damn it, I don't care how it gets done, long as it gets done."

Jorvis gave him a hard glare. "Where is he then?"

"He's close. Follow his horse. It's bound to go back to him."

Nodding, Jorvis turned on his heel and jogged in the direction Blaze had gone. Jewel sighed in relief, knowing the cave wasn't visible from where they stood, but she hoped against hope Blaze wouldn't wander back there.

Oh God, Sebastian! He was helpless lying on the floor of the cave. If Jorvis succeeded in finding him, he could easily kill him. A cry of desperation ripped from her throat and tears flowed down her cheeks as she watched Jorvis jog away.

"Whatcha got there?" another voice said behind them.

"I've got Lord Merric's betrothed," her assailant said proudly, turning to face the speaker. Jewel saw a young man staring at her in appreciation. He would have been handsome if the lines of his face hadn't been so hard. Wispy blond hair fell to his shoulders and a nasty smile tugged at his mouth.

"Seems a shame we should give her untouched to Merric," he said. "She's already had one man. What's a few more?" As he talked, he strode forward, unbuckling his sword belt purposefully. Jewel knew full well what he was about to do.

Fear rose inside her as she struggled to free herself, but the hand on her mouth prevented her from taking the deep breaths she needed. It wasn't long before she fainted, taking refuge in the blessed darkness.

ဆၟၒၷ

"Sir Sebastian. *Sir Sebastian!*" A voice whispered frantically in his ear. "Wake up!"

It took a few moments for Sebastian to regain his bearings, his senses returning to him one by one. He was lying on the hard ground, his skin wet and his clothing clinging to him. He smelled the dirt underneath him and heard the feminine voice.

"Jewel?" he croaked, surprised at the hoarseness of his voice. Licking his lips, he found them dry and cracked. He was unimaginably thirsty. "Jewel?" he asked again. The voice didn't sound like his wife.

"No, Sir Sebastian. You must get up. Jewel has been taken!"

Those few words finally got his attention and his eyes snapped open. The sight that greeted him made him gasp and scoot away on the floor of the cave in shock. There, gazing down at him with concern, was a small green dragon.

It took him a moment to compose himself before his eyes widened in recognition. "Good God! *Malnan?*"

Chapter Twenty-Five

Sebastian tore his gaze away long enough to glance at his surroundings. He was in a large empty cave—alone with the dragon. Not even his horse was with him.

"Where am I? Where is Jewel?" He tried to stand, but sat back down due to the dizziness in his head.

"Easy, Sir Sebastian," the dragon said, tilting its small head to the side. "I have healed your fever, but your body is weak from not eating."

"Fever?" Sebastian said in confusion, running his hands through his hair. "I had a fever? How did I get here?"

"Jewel found this cave in the foothills of the King's Mountains," she answered him.

"How did you..." he began, taking another long look at her small frame. She was beautiful, her green scales shining in the sunlight, her eyes bright and brimming with life. Her petite wings were folded on her back, making Malnan look regal with her head held high.

She smiled, as if seeing the question in his eyes. "There are eggs in this cave."

Sebastian stared back at her dumbstruck. "Dragon eggs?" he whispered.

"Yes."

Shaking his head, Sebastian finally recalled what Malnan had first said to him. "Where is Jewel?"

"She's been taken."

"Taken?" Sebastian yelped, this time succeeding in climbing to his feet. "*Taken?* By Lord Merric?" Instantly, he grabbed the hilt of his sword and scanned the countryside outside the cave. "Where is she?"

"Sir Sebastian—"

"Damn it, Malnan, *tell me!*"

"She has been taken east, farther into the King's Mountains."

"I've got to find her," he said, lifting the saddle. "Where is Blaze?"

"She had Blaze with her when she was taken."

He dropped the saddle in frustration. Without another word, he glared at the dragon, then walked purposefully out the mouth of the cave. Malnan followed.

Sebastian only managed to walk a few paces before he saw a familiar shape in the sky. The steady drumming of wing beats resounded off the nearby hills and he looked back at the small green dragon behind him. He wasn't sure, but it seemed as if Malnan had grown slightly bigger.

"Mynos is coming!" The air crackled around her as she began to change shape into her human form. Long green hair cascaded down her back, covering pale skin with a greenish hue. Her eyes remained draconic: the vertical slit much like a cat's eye apparent even from where Sebastian stood. Malnan held her hands to the sky as if wanting to embrace Mynos despite the fact he was still far away.

However, it didn't take long before Mynos was upon them, his large golden wings bringing him so close, dust and small

151

rocks flew all around. The instant his feet touched the ground, he began his transformation into a man. Once it was complete, he captured Malnan and crushed her to him, both of them sobbing, apparently unaware of their surroundings as they dropped to their knees.

Sebastian's heart was in his throat as he watched them, eager to chase after Jewel yet knowing Mynos and Malnan had been separated by millennia. They were touching each other everywhere, as if not believing the other was real. Mynos kissed her deeply and sobbed with a smile on his face.

"I thought I would never be able to hold you again." He ran his trembling human hands through Malnan's hair.

She smiled as her eyes shone. "I never left you, Mynos. I knew, even when I was going to die, that I would come back to you."

Long moments of silence stretched out before them as Mynos held Malnan close to him. Sebastian could stand it no longer.

"Mynos," he growled, "Jewel has been taken by Lord Merric's men. We must find her!"

"Is this true?" the dragon asked, gazing down at Malnan.

She nodded forlornly. "I could not help her, my love. I was transforming in the egg I found, bonding my soul to the ancient baby dragon inside. It was my one moment of helplessness. Sebastian was sick with fever, unable to protect her."

Mynos looked from his mate to Sebastian.

"We have to find her, Mynos." Sebastian drew a ragged breath. "I know what Arianna and Malnan have seen in their visions. I have seen them myself. It will happen if we don't find her soon."

Mynos nodded gravely, still clutching Malnan as if he would somehow lose her again. At that moment, Sebastian realized he had the help of not one, but *two* living dragons.

ঙ০৪০৫

When Jewel finally awoke, she was on the back of a horse. Strong arms held her and she wondered if it had all been a dream. Was she still traveling with Sebastian through the mountains? Slowly, however, she understood they weren't riding Blaze. The horse was jet black. Jewel stiffened, letting her captor know she was awake.

"Nice to have you join us, *Jewel*," the voice sneered behind her, mocking the name Sebastian had given her.

It was *his* voice. Lord Merric himself held her. *Oh God!* Panic such as she'd never known seized her, making her strain and push against him, trying to wiggle her way off the horse. Too late she realized her hands and feet were bound with rope.

"None of that now." Merric laughed at her, tightening his arms. "You are mine. You have always been mine. I'm merely taking back what has been stolen from me."

Jewel laughed shrilly, the sound of her voice foreign even to her own ears. "I am not yours. I am the wife of Sir Sebastian of Tabrinth."

Lord Merric squeezed her so hard, Jewel was sure she wouldn't be able to take another breath.

"Your husband is dead."

His words stunned her. "You lie!"

"Jorvis himself returned to camp not an hour after we found you with blood on his sword and your *Wolverine's* horse in tow. Yes, Isabella, your precious Sebastian is very much dead. See for yourself."

Jewel's eyes widened as she looked behind them at Jorvis riding off to their left—riding Blaze. A cold ache settled in her heart as hot tears fell from her eyes. She began shaking violently, unable to stop the sobs silently wracking her body. When she found her voice, she screamed.

"No! Sebastian, no! Please, God, *no!"*

Merric laughed at her heartache. "It is no less than you deserve, my lady," he said. "You will now honor our betrothal contract. Fortunately, you still wear this necklace." As he spoke, he fondled Malnan's Jewel on her chest. "I've no doubt you figured out how to harness its power to run from me once. But you will no longer be so lucky." With one yank, Merric ripped the gem off her neck, leaving a line of blood.

Jewel barely noticed. She was remembering Sebastian's words to her not too long ago. *"If they find us again, I will fight every last one of them to keep them away from you. They will have to kill me first before they lay one hand on you,"* he had said.

And they had succeeded. *Oh sweet, merciful God, they succeeded!* Jewel couldn't stop the deep heart-wrenching sobs that wracked her body.

Her Sebastian, her beautiful, loving Sebastian, was dead.

Chapter Twenty-Six

Overwhelmed by worry and guilt, Sebastian dropped to his knees, covering his face in his hands. "They'll hurt her." Never in his entire life had he felt so helpless. Tears gathered behind his eyes and blurred his vision. "They'll hurt her and there is nothing I can do to stop it!"

Sebastian let out a loud cry of rage that echoed off the surrounding foothills. He stood once again, his blood boiling as he walked straight to Mynos.

"Tell me what we can do to find her," he growled.

The dragon laid an understanding hand on his shoulder. "She was wearing Malnan's Jewel, my son. We can follow its call."

"I thought it wasn't enchanted like your Crystal?"

"That is true," Malnan answered. "Now that I've returned to flesh, it has no enchantment save one. My soul is still bound to the Jewel, Sir Sebastian. If I die in this body, my soul will once again find the Jewel. Because of that bond, I can locate it."

"Rest easy," Mynos said. "We will find her."

Sebastian's breathing was shallow as he hung his head. He still didn't feel as well as he should. His illness had sapped most of his strength. A brisk rush of wind pulsed over his body in that moment, pushing him back, and he felt refreshed and renewed. Sebastian arched his brow at the golden dragon.

Mynos smiled and nodded, his slitted eyes twinkling. "Let's go find your wife."

৪০৪০০৪

"Look at her, Merric," the blond man said in disgust as he sat on a fallen log. "How is she supposed to use the Jewel like that?"

"Patience, Bryce." Merric shoved Jewel down by the fire. "Once she completely forgets Sebastian, she will be ours to control. You are lucky I found you before you had your way with her," he said with murder in his thoughts. "I am the only one she will bow to. Do you understand?"

Bryce wiggled under his gaze. "She's beautiful, boss. How could I not want a taste of that?"

Without warning, Merric backhanded Bryce, making him topple off the log to fall face down in the dirt.

"*That's* how." Merric looked back at Jewel. She was staring into the flames, rocking back and forth, singing softly to herself. "You will stay away from her or I will kill you. It's that simple."

Bryce nodded once, hatred clearly in his eyes.

The other men kept a wide berth around Jewel, apparently not wanting to be the next victim of the back of Merric's hand. He shoved a plate of something hot near Jewel's foot. She did not move to pick it up.

"You must eat, Isabella," Merric said as he sat beside her. He lifted up a small biscuit to her lips. She turned her head from him. He tried again and she smacked the biscuit out of his hand.

Anger suddenly boiled inside Merric. "You will forget him, Isabella."

Jewel began rocking once again. *"Sleep and dream of me,"* she sang.

Grabbing her bound hands, Merric screamed, *"You will forget him!"*

Jewel lost her balance and landed in Merric's lap. She suddenly found the strength to fight him. *"No!"* She punched him as best she could with her bound wrists. "I will *never* forget him. *Never!"*

"Yes, you will," he retorted, slapping her hard enough to daze her before dragging her within the privacy of the trees.

"Watch the camp," he called back to Bryce. "We are not to be disturbed for any reason."

"Yes sir." Bryce averted his gaze.

When Merric tossed her to the ground, Jewel clutched handfuls of dried leaves in a desperate attempt to crawl away. Crying out, she realized there was nowhere to go. Merric's entire weight bore down on her, making her breath leave her body in a rush.

"You will forget him," he yelled once again, like a man obsessed. "You are mine. You will love only me."

Shaking her head from side to side, Jewel was only barely aware Merric had ripped her dress open until the cool night air stabbed her bare skin. He pressed her wrists hard into the dirt with one of his hands while he worked to rip her dress with the other. She tried to buck him off, she tried rolling and squirming, but nothing could unseat him. Lord Merric meant to rape her—and no one would stop him.

"No," she cried out, choking on her sobs. "You killed him. *Sebastian!"*

Merric gave Jewel a cruel slap across her face, making her mouth bleed. "Shut up, you stupid bitch!" Fumbling with his breeches, he concentrated on his task.

Looking at the sky, Jewel couldn't believe this was happening to her. A shape flew low over the trees, something large. She gasped at the sight, yet Merric seemed completely unaware of it. His hand clutched her breast, bruising it with his painful caress.

Jewel heard the sound of beating thunder. Was it her heart? It must be. She was still crying as she felt Merric hard against her as he slit the ropes binding her ankles. He was forcing her legs open.

Screams came from the camp. Jewel's eyes widened and Merric stopped for a brief instant.

"Think I care what my men are doing?" he growled at her. "They will not interfere, Isabella. Get that hope out of your eyes!" Once again Jewel began her futile twisting and bucking. "Lie still!" Merric ordered, slapping her again.

"Bastian!" she yelled through her tears.

Suddenly, Merric's weight was miraculously gone. Jewel was stunned at first as she glanced around, but in the darkness she could only see the outline of two shapes as they struggled.

Gathering what she could of her dress, she huddled against the nearest tree, sobbing and trembling violently. Sounds of brutal punches were close, but she was too overwhelmed by what Merric had almost done to her.

Strong arms scooped her off the ground and Jewel let out a shriek. Golden hair shone in the moonlight and strange slitted eyes regarded her.

"Mynos!" She sighed in relief and hugged him fiercely. "Oh God, Mynos! My Sebastian..." She couldn't go on through her tears, hearing punch after punch behind her. Mynos carried her through the trees and sat her in front of Merric's fire. All the men were dead, their bodies smoldering as if they had been set on fire themselves.

Jewel saw a woman through her tears. *A woman?* Then she recognized her. "Malnan," she said in shock. "They killed him!"

Malnan told Mynos to put Jewel down as she embraced her. "Killed who, Daughter?" The green dragon brushed Jewel's tousled hair from her face.

"Bastian. They killed him." Sobbing, Jewel collapsed against her and moaned. "Lord Merric, he…he…has…"

"I know what he did, Daughter," she said, glancing at Mynos. "But Sir Sebastian is not dead."

Suddenly they heard loud cursing from the trees. *"Bloody everlasting hell!* Where did he go? Mynos!"

Sebastian looked everywhere. Lord Merric was nowhere to be found.

"What has happened?" the dragon asked when he broke through the trees.

"He's just gone. I had him. I had the bastard and he disappeared in front of me!"

"What?"

"It's like he winked out of existence. He's gone, Mynos. I cannot find him anywhere. That son of a bitch was raping my wife!" At that comment, Sebastian suddenly raked his fingers through his hair and sucked in his breath. "Oh God. Jewel!"

Racing back through the trees, he found Jewel sobbing uncontrollably on Malnan's human shoulder. Malnan gazed at Sebastian. "They told her you were dead."

Ever so gently, Sebastian peeled Jewel's arms from Malnan and turned her to look at him. The sight of her face broke his heart. She had a black eye and a split lip, and her face was swollen from her sobbing.

"Look at me, my lady Jewel," he said tenderly. "I am not dead, sweetheart."

Jewel was silent for a few moments before she spoke. "Did he finally kill me?" She touched Sebastian's face.

Tears stung his eyes as he gazed at her, noticing her dazed expression as well as the reflection of a crushed spirit in her eyes.

"You are not dead, my sweet wife. Neither am I. I'm very much alive." Taking both of her hands, he pressed them firmly to his cheeks to convince her.

"You're alive? Bastian?" She finally understood he was truly standing in front of her. "You're alive!" she shrieked, jumping into his arms. Sebastian held her to him as hard as he could without hurting her, lifting her feet off the ground.

Sebastian turned and carried her through the forest. He stopped near a large tree before he sat down, holding Jewel on his lap. She continued to cry as she clutched him, unaware that he had taken her beyond the firelight for some time alone.

He tried to soothe her with his hands as he ran them slowly through her hair, something that had become quite a habit for him to do. After long agonizing moments, Jewel finally calmed until she was sniffling, but she never eased her hold around his neck. Her face still pressed firmly into his neck and every breath was ragged.

"I'm so sorry, Bastian."

"Sorry for what?" he asked gently.

"I'm sorry for leaving you...for getting caught...I'm sorry for letting him touch me..."

She was crying again, but he knew she was trying to hold back the sobs that wanted to come. Hugging her closer, Sebastian let out a tortured sigh.

"Don't you dare blame yourself for that monster's actions. Do you hear me, my lady Jewel? You are not to blame."

An anguished cry escaped her and she tried to crawl even closer to Sebastian. "He...he was going to ra—rape...me..."

"Baby, hush."

"I felt him, Bastian. Oh my God, I felt him!" Jewel began shrieking and it took all of Sebastian's strength to hold her as her entire body reacted to the pain.

Both of them were crying now, Jewel for her pain and Sebastian for his wife. He damned himself for not running Lord Merric through when he'd had the chance. He hadn't had time to think when he came across them in the trees. His vision had turned red as he heard Jewel screaming for him and all rational thought had left at that moment. He had done nothing more than give Merric a sound thrashing before the man had miraculously disappeared from in front of him. How Merric had accomplished that, he had no clue.

"He will never hurt you again." Sebastian's voice cracked. "Never. If I have to move heaven and earth to keep that promise to you, so be it."

Jewel nodded on his shoulder as her breathing came in great gulps. "Don't let go, Bastian, please don't ever let go of me."

Leaning back to look into her eyes, Sebastian lightly held her face in his hands. He gazed at her, pleading silently for her forgiveness. He felt so damn guilty for not being able to protect her. How could she still love him?

"Listen to me," he begged. "You are my wife. You are my heart. I promise to protect you until my last breath. I'm the one

161

who should be sorry, my lady Jewel. I didn't protect you when you needed me most."

"Bastian, they told me they had killed you. That man had Blaze. He had blood on his sword. I thought you were dead! I thought I had lost you. You were so sick in the cave. He could have killed you so easily."

"He must have found Blaze but not the cave," he told her. "Knowing Lord Merric's temper, he probably killed some creature and only claimed it was my blood."

"I was so scared when I thought you were dead, Bastian," she sobbed. "I was terrified. My whole world collapsed."

"I am here now, Jewel, and I will never let you go again. Mynos and Malnan will help me to keep that promise, now and forever."

He kissed her, trying to tell her with that one gentle kiss how much it had cost him when he found her gone. He was feeling so guilty—he needed to atone to her somehow. He found the solace he needed in her fierce embrace.

Chapter Twenty-Seven

Malnan turned back to Mynos once Sebastian and Jewel had disappeared into the trees. She was silent for a few moments. "I must tell you something."

Mynos grasped her hand and held it in both of his. "What is it, my love?"

"I felt...a tugging when Lord Merric disappeared."

"A tugging?"

Malnan nodded.

"What do you mean, 'a tugging'?" Mynos asked.

"Lord Merric has the Jewel now," she said quietly. "He's figured out how to use it."

Mynos stared at her with his golden eyes. "Your Jewel is only enchanted by your bond to it. He wouldn't be able to use it like my Crystal."

"No, he wouldn't. But he has figured out a way, Mynos. I didn't think it would be possible, but it is. Merric disappeared by using the Jewel's power."

"But how can that be?" Mynos gazed at her in confusion.

Malnan lowered her eyes before she said, "He is a magic user. Of that I have no doubt. He knows the necklace whisked Jewel away from him when he beat her. I believe he tried to use it for himself when Sebastian was beating him. The Jewel can be used, Mynos. By tapping into it with his magic, he followed the bond to me and drained some of my own power for his needs."

"He is able to wield your magical power himself through your bond with the Jewel?"

"Yes. I felt my magic weaves pulling on me, Mynos, the moment he disappeared."

"How often can he do this?"

"I would say every time he channels into the Jewel he would be able to tap into my abilities. The more he does, the weaker I shall become. I can already feel an infirmity settling in my heart. If this continues, my new body will eventually die, and my soul will once again be trapped in the Jewel."

"Then we must find him. He will not succeed in killing you!"

"We need to hurry, my love." Malnan gasped as she doubled over in pain. "He is using the Jewel as we speak!"

Mynos rushed to help her sit on a fallen log. Malnan sat straining for breath, looking worriedly into Mynos's golden eyes.

"He is testing its power," she said through gritted teeth. "I don't know what he's doing, but he's trying to find out what he can do."

As soon as it had come, the pain was gone and Malnan sat up once again, panting.

"Do you know where the Jewel is?" Mynos asked with white-hot anger in his ancient eyes.

"I believe he has returned to the castle."

"Then I will send word to Arianna. He must *not* be allowed to use it."

"Arianna will be no match for him if she doesn't use your Crystal. Even her own magic isn't as strong as mine. Only when she is wielding her magic through the Crystal is she stronger."

164

"Then we must convince her to use the Crystal again," Mynos said.

"I only hope we can." Worry settled into Malnan's heart. "She's not likely to forget losing her only child to the Crystal's power."

଼ଠ଼ଠଡ଼ଠଃ

Arianna sat in the alcove of her bedroom window and looked out at the inky blackness. Her husband lay in bed a few feet away, breathing softly in sleep. She sat there often at night, unknown to Geoffrey, gazing out at the black, rubbing her now-flat belly with sadness. Geoffrey would worry if he knew it was a nightly routine; he would try his hardest to make her happy and sit up all night with her if she needed him. A few times, Arianna had been tempted to wake him.

Losing her daughter had been so very painful, bringing back the memories of losing her family years before. Even Geoffrey had died long ago, though she'd managed to bring him back to life through the power of the Crystal. Every thought she had of the Crystal made her painfully aware of it, tucked safely in the cave below Castle Templestone, softly calling her name. It had bonded itself to Arianna, and no matter how much she wanted it out of her life, only the Crystal would decide whether or not it would let her go.

She desperately wanted to run to it, to pick it up and channel through it, to feel the energy she could wield with it. It was almost a need inside her and she was afraid. Perhaps that was why she sat in the alcove staring out the window, to keep herself from descending the spiral staircase to Mynos's lair and retrieving it. The pull was so strong to get up and leave the room that she forced herself to sit there, forced herself to stare

Rebecca Goings

at nothing, and wondered once again if she really should wake Geoffrey.

At that moment Arianna heard the voice of Mynos in her head.

"Daughter!"

Drawing her knees to her chest, Arianna dropped her head on them and refused to answer.

"Daughter!" he called again, louder.

She sensed an urgency about him, and with a heavy heart, knew what he was going to ask her.

"Mynos, no," she answered silently before he could even form his question. *"You ask too much of me."*

"Arianna, you must try to stop Merric. He has returned to the castle with Malnan's Jewel, but Malnan's soul is no longer inside it. Sebastian and Jewel found dragon eggs in the King's Mountains. Malnan is alive! But her soul is still bound to her talisman. He can follow that bond and wield Malnan's magic through it."

"I cannot, Mynos. I will never touch your Crystal again. I served my purpose by killing Iruindyll. I will continue to be a healer with my own magic. But touching that Crystal is denying me what I want the most. You cannot ask me to sacrifice that."

"What's wrong, Rose?" Geoffrey yawned. Lying on his stomach, he gazed at her with his eyes half open, his head still on the pillow. He was so incredibly handsome with his tousled blond hair and blue eyes filled with concern.

Arianna drew a deep breath. "Lord Merric has stolen Malnan's Jewel." Geoffrey rolled over and sat up, the sheet falling away from his bare chest.

"And Malnan?" he said with alarm.

Shaking her head, Arianna told him what Mynos had told her about the dragon eggs that had been found. "She is alive, Geoffrey. But Mynos has told me Lord Merric has returned to the castle. He knows how to tap into Malnan's power through the Jewel. He wants me to try and stop him."

"Stop him how?" Geoffrey's eyes darkened. She'd seen that look before. She knew her husband well enough to know he was about to refuse whatever idea Mynos had been planning.

Arianna lowered her eyes. "I told him I wouldn't do it."

"Rose..." He crossed his arms over his chest. "What did Mynos say?"

"He wants me to use the Crystal to stop Merric."

"Absolutely not!" Geoffrey stood fully now, making his way to the window. Grabbing her chin in his hand, he forced her to look at him. "You will not," he said sternly. "I've already lost a daughter to its power, Arianna. I am *not* about to lose you as well."

Arianna moved his hand from her chin and brought it to her lips. "You have nothing to fear," she said, holding his hand to her cheek. "I will never touch the Crystal of Mynos again."

Looking down at her, Geoffrey's eyes filled with tenderness. "Once, I forbade you to retrieve the Crystal, Rose, but I had no right to forbid you then." Arianna opened her mouth to say something, but he stopped her with his finger on her lips. "Now, I am your husband—I *do* have that right." Bending over so his face was inches from hers, he whispered, "You tell that dragon your husband has forbidden it. If he persists, he will take it up with me."

Nodding, Arianna sighed with relief. Geoffrey gave her a sleepy grin. He had known she'd needed him to support her, be her strength when she was so tempted to do otherwise.

"Thank you."

Geoffrey took her hand. "Come back to bed, Rose, where you can thank me properly."

Arianna smiled. Geoffrey still had the power to make her blush.

Chapter Twenty-Eight

Lord Merric smiled to himself as he padded silently up the grand staircase of Castle Templestone. He finally had Malnan's Jewel in his hands. After all these years of searching, he hadn't even been sure it was real until he found a beautiful young girl wearing the gem in Evendria. He'd heard stories about it—rumors whispered that another stone existed after the Crystal of Mynos had been discovered. Even Queen Darragh had known about it, yet refused to search for it. She had been a fool.

Queen Darragh had always scorned Malnan for being the one Mynos picked to be his mate. She had never given a thought that Malnan's Jewel might be just as powerful as the Crystal. She had even laughed when Merric suggested she find the Jewel. But Merric hadn't known Queen Darragh's motive was to obtain both the Crystal—and Mynos himself.

No one had known Queen Darragh was truly the dragon Iruindyll, filled with hatred and intense jealousy for Mynos's mate though Malnan had died millennia before. The fact was, even though she was dead, Malnan still lived on in the heart of the ancient golden dragon. Iruindyll would never have been able to make him hers.

After Iruindyll's death, Merric had fled Shadow Mountain, intent on searching for Malnan's Jewel himself. For years, being a Dark Knight was all he had ever known. His family was from

Westchester and he truly was a lord. Changing his identity back to Lord Merric had been easy for him, explaining his years away as spending them in King Brennan's court. His family had readily accepted that explanation, knowing their son couldn't possibly have been one of Queen Darragh's Dark Knights, much less her Captain of the Guard.

Charming Isabella's father had been so simple, as Merric was very familiar with the magic of brainwashing. He'd had the betrothal contract written up the very day he met Lord Andrew of Evendria. Isabella had been another matter altogether. For a reason that still eluded him, Merric had been unable to contact Isabella's mind. He figured it must have been due to the Jewel she always wore. Her father explained it had belonged to Isabella's mother and had been given to her after her mother's death. No one had known the tear-shaped lavender Jewel had been made by the dragon Malnan eons ago. Merric almost laughed at the thought of it being merely a trinket for all these years.

On the day of their wedding, Merric had tried to charm Isabella, with no success. He had planned on using her to wield the Jewel's power, but if he couldn't control her, how could he control the Jewel? He had heard the Crystal of Mynos could only be held by the hand of a woman and thought the same might be true for Malnan's Jewel. But in his frustration, he had beaten Isabella so badly she had left quite a bloodstain on the carpet. When she had miraculously disappeared in front of him, it had confirmed the gem around her neck was the legendary Malnan's Jewel.

He had searched Evendria high and low, looking everywhere for her, until a runner from the castle arrived many days later. All this time, Isabella had been at Castle Templestone and couldn't remember who she was. It had been too perfect. But Lord Merric hadn't counted on Sir Sebastian.

The man was a brick wall. And damn Jorvis for lying about his supposed death! Even thinking about his deceit made Merric's blood boil. Merric knew damn well in order to get to Isabella, Sebastian must die. But now he knew Malnan's Jewel could be touched and used by anyone after his fight with Sebastian in the forest. He'd been taking a chance channeling his magic through the gem, but Sebastian had been a hair's breadth away from killing him. Merric had been frantic to get away. Now, he didn't need Isabella any longer to wield the Jewel. But he still wanted her for himself.

That one little taste of her in the glade made his loins burn and ache, and he knew, even if he no longer needed her to use Malnan's Jewel, he would still have her. He had been scorned and he wouldn't let it lie. As a Dark Knight, Merric had *killed* men for less. He was going to kill Sebastian himself now, of that he was sure. And Isabella would be made to watch. Surely her resolve would crumble as she watched her husband die, knowing there was absolutely no hope for her escape.

But for now, Merric's plan was much, much bigger. The Crystal of Mynos was no longer a threat, as he had overheard much of the gossip floating about the castle regarding Lady Arianna and her stillborn daughter. She had vowed never to touch it again. Mynos himself posed a much bigger problem, however Merric was confident he could fight the dragon with Malnan's Jewel. Perhaps he could even blackmail him with the gem, for the dragon must know about it. It was the last remaining relic of his mate. Who knew what length a dragon would go to for love? And a dead love at that. Merric laughed to himself at the absurdity of it.

Queen Darragh had wanted Lyndaria for herself. She had wanted to rule absolutely over the land with Mynos and restore dragonkind to its former glory. But she had failed. Merric had no such ambitions regarding dragons. But power he craved above all else.

With Malnan's Jewel glittering wildly in his hands, Lord Merric walked silently and purposefully toward the royal apartments.

ᏘᏘᎻᏘ

Mynos hung his head as he spoke to Malnan. "Sir Geoffrey has forbidden Arianna to touch the Crystal ever again."

Malnan moved to place an understanding hand on his cheek, running her hand up through his hair. "Did we expect any less?"

"We must leave now," Mynos said. "If Arianna will not fight, we must return as soon as we can. Who knows what Lord Merric can and will do with the Jewel?"

Malnan nodded, worry creeping into her eyes.

Mynos walked into the trees, intent on finding Jewel and Sebastian. He found them not far from the camp leaning against a tree, embracing each other, not saying a word.

"We must leave," Mynos said. Neither one seemed to hear him. "Sir Sebastian?" He gazed down at them.

Sebastian finally looked up, his face haggard, his eyes red rimmed from crying. "He hurt her, Mynos."

Kneeling, Mynos laid a hand on both of them. Jewel's scrapes and bruises magically disappeared and she sighed in relief.

"Lord Merric has returned to the castle," Mynos explained. "He has learned how to channel Malnan's magic through her bond with the Jewel. That is how he vanished. We must stop him."

"What of Arianna and the Crystal?" Sebastian's voice was hoarse.

Mynos shook his head. "Sir Geoffrey will not allow her to use the Crystal again. We must return."

"I cannot go back there, Bastian," Jewel said in a small voice. "Not if *he's* there."

"You will be safe, Daughter." Mynos squeezed her shoulder. "You will stay in my lair underneath the castle. It's doubtful Merric knows of its existence. And even if he does, he couldn't find the entrance."

Jewel glanced at Sebastian with imploring eyes.

"Even I don't know how to get to Mynos's lair, my lady Jewel," Sebastian said candidly. "Only those who need to know are allowed to see it."

Suddenly, a shout came from the camp.

"Mynos!"

Without a word, the dragon leapt up and sprinted through the trees, Sebastian and Jewel right behind him.

Malnan lay writhing on the ground, fighting for a breath. Immediately Mynos was by her side, placing a hand on her chest. A white light emanated from his palm and into her body making her convulsions weaker and her breathing easier.

"Merric?"

Nodding, Malnan tried to sit up but fell back. "Mynos!" she wailed. "I saw what he's done. I saw it all."

Jewel pressed closer to Sebastian's side, fear coursing through her with one look at Malnan on the ground. What had Merric done?

Mynos smoothed Malnan's hair away from her face and cooed to her, trying to calm her. It worked somewhat, but she refused to lie down.

She put her face in her hands. Her words were muffled. "He's killed them, Mynos. Every single one of them. There's no one left to claim it. Oh God, there's no one left!"

"Claim what?" Jewel asked.

Malnan's green slitted eyes glittered with tears as she glanced up at her. "Claim the throne," she choked. "Lord Merric has killed the entire royal family!"

Chapter Twenty-Nine

Sebastian stared at Malnan in shock. His mouth fell open as Jewel clutched him even harder. He was barely aware of her crying against him. Mynos regarded his mate, his golden eyes filled with concern.

"Everyone?" he asked in a small voice. "Brennan and Lily?"

"Gone," Malnan breathed.

"Nicholas and his wife, Princess Derekah?"

"Gone."

"Even their baby son, Ryon?"

Malnan nodded, a look of horror on her face.

"Good God," Sebastian whispered, the severity of what Lord Merric had done hitting him in full force. "He's after the throne."

"But how can he be?" Jewel asked. "Everyone will know they were murdered!"

"With Malnan's Jewel," Mynos told her, "he can convince the people with his magic. Who knows what story he will come up with?"

"Then what are we waiting for?" Sebastian asked, a murderous gleam in his eyes. "I may be a Wolverine no longer, but Brennan was my king and I will defend him even in death. That bastard Merric will feel the sting of my sword, mark my words."

ജ്ഞോ

Jewel marveled at how high they were flying. Sebastian sat behind her, holding on hard—regardless of the magic holding them astride. She had never seen Mynos in his dragon form, and she was still reeling from watching him change his shape right in front of her. Malnan had changed too and before she knew it, Jewel was staring at two magnificent dragons.

"You look bigger, Malnan," Sebastian exclaimed at his first sight of her.

Malnan smiled. "I am, Sir Sebastian," she said. "I do not have to age again as a hatchling. My body will grow to the size it once was when I died."

Lowering a wing, Mynos said, "Climb up, children. You will not ride Malnan. If Lord Merric uses the Jewel again, she might falter in the sky and we cannot take that chance."

Sebastian had let the horses loose. He'd said returning to the castle was more important than bringing Blaze back. It was a sad moment, as Sebastian had ridden Blaze for a good many years. He'd been sired by Sir Geoffrey's own stallion, Noble, and was the pride of the stables at Castle Templestone. Jewel hugged Sebastian as he turned away from his horse, slapping the animal on the rump to get him running.

Now they were high above the countryside on the back of the ancient dragon, the wind whipping about them. At any other time, Jewel would have reveled in this ride, laughing and feeling free as a bird. But she couldn't help but be miserable. Mynos had healed her bruises, but she could still feel Merric's touch on her everywhere.

His crushing weight on her chest played over and over in her head, making her breath catch in the back of her throat.

Whenever Sebastian's hands came close to brushing one of her breasts, she tensed, wanting to scream at the memory of Merric's painful hands.

She knew it was silly, that Sebastian would never hurt her, but her anxiety rose as he nuzzled her neck from behind. It was a strange feeling, wanting him to hold her and then wanting to run from his touch at the same time. Sebastian was her husband. She loved him truly, so why did her heart race at the thought of making love to him again?

Sebastian somehow noticed her stiff frame, noticed her body trembling with a sudden fear. "What's wrong?"

Jewel's heart fell. She had hoped she could keep her distress a secret but she'd apparently failed miserably. What was he to think? Would he be angry at her? Would he think she blamed him for what Merric had done?

Her mouth suddenly dry, she said, "Nothing."

His arms squeezed her, telling her without words that he didn't believe her.

"What's wrong?" he repeated, concern lacing his voice.

Closing her eyes to the wondrous sight of the star-filled sky, Jewel sighed and bowed her head.

"Jewel?"

"I... I..." she stammered.

"What is it, my sweet wife?" He rested his chin on her shoulder, his cheek against hers.

"When you touch me, Bastian," she began, pausing to take a deep breath. "When you touch me, I can only think of Merric. I can only remember *his* touch and the way he..."

Unable to say more, Jewel hid her face in her hands, ashamed to confess to Sebastian she was terrified of his caresses.

Sebastian nodded. "It is to be expected," he told her with regret in his voice. "Do you believe me when I say I will never hurt you as he has?"

"Yes, Bastian. You have never hurt me. But I can't seem to tell my body that."

Sebastian kissed her neck and she shied away. "It seems I've got a lot of work ahead of me to erase his touch from your mind," he said with a pang of guilt. "I'm so sorry, my lady Jewel."

Turning in his arms, Jewel looked into his eyes. "You're not mad?"

"At you? Of course not!" He shook his head. "Do not even think it. It's Lord Merric who needs to pay for what you've been through."

They stared at each other for long moments before Jewel whispered, "I love you, Sir Sebastian of Tabrinth."

He caught her lips in a tender kiss before she warily pulled away. "And I love you, Lady Jewel of Tabrinth."

Sebastian didn't care that their titles meant nothing. Holding her close, he silently wished he could take all her pain on himself. Jewel was now haunted by memories of Lord Merric's hands on her, and Sebastian had to rid her of them. Somehow, he had to ease her fears and get her to trust him again.

He wanted, no, he *needed*, his sweet, passionate wife back. He needed the woman who welcomed him into her arms and begged him to make love to her. But how? How could Sebastian overcome those fears? He had to find a way. He loved her too much not to.

Chapter Thirty

Mynos and Malnan flew high in the sky as the sun peeked over the horizon. The air was frigid and almost too painful to breathe. It was a precaution. Those on the ground wouldn't immediately detect them as they approached Castle Templestone, despite the loud beating of the dragons' wings.

Jewel shivered, making Sebastian's grip around her tighten. His face was buried into her neck and shoulder, she assumed to ward away the sting of the cold air. Jewel lowered her face into the crook of Sebastian's elbow as one of his arms held her around her shoulders. It wasn't comfortable, but it offered protection against the chill, if only a little.

Mynos sailed over the cliffs and far across the open ocean beyond, only turning around when they wouldn't be seen from the castle. Descending, the dragons soared until they were mere feet above the ocean. Their wingtips touched the water with every beat, leaving a strange dotted trail behind them. Soon they caught the wind and floated on the current. Mynos explained the closer they were to the water, the harder they were to see. No one was expecting to see two dragons flying so close to the surface of the water.

The cliffs of Lyndaria loomed close, and Mynos didn't pull up until he almost collided with them. It brought a frightened shriek from Jewel who closed her eyes and held her breath as they flew upward, almost vertically.

Before she knew it, they had alighted inside a very large cavern located in the cliffs above the ocean, directly underneath the castle. The waves boomed as they crashed on the rocks below.

"We are here." Mynos lowered his wing, releasing the magic that held Sebastian and Jewel astride. As soon as they had jumped off, both dragons once again shifted into their human forms. Jewel was fascinated watching it. She never would have imagined such powerful magic existed if she hadn't witnessed it for herself.

An eerie glow filled the cave as tiny rainbows danced everywhere. What sounded like soft little chimes whispered throughout the cave. Glancing around, Jewel noticed the source of the light. Sitting in a niche in the far wall was the Crystal of Mynos. Without hesitation, the golden dragon walked straight to it and lifted it from the alcove.

Suddenly the light of the Crystal began to pulse, as if it were happy at being in the hands of its creator. Happy? *How could it possibly be happy?*

Sebastian took her hand, making her look at him. She was still ashamed of what she'd told him earlier, but his gaze wasn't accusatory in the least. If anything, his eyes seemed filled with sorrow as he smiled at her.

"If I were a real man," Mynos said, looking at Jewel and Sebastian, "the Crystal would have struck me down. However, it knows who I am and therefore will not."

Jewel felt a fluttering in her mind. She didn't understand what it was, but saw Mynos staring intently at her. *"The Crystal can only be touched by the hand of a woman."* She jumped at the sound of his voice in her head. *"It has bonded itself to Arianna, but I will break that bond, Daughter."*

"What does that have to do with me?" Jewel asked out loud.

Sebastian looked at her sharply. "Jewel?"

Mynos continued. "If you touch the Crystal after the bond with Arianna is broken, it will bond itself to you, Jewel."

Sebastian whipped his gaze back to the dragon. He stepped in front of Jewel. "Mynos, you can't possibly be suggesting..."

"No, Sir Sebastian," the dragon said, his gaze falling on him. "Jewel must not touch the Crystal. Arianna has magic in her family—in her blood. Jewel does not. I have confirmed it by touching her mind. If Jewel were to attempt to bond to the Crystal, it would crack her fragile mind like an egg."

At his words, Jewel took an involuntary step toward Sebastian, squeezing his hand. "I will not touch it."

Mynos nodded and glanced at Malnan. "I've never broken the Crystal's bond before."

"Will it cause Arianna pain?"

"I do not know."

ಜಇಞಗ

Without warning, Arianna sat straight up in bed and screamed. Geoffrey shot up, staring at his wife for a moment before realizing she was screaming. She clutched her head in both hands, shaking violently, shrieking at the top of her lungs.

"Arianna!" He seized her wrists and pulled her to him.

Wild eyed, she gazed at Geoffrey as if she had never seen him before. Tears fell freely and she began whimpering.

"Rose, sweetheart, what's wrong?" Geoffrey knelt in the middle of the bed, holding her close. "Rose?" He felt helpless. Without knowing what else to do, he stroked her hair and cooed to her. *"Can you hear me, baby?"*

"Geoffrey?" she asked silently, as if shocked he was even there.

"Yes, it's me," he told her, kissing her temple. *"What happened, do you know?"*

Arianna was still shaking and it was all Geoffrey could do to hold her still. But soon, she calmed down, taking in great gulps of air. *"I can't feel it anymore."*

"Can't feel what?" he asked, taking her face in his hands.

"The Crystal," she answered. "Geoffrey?" Her voice sounded confused.

"Hush yourself, now," he whispered.

"I can't feel it. I can't feel it."

"Hush." Lowering his head, he tried to calm her the only way he knew how. Brushing his lips against hers, he kissed her tenderly. He didn't stop until he felt her arms circle him. When they did, he held her in his firm embrace.

"He broke the bond," she breathed after long minutes.

"Who?"

"Mynos. I am no longer bonded to his Crystal."

Geoffrey found himself smiling with relief. He had never realized how much of a burden it had been for him to know that Arianna, the woman he loved more than life itself, had been bonded indefinitely to the whim of a magical talisman.

"Are you hurt?" He smoothed her hair.

"I have a headache and I feel as if I haven't had any sleep," she confessed.

"Well, you didn't get much." Geoffrey bent her head back to gaze at her with a teasing smile. "I seem to recall your thanks to me earlier keeping us up well into the night."

Arianna blushed as she gave him a tired grin. Looking out the window, she noticed the sunlight streaking the sky and knew Geoffrey would be leaving soon for his duties about the castle. "Will you stay with me?" She hugged him again, burying her face into his neck.

Laying her back into the pillows, Geoffrey leaned over her and smiled, taking her breath away. "I'll stay, Rose," he whispered as he bent to kiss her neck and shoulders. "But I'm not sure how much sleep you'll actually get."

Arianna sighed, reveling in the feeling he was giving her. She loved her husband with all her heart.

Geoffrey chuckled. "I love you too, sweetheart."

Chapter Thirty-One

"It's done." Mynos hung his head. "Arianna is no longer bonded to the Crystal."

Jewel noticed the gem, which had once flickered with a white light, now pulsed with a dark blue hue.

"How do we stop Merric?" Sebastian asked.

"We need to retrieve Malnan's Jewel and sever the bond holding Malnan to it. Once that is done, it will be useless to him."

"How will we obtain my Jewel?" Malnan raised a brow. "He can use my power at his whim. We will never get close to him."

"None of us can stand against the power of a dragon," Sebastian argued. "Even you, Mynos. If you fight Merric, he'll drain Malnan dry and kill her!"

Mynos regarded everyone, then looked down at his Crystal thoughtfully. "I made this talisman, not for myself, but for men. It is a tool to learn about magic, to enhance your own magical ability and do things beyond your wildest imaginings. Yet I've never used it myself."

A stunned silence hung in the air. "You've never used it?" Jewel asked.

"Never," Mynos answered. "My powers are strong enough. I've never had the need. Perhaps now I do."

"Are you saying your Crystal will enhance your own powers?" Sebastian asked in awe.

Mynos quirked a smile at him. "Exactly."

At that moment, a swirling wind picked up in the cave. In almost the blink of an eye, Mynos and Malnan had both changed their appearance, shockingly, to look exactly like Sebastian and Jewel.

Jewel gasped, as well as Malnan, who now looked exactly like her. "How did you do that?"

"I merely channeled my magic through the Crystal to see if it would work," Mynos said, an exact copy of Sebastian. Looking closely, Jewel couldn't even see a trace of the dragon's slitted eyes.

"This will do nicely," Mynos said, obviously proud of himself. "Merric will not suspect a thing."

"You're going to pretend to be us?" Sebastian asked with wide eyes.

"Indeed, Sir Sebastian. But there's one more thing I need." The dragon closed his eyes and concentrated. A sparkling light began to take shape on the ground before his feet, and within moments, a sword of a Wolverine lay there.

Sebastian recognized it immediately. "Fleetfire!" he exclaimed as he bent to pick up his weapon.

"You no longer need Quicksilver," the dragon told him.

Handing Fleetfire to Jewel, Sebastian immediately unstrapped Quicksilver from his waist. Once it was off, he handed Arianna's sword to the dragon.

"Perhaps we can convince Lord Merric that whenever he uses the Jewel he will be harming his Isabella," Mynos suggested. "He doesn't know exactly how the Jewel works so it wouldn't be hard to convince him."

Jewel was still too in shock to say a word.

"I hope this works," Sebastian said, strapping on his true sword.

"I hope so too," Mynos agreed as he looked at his mate and then back at Sebastian. "I want you two to stay down here. Do not come above unless instructed, is that understood?"

"Yes." Sebastian took Jewel's hand. She merely nodded after Mynos's words sank in.

Whatever the dragons planned to do, she hoped it would work.

ಬಿಕಿ

Malnan and Mynos had just reached the secret door at the top of the spiral staircase when Malnan fell over, screaming in pain. Mynos held her to him, knowing Merric was once again using the Jewel.

They both felt it at the same time, an overwhelming urge to believe there never had been a King Brennan, that Merric had always been king of Lyndaria. Mynos fought the urge, warded it off with magic he channeled through the Crystal. He shielded Malnan from it as well while she trembled from the force of Merric's own magic.

"He's learning how to pull more power from me, Mynos," Malnan whispered. "I'm so tired."

Mynos gave her more energy through his Crystal and helped her to her feet. "It would seem Merric is brainwashing the castle into believing he's the true king."

"We must hurry, Mynos," Malnan gasped.

"Indeed."

ℰℐℰℂ

As the dragons raced up the stairs from Mynos's lair, Sebastian turned and smiled tenderly at his wife.

"We're alone now, my lady Jewel." He held out his hand to her.

"So it would seem," she answered, taking his hand yet resisting his pull into his arms.

"Come here," he said, tugging a little harder.

"Bastian..."

"I only want to hold you." His eyes pleaded with her, telling her the truth of it. She conceded, leaning on him, feeling safe and secure. "We should sleep," he said in her ear. "I don't know about you, but I didn't get any rest last night."

"I can't sleep. Not when Merric is so close."

"Don't think about him." Sebastian ran his fingers through her hair.

Jewel shivered. "I can't help it. I can still feel him, I can still feel..."

"Shh." Sebastian pressed his lips on her cheek. "Let me help you forget about him."

Jewel wanted Sebastian to continue his caresses, she wanted to feel loved once again, but fear crept up her spine. The fear won out as she pushed away from him.

"I can't, Bastian." She walked away and braced herself against the far wall of the cave.

Jewel hadn't heard him walk up to her, but suddenly his presence warmed her back as he braced his hands against the wall on either side of her.

"We need to face this," he said behind her.

Jewel tried to duck under his arm to retreat again, but he wouldn't let her.

"Turn around," he implored.

"No." She buried her face in her hands. "I can't, Bastian."

"Look at me, sweetheart."

When she shook her head once more, Sebastian sighed, but didn't give up. Curling his left arm around her waist to hold her to him, he moved her hair away from her neck and kissed her there. Jewel shivered and whimpered at the same time.

"Bastian, please..." she choked out.

"You are afraid of me," he murmured as he made his way to her ear. "But you never were before. I need to make you forget this fear of yours, my lady Jewel. You have nothing to be afraid of, sweet wife. Let me prove it to you."

Turning her in his arms, he simply held her and did nothing more. Jewel stood trembling, resting her head on his chest. Her arms slowly curled around his neck and she clung to him as if she would fall if she let go.

"We need our sleep," he said to her, his deep voice thrumming through her body. "I will not touch you, my lady Jewel, not unless you want me to."

Jewel closed her eyes with relief, feeling a pang of guilt at her own cowardice. "I'm so sorry, Bastian."

Sebastian tightened his arms around her and rested his forehead on her shoulder. "We will get through this, I promise you. Together."

Tears collected in Jewel's eyes. "Please say you still love me," she choked. "Please say you aren't angry with me."

Sebastian sighed as he looked down at her. "Sweetheart, of course I still love you. What happened to you doesn't change my feelings in the least. I am not angry with you. You must believe that. I will be patient and wait, sweet wife. I know you are worth it."

Jewel's heart melted at his words. Pressing closer to him, she sobbed, deep, wrenching sobs, betraying the fear in her heart.

Sebastian slowly sank to the ground, still holding Jewel, and drew her against him. She scooted as close as she could, her face buried in his neck.

"I love you so much, Bastian."

She was still trembling as his arms held her tight.

"You are safe, Jewel, you are safe."

Chapter Thirty-Two

The newly crowned King Merric of Lyndaria sat on his throne and gloated to himself. Nobles and Wolverines alike bowed to him, carrying out his every whim, eagerly stumbling over themselves in order to be noticed. He fondled the lavender Jewel winking in the sunlight pouring through the high windows, despite the fact it had no facets to refract the light.

A low chuckle rumbled through him as he thought how easily he'd infiltrated the castle and killed the royal family. Queen Darragh had been a fool for not seeking Malnan's Jewel instead of the Crystal of Mynos. Merric held the true power in the palm of his hand.

Sitting on the raised dais, he could see the entire throne room and noticed instantly when a familiar couple entered through the wide open doors. Merric stood so suddenly he almost dropped the Jewel. With a harsh bark of command, he yelled, "Bring those two to me!"

Three young Wolverines standing at the bottom of the dais ran to do their king's bidding, hauling the offending couple through the throngs of courtiers.

Merric curled his lip in delight, his loins already hardening at his first glimpse of Isabella. His lust was almost doused, however, when intense hatred for Sebastian surged through him. He couldn't believe they'd *actually* dared return to the castle. But now, he was their king and sovereign. There was nothing they could do to stop him. Not when he held the power.

"Isabella," he purred, slowly descending the steps of his dais. "I've been thinking about you since our interlude in the forest. I think it's about time we finished what we started, don't you, my dear?"

"She won't be going anywhere with you," Mynos said confidently, his voice, sounding like Sebastian's, ringing throughout the throne room.

"Ah, Sebastian, the devoted husband." Merric's voice dripped with sarcasm. "I thought I had killed you once—I can kill you again."

Mynos smiled at him, delighting in the look of rage crossing Merric's features at the defiant gesture.

"You will bow to me before I kill you," Merric howled.

"No."

"What did you say to me?" Merric asked, as if not believing his ears. "I am your king, *boy*."

"Brennan was my king!" Mynos shouted. Everyone present whispered amongst themselves.

Merric laughed, holding his sides. "Who is this Brennan of whom you speak, Sebastian?" he asked with a sweep of his hand. "I always have been and always will be *king* of Lyndaria."

Many nods and rounds of applause followed his statement.

"Brennan was the king you killed." At that moment, Mynos used his magic to flash scenes through everyone's heads: of Merric hovering over a rotund, bearded man pleading for his life. By the gasps of the crowd and the strange look in their eyes, Mynos knew they had seen his vision.

"What kind of trickery is this, *Wolverine*?" Merric taunted. "Have you learned the powers of magic since last we met?"

"Perhaps."

Another scene flashed through Mynos's magic, this time showing Merric standing over a crib, crushing the life out of a tiny baby.

Women wept, and many of the courtiers didn't know what to make of what they were seeing. Yet none of them had the courage to question their king.

"Enough," Merric bellowed. "You will die, Sebastian, but not before you kneel!"

"No!" Mynos growled, suddenly furious himself at seeing the scenes. He too had loved the royal family. Merric must pay for what he had done.

The incensed lord suddenly held the Jewel in front of him and began to channel his magic through it. A wave of force focused on Mynos, and in a split second, the dragon countered it with the Crystal. An invisible shield erected around him, making Merric's attack fizzle and curl around the shield as if it were searching for a way in.

Malnan gave a shriek and fell to the floor, writhing. While Merric had channeled into the gem, her disguise had faltered ever so slightly, showing her true form.

"What is the meaning of this?" Merric shouted, his eyes wild. "You are not Isabella!" Pointing the Jewel at Malnan, he channeled into it once again, her disguise finally melting away. Malnan lay panting at Merric's feet, terror shining in her green slitted eyes.

Merric glanced back at Mynos. "Who are you that you can hold the Crystal and live?"

Mynos saw no use in keeping up his disguise any longer. He once again took his golden human form and bowed slightly.

"King Merric,*"* he mocked, "I am the dragon Mynos."

Merric looked back and forth between the dragon holding the Crystal, and the one on the ground. He quickly climbed the stairs of the dais to put some distance between them.

Mynos bent and helped Malnan off the floor. "And I believe you just met my mate."

ഇൽൽ

A loud banging finally woke Geoffrey out of his exhausted sleep.

"Go away!" he yelled.

The banging continued. Someone was calling for him beyond the door to his chambers.

"They're not going away," Arianna murmured. She flung an arm over her eyes to shield out the offending sunlight.

With a growl, Geoffrey sprang out of his warm bed, scrambling to put on his breeches. Once he had them on, he grabbed his sword and pulled it out of its sheath with an ethereal *tang.*

Yanking open the door, Geoffrey pointed the weapon at Briand, who stood wide eyed on the other side of the door.

"Sir Geoffrey!" he yelped, obviously worried Geoffrey actually meant to skewer him right then and there.

Lowering his sword, Geoffrey sighed and leaned against the doorframe. "This better be good, boy. My wife and I have had a rough night."

"Sir... Sir..."

"Out with it!" Geoffrey snapped, running his fingers through his unruly hair.

"It's Mynos, sir! He's attacking King Merric!"

"Attacking the king?" Geoffrey said in disbelief. Arianna sat up with a gasp. "Are you sure?"

Briand nodded vigorously. "He disguised himself as Sebastian and defied the king. He would not kneel! He then pulled out his Crystal, Geoffrey. I came to get you as fast as I could. I thought maybe since you and Arianna know Mynos better than any of us that you might be able to stop him."

Geoffrey glanced at Arianna who stared back at him with wide eyes.

"King Merric?" she said in a small voice. "That doesn't sound right."

"It is confusing to me as well, my lady. Mynos has long been allies with the king," Briand said from the hallway, making Geoffrey close the door just enough to hide his naked wife from the boy.

"I know," she continued, "but that name 'Merric' doesn't seem right."

"I'll be right there, Briand." Geoffrey grunted as he closed the door in the boy's face. Mynos? Attack the king? Why would he do such a thing? He had been King Merric's ally ever since they awakened him years ago.

Geoffrey wasted no time in getting dressed. Shooting a knowing glance at Arianna, he said, "You're not going."

"But..."

"No, Arianna. Briand said he had the Crystal. I'm not letting you near it again."

They stared at each other in silence, Geoffrey's stony countenance telling her not to say a word.

Arianna didn't like being left behind, but she knew Geoffrey was right. In Sebastian's absence, her husband was now

Captain of the Guard. He would be able to handle it on his own. She hoped so, anyway.

Chapter Thirty-Three

Sir Ethan of Krey stood on the battlements and gazed across the lush green fields surrounding the castle. It was a beautiful day. The sun was warm and a light breeze ruffled his sandy hair. Leaning against a crenellation, he sighed and thought about Sebastian and Jewel. He silently hoped they found their way to Evendria unharmed.

His friend Duncan leaned next to him with a smile on his face. "You think Sir Geoffrey is ever going to show himself this morning?"

Ethan grinned and tucked a few stray hairs behind his ear. "I wouldn't be surprised if he didn't with a wife who looks like Arianna."

"Do you make it a hobby of lusting after everyone else's wife, Sir Ethan?" Duncan was teasing, but Ethan knew he was referring to Jewel.

"Not at all," Ethan scoffed. "I sometimes lust after Lady Arlington."

Duncan's face went as red as his hair.

"Oh, did I hit a nerve?" Ethan's grin widened. "Word has it you're her new favorite."

"What?" Duncan exclaimed as he laughed nervously.

"She's old enough to be your mother, you know." Ethan poked him in the ribs.

"I don't care." Duncan lifted his chin. "She's a wonderful woman."

"I heard she had to chase you down before she got you into her bed."

Duncan gasped, looking around at the other Wolverines walking to and fro in the courtyard. "Where did you hear that?"

Ethan shrugged. "Does it matter?"

"I'm not ashamed, you know."

"Nor should you be, dear boy," Ethan said, patting Duncan on the back. "There's nothing wrong with having fun with a woman."

Both men stood there in silence for a few moments before Duncan said, "Do you ever get the feeling something bad might happen to you?"

"Like what?"

"Oh, I don't know. I sometimes get a feeling of dread creeping up my spine and I don't know where it comes from."

"I'm sure it's nothing." Ethan smiled as he turned to look back out at the fields.

After more long moments, Duncan said, "Ethan, I want you to promise me something."

Ethan turned to look at his friend, giving him a critical stare. "What?"

"I want you to promise that if anything happens to me, you'll look after my sister."

"Your sister?"

Duncan nodded. "She lives in Marynville. Her name is Meghan. I'm the only family she has left. If something were to happen to me..."

"Nothing is going to happen to you, Duncan," Ethan exclaimed.

"But if something were..."

"Duncan! Stop with these horrid thoughts."

"Just promise me, Ethan," Duncan stressed.

Ethan glared long and hard at his friend before turning away. "All right. I promise," he growled.

"Thank you." Duncan sighed as his body relaxed once more.

At that moment, Ethan stood up straight on both feet, staring out at the fields. "What the hell?"

As Duncan turned to look over the wall, a bright, thin line materialized in the air above the fields before ripping a hole in reality itself. Many Wolverines gasped and pointed at the spectacle as they watched what appeared to be an army of elves streaming through a magical portal. The men glanced about nervously.

Most of the Wolverines on the walls recognized King Kaas himself riding a horse in the front, along with Rowan riding next to him, who was both Arianna's uncle and the escort to the king of the elves.

However, coming unannounced with a large army was rather unsettling, even if they were allies to the king of Lyndaria. An aging Wolverine named Quinn, with salt and pepper hair and a bristling mustache, ordered the gates of the castle closed as a precaution.

Once Rowan saw this, he bellowed, "Open your gates, Castle Templestone. We are allies!"

"You come unannounced with an army at your back. State your business!" Quinn yelled from above.

"We are the entourage of King Kaas of the elves. We are here to see King Brennan."

"There is no King Brennan here," Quinn shouted as he glanced around at the other Wolverines on the wall. "What sort of game is this?"

Rowan and Kaas looked at each other in confusion. "We are here to seek an audience with the king. It is urgent!"

"The king has said nothing of your coming."

Kaas yelled up this time, "Open your gates at once! This is an outrage! I demand we be shown the hospitality that is our due as allies!"

"No," Quinn said. "I will send a man to tell King Merric you are here. If he should decide to let you in, then I will open the gates."

A dark look came over Kaas's face and he roared in frustration. "King Merric?" he yelled. "What goes on here? Brennan is your king!"

"*Merric* is our king, Your Majesty. How is it you do not remember?" Quinn shouted.

Kaas seethed at the aging Wolverine and did not answer him. "My daughter, Princess Derekah, and my grandson have been killed, boy! *Open these gates!*"

Quinn bristled at the insult. "Now see here..." he began, but Kaas yelled over him.

"If you refuse to open these gates, then we will open them for you!"

At that threat, Wolverines scrambled in the bailey to pull out bows and arrows from the armory along with heavy beams to brace the gates.

"You dare lay siege to Castle Templestone?" Quinn shouted in disbelief. "We are protected by a dragon!"

"Mynos is my ally as well," Kaas yelled. "If I cannot speak with your king, then send out your dragon and I will talk with him."

"You think me daft, man?" Quinn asked. "I cannot order a dragon about."

"Have you no respect for the king of the elves? Have you no respect for the father of the woman who would have been your future queen?"

"I know not of what you speak, sire," Quinn said. "There is no Queen of Lyndaria. But you are not entering these gates until King Merric has told me otherwise."

"Your king is Brennan!" Kaas yelled again, exasperated. "Where is Sir Sebastian? I will speak with your Captain of the Guard."

"He is Captain no longer," the Wolverine answered. "Sir Geoffrey of Emberdale is our new Captain."

Rowan sucked in his breath at that news, wondering what on earth was happening.

"Sire, something is very wrong here," Rowan whispered to Kaas. "They will not open their gates no matter what we say."

Kaas frowned. "I will not just sit here, Rowan. My daughter is dead!"

Rowan saw his shimmering eyes and nodded gravely. Rubbing his arms, he could feel powerful magic in the air around the castle. "What if Mynos is under this spell? He could decimate us easily."

"He is not," Kaas said. "It takes much more than simple magic to sway a dragon."

Closing his eyes, Rowan concentrated on touching the dragon's mind with his. After a few moments, he gasped and snapped his eyes open, gazing at Kaas with a look of disbelief.

"He wants us to hold our position."

"What has happened here, Rowan?"

"A man named Merric has killed the entire royal family and claimed the throne as his own. He is using his magic to brainwash the castle to believe the lie."

"He killed the *entire...*royal...family?" Kaas whispered.

Tears collected in Rowan's eyes. He let them fall. "This Merric has Malnan's Jewel."

Kaas was silent for a moment. "*Malnan's Jewel?* I thought it had been destroyed."

"No, Sire, it was not." Rowan sat in silence for a few more moments before he turned back to the king. "Mynos doesn't want us to lay siege to the castle. He doesn't want any innocent lives to be lost. But he has asked us to band together and lift the spell that has been placed on the castle."

Setting his jaw, Kaas sighed. "So be it. Tell Mynos I want to see him shortly. In the meantime, tell this young puppy guarding the gates that we will wait for word from his so-called king."

"You there!" Rowan yelled back up at Quinn. "Send your man to the king and tell him King Kaas, ruler of the elves and leader of the Army of Magi, will be waiting for his word."

Turning their horses, the two elves rode back out to their men and relayed what must be done. A few elves were saddened and in shock while even more were angry at the death of Princess Derekah and her family. They banded together however, as they chanted their magic to break the castle of Merric's spell.

ಜಿಜಿಂಛ

Ethan and Duncan stared at each other in astonishment. Was the elven king mad? Who was this King Brennan he spoke of? The hair on the back of Ethan's neck stood on end as he remembered all too well the battle to defend the castle from Darragh's army years ago. Would the elves truly march against their own allies? And if they did, would the Wolverines even stand a chance?

"You there!" Quinn yelled at Duncan.

Duncan snapped to attention in front of the old man, wide-eyed and trembling. "Y-yes sir?"

"Go tell King Merric that the king of the elves demands an audience."

Duncan merely stood there, staring at Quinn with his mouth hanging open.

"Now, lad," Quinn bellowed. "There's an army out there!"

Duncan didn't have to be told again as he bounded down the steps of the battlements and raced toward the castle.

Chapter Thirty-Four

Merric stood at the top of the dais and glanced uneasily at the two dragons standing before him. Mynos held Malnan at his side as she panted against his shoulder. Malnan was alive. But how was that possible? Her soul was trapped in the Jewel—wasn't it?

Holding up the lavender gem, Merric examined it in the light. A sudden smile spread out upon his face as he gazed back down at them.

"Greetings, Malnan," he said. "Indeed you are every bit as beautiful as the stories say."

Mynos scowled at him and took a step forward.

"I wouldn't if I were you, *dragon*," Merric spat.

Holding up his Crystal, Mynos gave him a wicked grin. "I am not afraid of you, Your Majesty."

"Nor I of you. Not when I now know your weakness."

At his words, Mynos glanced back at Malnan. "I am through playing with you, Merric." Mynos began to climb the steps of the dais.

Merric grinned and channeled through the Jewel, making Malnan shriek and double over on the ground once again. A huge ball of fire suddenly materialized in front of him and shot through the air toward the golden dragon. Mynos only had a moment to be surprised before he safely shielded himself. The fireball exploded against his own magic.

But Merric didn't stop there. Time and time again he pelted Mynos with the magical fire that spewed from the Jewel. Harder and stronger the magic became as Merric channeled all the energy he could, knowing full well he was sucking Malnan dry.

With a cry of desperation, Mynos concentrated on the Crystal and threw a thick wave of magic back at Merric. It flew through the air as if it were a wave on the ocean. It succeeded in hurling Merric backward, and he stumbled, falling over the throne.

"Mynos, stop!" a familiar voice yelled from the bottom of the dais.

Chancing a quick glance over Mynos's shoulder, Merric saw Geoffrey, his sword drawn, a look of confusion on his face. "Step away from the king, Mynos."

"Seize him!" Merric pointed at Mynos, struggling to stand.

No one moved at all. Mynos stood his ground with the Crystal flaming magical fire in his hand. The Wolverines in the throne room looked on, too afraid themselves to approach the dragon.

Geoffrey was the only Wolverine in the room who moved to obey his king. Cautiously, he climbed the steps toward the dragon, his sword drawn and leveled at him.

"Don't make me do this, Mynos."

"Merric is not your king, Sir Geoffrey," Mynos told him. "What does Flameblade tell you?"

Geoffrey's sword was glowing wildly, screaming inside his head, pleading for him to listen to the dragon.

"I will not listen to you or your treachery," Geoffrey said in a pained voice. "You have been a friend, Mynos, a good and trusted friend. But you have betrayed that trust by attacking my king!"

Mynos unexpectedly channeled his magic through the Crystal. Geoffrey's sword suddenly glowed red-hot. Geoffrey cried out and dropped it to the ground with a loud clang.

Staring at Mynos with a look of shock, Geoffrey took a step back in spite of himself. His heart ached at the thought of the dragon's betrayal. "What is the meaning of this, Mynos?"

"Sir...Geoffrey," a gritty voice panted behind him.

Turning to look, Geoffrey saw Malnan crawling to him on the floor, pain in her slitted eyes as she took hold of his ankle. Suddenly, images and scenes of King Brennan's death fluttered in his head as she showed him with her magic every last detail of what Merric had done to the royal family.

"Oh my God," Geoffrey whispered, glancing back at Mynos. "King Brennan!" He sobbed in grief before sinking to his knees, weeping there on the steps.

"What are you waiting for?" Merric yelled once again, looking around at everyone present. "Seize the dragon, I command you!"

The Wolverines in the room glanced about at each other, all apparently shocked at the sight of their Captain weeping in front of them.

Sir Duncan ran into the throne room at that moment, breathless. "Your Majesty!" he squawked as he made his way through the crowd. He stopped short upon seeing Mynos holding the flaming Crystal aloft with Geoffrey crying on the steps. "Your Majesty?" he said again, this time raising his eyes to Merric.

Malnan's Jewel glittered in Merric's hand as he seethed with rage. He seemed to focus all his energy on the red-headed man.

"What is it?" he asked in a deceptively calm voice.

"King Kaas of the elves is awaiting an audience with you, demanding the reason for his daughter's death."

"Get rid of him," Merric commanded, turning back toward the dragon.

"I cannot. Sire, he's brought an army. He is threatening to lay siege to the castle if we do not open our gates!"

"What?" Merric screamed as he channeled through the Jewel recklessly. Only this time, his magic hurled through the air and pitched Duncan back with such force, he flew through the wide open doors of the throne room. Slamming into the wall on the far side of the hallway, Duncan's body broke some of the stones in the wall with a sickening crack. He slid down the wall and crumpled to the floor, his eyes rolling back as he lay silent and bleeding.

Geoffrey let out a roar at the sight and grabbed his sword, now cool to the touch. Without a thought, he sprinted up the steps, intent on running Merric through. However Merric suddenly disappeared into thin air. Geoffrey wasn't able to stop his charge in time and only succeeded in putting a fine hole into the back of the king's throne.

With a broken sob, he wrenched his glowing sword from the back of the gilded chair and looked around frantically. But Merric was nowhere to be seen.

"Malnan!" Mynos ran to her. She was unresponsive as he turned her over. Her green eyes were dilated and unfocused, telling Geoffrey beyond the shadow of a doubt Mynos had lost her once again.

"No!" came the dragon's anguished cry. Still holding the Crystal, Mynos was unaware of the power of his grief as he unwittingly channeled his magic through it. The walls of the

castle shook violently and the courtiers ran screaming from the room.

Geoffrey raced back down the stairs and grabbed the dragon, forcing him to look him in the eye. "Mynos!" he yelled into his ear. "Mynos, you must stop."

Geoffrey was taken aback by the tears in the dragon's eyes as he turned his tortured gaze upon him. The rumbling through the castle ceased.

"He has taken her," Mynos whispered. "He has killed Malnan and taken her!"

"Her soul is still bonded to the Jewel, is it not?" Geoffrey asked.

Mynos nodded as tears fell from his eyes, embedding themselves into the stone floor as veins of gold.

"Then you haven't lost her, Mynos. She will find her way back to you. Merric hasn't won that easily."

Nodding, Mynos dried his eyes and began chanting, his hands weaving intricate patterns in the air. After a few moments, Malnan's body faded away.

"What is happening?" Geoffrey asked in alarm.

"Do not be frightened, Sir Geoffrey," Mynos said as he wove his magic. "This is how we consecrate our dead. A dragon's body should never be wasted." With that, Malnan's body completely disappeared, leaving a glittering green gem winking innocently at them on the floor.

Geoffrey looked back at Mynos, glanced at the Crystal, and back at the gem in front of him. "Mynos," he said in awe, "is this how you made your Crystal?"

Giving Geoffrey a smile, Mynos bent and picked the gem off the floor. "Not every dragon is consecrated in this way, Son," he told him. "But when we die, our wish is to become an instrument of teaching magic to future generations. Our bodies become magic itself when we are consecrated, and the Jewels that result are clean slates, to be enchanted by the whim of the dragon who consecrated it—as they see fit."

"What are you going to enchant this one with?"

Mynos said nothing, slipping the smooth and perfectly round green gem into his pocket.

"Sir Geoffrey!" Briand's voice cracked as he ran forward.

Geoffrey stood and lifted his sword, expecting to fight Merric right then and there. "What is it?" he asked, his eyes blazing.

"It's Duncan," the boy choked out. "Sir Duncan of Marynville is dead."

"Oh...God," Geoffrey groaned as his shoulders sagged in grief, dropping his sword. "Not poor Duncan!"

Mynos placed an understanding hand on Geoffrey's shoulder as he crumpled to the floor, weeping for Duncan, for Malnan, and for King Brennan, who had been both his sovereign and his friend.

Chapter Thirty-Five

Jewel awoke with a start. Her heart raced as she looked around frantically, half-expecting to see Merric kneeling over her with a sadistic grin pasted on his face. Relief flowed through her when she saw Sebastian lying next to her, his arm loosely wrapped around her shoulders, his breathing even. He was asleep, and regardless of the horrid dream she had just awoken from, she found herself staring at her husband.

He seemed so at peace with his unruly hair falling over his forehead and his eyes shut tight. His mouth was slightly open as he breathed and Jewel found herself wondering what he was dreaming of. He was such a handsome man, and she couldn't resist the urge to softly touch his cheek. After a few days of not taking a blade to his face, Sebastian's chin was prickly with dark stubble. A full beard would make him look older. She was so involved with studying his strong chin that she jumped with surprise to see his stormy blue eyes open, regarding her.

Neither one of them said a word as Sebastian reached his hand out to stroke her face as well. His eyes never left hers, making her feel uncomfortable under his scrutiny, but she did not look away.

"Did you sleep?" he asked in a whisper.

Jewel nodded and pushed his hair away from his face, feeling its texture.

"Did you dream?" His deep voice rumbled through her.

She nodded again, still holding his gaze.

"About Merric?"

Jewel bit her lip, but still she did not look away. After long moments, she nodded once more.

Sebastian said nothing else, continuing to stroke her face, every now and then running his fingers into her hair.

"Did you know you're the most beautiful woman I have ever seen?" he asked, taking her off guard with his thoughts. Jewel smiled and blushed, finally looking away from his eyes, but only to rest her gaze on the beating pulse in his neck.

"I have never seen eyes the color of yours, or hair quite so silky." He brought a dark lock to his lips and kissed it. That simple, innocent gesture sent a sudden and unexpected shock of desire through her. Closing her eyes, she whimpered.

"Jewel?" he asked in concern, pulling his hand away. "Are you all right?"

Sebastian was no longer touching her, except for his arm around her shoulders, and Jewel felt the loss of his contact with a pang of regret.

"I am sorry, sweetheart," he said as he tried to sit up. "I didn't mean to scare you."

"No!" she yelped. "No, Bastian, please don't go." Jewel held onto fistfuls of his shirt and buried her face into his shoulder. Sebastian lay back down, but made no move to touch her again.

Looking up at him, Jewel grabbed his hands and brought them to her cheeks. As her tears fell, she held his hands there with her own.

"Please don't give up on me," she pleaded with him. Turning her head, she placed a soft kiss on each of his palms.

Sebastian sighed and gazed at her tenderly. Wiping away her tears with his thumbs, he sat up just enough to kiss her wet eyelids. He pulled her into his embrace and she curled her arms around his neck.

"I will never give up on you, my lady Jewel," he breathed into her ear.

Jewel sat back and ran her fingers over his bottom lip. Without another word, she urged his head to hers and gave him a gentle kiss. Sebastian pulled away first, but she didn't mistake the warm glow in his eyes as he gazed at her.

"We cannot rush things," he told her. Jewel nodded, yet she couldn't help but feel disappointed.

"You are right." She sighed, laying her head back down on his chest. She heard his steady heartbeat as she held him and wished things were different. She wanted so much to share her love for him as they had done many times in the past, but rushing things before she was ready was not the answer.

At that moment, a loud humming noise echoed throughout the cavern.

"What is that?" Jewel looked around.

"It's Fleetfire," Sebastian said in surprise. He stood, pulling the sword from its scabbard. The weapon glowed bright white, casting long shadows on the walls. Sebastian and Jewel covered their eyes.

Jewel stood as well and watched as shock and horror crossed Sebastian's handsome features. With trepidation, she wondered what his enchanted sword was telling him.

"Bastian?" she murmured, noticing the pools collecting in his eyes. They fell down his cheeks, leaving wet trails as he continued to stare at his sword.

"Oh no," Sebastian cried, clutching the hilt with both hands as if he were going to drop it. "No!"

"Bastian," Jewel asked, frightened. "What is happening?"

"Oh God, Jewel, he's killed Duncan. The bastard killed Duncan!"

The cave suddenly shook as clumps of dirt and rocks fell from the ceiling. Jewel lost her footing and fell back, yet Sebastian stood fast, holding his sword aloft, crying all the more.

"*Malnan,*" he moaned. The violent shaking stopped as swiftly as it started. "He's killed her too."

Jewel couldn't speak. She couldn't even breathe. After several attempts, she found her voice. "Are you sure, Bastian?"

Fleetfire's light diminished. Sebastian closed his eyes and tried for all he was worth to get the scenes out of his head. He'd seen it all—Duncan being hurled back only to slam against the wall, and Mynos cradling the still form of Malnan lying on the floor of the throne room. He couldn't answer her. All he could do was nod as he stumbled over to the wall to brace himself.

Neither one of them spoke for what seemed an eternity as Sebastian sheathed his sword with a shaky hand.

"Merric is gone," he finally said, regaining his composure and wiping his eyes. "He's disappeared once again to God knows where."

"Does...does he still have Malnan's Jewel?"

"Yes, and her soul should have returned to it. I'm not so sure he'll be able to wield its magic as he has before." Walking over to her, Sebastian helped her wipe the dirt from her dress before saying, "Mynos has summoned us to the castle. Are you ready?"

"If Merric is gone and you stay close to me, Bastian, I'll be fine." Jewel pressed her trembling hand into his.

"Come," he urged, stepping toward the spiral staircase. "Let's hope the death of King Brennan won't be the downfall of Lyndaria. I don't know what we're going to do now."

Chapter Thirty-Six

King Kaas of the elves stood stoically at the large paned windows in King Brennan's study, brooding as he stared at the crashing ocean far below. His mages had lifted Merric's spell on the castle with little effort, regardless that the spell was drawn from a dragon's power.

A young Wolverine named Sir Ethan of Krey had finally opened the gates of Castle Templestone to Kaas's entourage after the spell had been broken, and Kaas wasted no time in seeking Mynos out. The two agreed to convene in King Brennan's study, as King Brennan himself would have had it no other way.

Stepping ever so slowly away from the windows, King Kaas turned toward the dragon. Mynos sat in an overstuffed chair near the enormous desk piled high with paperwork. He looked bone weary and full of sorrow, and also full of the knowledge he had once again lost his mate.

"King Brennan has left no living heirs," Kaas said. "His son and his grandson were killed with him, as well as his wife. He has no brothers or sisters." Kaas paced the room. "Not even any distant living relatives."

Mynos nodded with a sigh. "None."

"Then *we* must choose a new sovereign for Lyndaria," Kaas said sorrowfully, pinching the bridge of his nose.

"This is not the first time Lyndaria has had to pick a new ruling family," Mynos declared. "After the first war for my Crystal millennia ago, King Timothy died because he was no longer being sustained by the Crystal's power."

"I remember hearing stories about this from my father." Kaas continued pacing back and forth. "My grandfather was king of the elves at the time. The people had chosen you to crown the new king, did they not?"

"Yes," the dragon said. "I chose a Wolverine named Sir Benjamin. King Brennan himself was descended from him."

"Then we must do the same. It seems history is repeating itself."

Nodding his agreement, Mynos stood from his chair. "I have already made my choice." He looked at Kaas with a gleam in his eye.

The king of the elves stared at the dragon for long moments before he demanded to know who. As Mynos indulged him, Kaas smiled in approval, knowing Mynos had made a fine choice. A fine choice indeed.

ƒ蔥XC&#x8;

When Sebastian and Jewel were let into King Brennan's study a few hours later, they were greeted by the smiling faces of King Kaas and the dragon Mynos, as well as the stunned faces of Sir Geoffrey and Lady Arianna of Emberdale.

Sebastian glanced nervously around the room and urged his wife to sit next to him in a large chair. Jewel clutched his hand. She looked at him every few moments.

"Sebastian," Mynos began, "do you know what has happened at the castle today?"

"I only know what Fleetfire has told me. Sir Duncan is dead, as well as Malnan." As soon as he said it, Sebastian wished he could take it back for the look of pain that crossed Mynos's face.

"King Kaas has arrived to avenge the death of his daughter, Princess Derekah, the wife of Brennan's son, Prince Nicholas. His mages lifted a spell Merric had placed on the castle that made the people believe he was the true king."

Sebastian spared a glance at Geoffrey, who still had a dazed look on his face, not really focusing on anything at the moment. Geoffrey's arm was firmly locked around Arianna's shoulders and it was a good thing too, for she seemed she would crumple to the floor without his support.

A few moments of uncomfortable silence passed before Sebastian finally asked, "What is going on, Mynos?"

"King Brennan has no living relatives. Therefore, King Kaas and I have chosen one of the king's own Wolverines to be crowned as king of Lyndaria."

Sebastian remembered the old stories, the ones of Sir Benjamin, who'd been like a son to his king when the Crystal was stolen from the castle all those years ago. The king had later died without the power of the Crystal and Sir Benjamin had been crowned king.

Sebastian stared at Mynos with wide eyes. "Mynos, are you saying..." He was unable to finish his sentence.

"Yes." The dragon smiled. "Sir Geoffrey wanted you to be the first to know, since you will be reinstated as his Captain of the Guard."

It took a few moments before those words sank into Sebastian's befuddled brain. "I'm going to be reinstated as the...*Geoffrey?*" he shouted as he stood with a look of amazement on his face. "*King Geoffrey?*"

216

Without another word, Sebastian hugged both Geoffrey and Arianna, laughing joyously. His friends hugged him back, obviously not wanting to fall over from the force of his enthusiasm. Soon, there wasn't a dry eye in the room as Jewel also stood to embrace the new royal family.

"Their coronation will be held tomorrow morning, and as his first act as king of Lyndaria, Geoffrey wanted to give you back your title as Wolverine *and* Captain."

Words failed them both as Sebastian and Geoffrey gazed at each other. Sebastian gave him a wide grin.

"I'll serve you with my life, Geoffrey, you know that, don't you?"

Geoffrey merely nodded as he hugged his friend, patting him unmercifully on the back. "Your titles and your lands will be restored to you, Sebastian," he choked out through his tears, "as well as Jewel's estates in Evendria. Don't be late to the coronation. You are my closest friend. I need you there."

"Don't you worry," Sebastian said with a grin as he turned to hug his own wife. "We'll be there." After a short silence, Sebastian asked, "Should I start calling you 'Your Majesties' now?"

"You do, and I'll smack you," Arianna teased, wiping the tears from her lashes. "Never in a million years would my father have seen this coming," she said in a wavering voice. Geoffrey looked at her with obvious love in his eyes. "I can't stop trembling. This is a dream. It must be a dream. Geoffrey, are we dreaming?"

"We're not dreaming, Rose," he said, shaking his head with a gentle smile. "We are now, truly, the king and queen of Lyndaria."

Chapter Thirty-Seven

Jewel grinned with pride as she watched her husband knighted once again by the newly crowned King Geoffrey, ruler of the Four Realms and leader of the Order of the Wolverine. The sword known as Quicksilver blazed in King Geoffrey's hand as he knighted Sebastian, who was visibly nervous.

Glancing down the pew she was sitting on, Jewel noticed the imposing visage of the man who had stopped them before the ceremony, just as they were entering the sanctuary. A full beard adorned his face and long hair spilled down his back, tied at the nape of his neck by a small piece of leather. He was at least a good six inches taller than Sebastian and had looked down at him with a disapproving glare.

"And where do you think you're going, boy?" she heard him say as he stood directly in their way, in front of the chapel's double doors. His dark eyes were as hard as agates as he stared severely at Sebastian, both arms crossed on his chest. For a split second, Jewel didn't know what to think or what Sebastian would do, as his entire body tensed. If it weren't for the beautiful blonde elf next to the burly man, Jewel might have thought the two men would fight each other right then and there in the hall.

However, a grand smile suddenly dawned on Sebastian's face as he grabbed the big man in a hug so strong, Jewel wondered if he could even breathe.

"Cederick!" Sebastian smacked the man on his back. "How's life with the elves been treating you?"

"Wonderful," Cederick barked, hugging the small, beautiful elf at his side. "Meliena has given me two gorgeous little girls, but I'm hoping the next will be a boy."

"The *next*?" Sebastian asked. Gazing at the elf, he whispered, "Are you..."

"No." She chuckled, slapping Cederick's shoulder.

"We'll have to remedy that, now won't we?" he teased with an exaggerated wink.

Sebastian tossed his head back and laughed.

"I apologize for my rudeness, my lady Jewel." He placed his hand on the small of her back. "This is my good friend, Sir Cederick of Breckenwood, and his lovely wife Meliena of the elves. Cederick, Meliena, this is my wife, the soon-to-be-again Lady Jewel of Tabrinth."

Without warning, the robust man grabbed her in a hug not too unlike the one he'd given to Sebastian.

"Seb, you old dog! Why didn't you tell me you got yourself gelded?"

"I just did!" He chuckled at his friend as he rescued Jewel from Cederick's iron grip.

"How'd you do it, girl?" Cederick asked, a wide smile plastered on his face. At least he seemed approachable when he smiled. "How'd you get ol' Seb here to the altar?"

Sebastian blushed and took Jewel's hand. "There will be plenty of time for catching up, Cederick. We need to be seated."

"Indeed." Cederick grinned as he followed them into the chapel.

Ethan and Briand had saved seats for Sebastian and Jewel in the front pew, and Cederick succeeded in strong-arming his way into sitting next to them.

Now, Jewel was shocked to see Sir Cederick wipe his eyes as Sebastian once again became a Wolverine. Never would she have pegged Cederick for an emotional man.

Loud applause rang throughout the sanctuary when Sebastian stood and greeted his fellow Wolverines as their Captain once again. Jewel was so proud of her husband, she doubted she could feel any more love in her heart than she did right then.

Without warning, Sebastian bounded down the steps of the altar and snatched Jewel into his arms, hugging her close before swinging her squealing about the sanctuary.

৪০৪০৪

In the days that followed, King Geoffrey ordered the entire castle searched from the highest tower to the lowest dungeon in search of Lord Merric. But he was not to be found.

The bodies of King Brennan and his family were buried formally in the royal crypt, with all the flair and propriety deserved of the former royal house. Many nobles and townsfolk from far and wide came to give their last respects to King Brennan and swear fealty to King Geoffrey.

He declared the country in mourning over the death of King Brennan and wasted no time in signing treaties and meeting with his countrymen who were already beginning to love their new king.

The Wolverines buried Sir Duncan of Marynville in the cemetery behind the castle and grieved his passing. But none wailed louder than Lady Arlington. Sebastian truly felt sorry for her as she had to be carried away from Duncan's grave. Perhaps there had been more to their relationship than just a simple fling.

Standing on the battlements, Sebastian's thoughts were on Duncan as he breathed in the crisp morning air. There was so much death at Castle Templestone. He could only hope they would be able to move on and start anew.

Jewel had seemed contented enough for Sebastian to go back to his rounds on the castle walls after a few days, but she was still reserved. He didn't know how much longer she would be like this, or if she would ever change. Lord Merric had broken her spirit when he'd tried to defile her, and Sebastian was at a loss of what to do to help her through it.

"Woman trouble?" Sir Ethan grinned as he leaned against the crenellation next to Sebastian.

"Jewel and I are perfectly fine." Sebastian sighed, hoping he wasn't too easy to read.

"Then why are you scowling?"

Rubbing the hilt of his sword, Sebastian murmured, "I am thinking of Duncan."

At that admission, Ethan's face fell. "He was a good man."

"One of the best."

"He asked me to look after his sister. Made me promise, as a matter of fact."

Sebastian turned to face him. "Why would he say that?"

"I don't know. He said he had a bad feeling, like something terrible was going to happen to him."

"And something did," Sebastian mused.

"When can I go to Marynville?" Ethan held his breath, as if the entire world rested on Sebastian's answer.

"What for?"

"To find Duncan's sister, make sure she's well taken care of."

Sebastian pondered Ethan's words and ran his fingers through his hair. "I will not make you break your promise. But I do ask you stay at the castle until Lord Merric has been found."

Ethan nodded, expelling his breath. "I hope it won't take too long."

"It shouldn't." Sebastian grunted. "King Kaas has his mages scouring the countryside."

At that moment, both men noticed a plume of dust rising on the road to the castle. It wasn't long before Sebastian spotted a single rider in the distance, racing as hard as he could toward them. He was bent low over his horse and did not carry a pennant of any sort.

"Ethan, round up a few men and intercept this rider," Sebastian ordered. "If he is a messenger, escort him in. If not...you know what to do."

Ethan bowed deeply. He wasted no time in bounding down the steps on the side of the curtain wall, whistling to two of his men to follow as he sprinted to the stables.

Chapter Thirty-Eight

The boy felt like a cornered animal as his eyes darted back and forth between the angry men. He stood next to his lathered gelding in the bailey of Castle Templestone and wished he could be anywhere else at that moment. The fifty gold ladies jingling in his belt pouch didn't sound like such a king's ransom after all.

"Who gave you this?" asked the dark, forbidding figure in front of him, waving the missive in the boy's face.

"A...a man did, sir," the boy squawked, his voice trembling. "Told me he'd make me rich if I'd bring this note to the Captain of the Guard at Castle Templestone."

Sighing loudly, Sebastian studied the boy with a critical eye. He couldn't be older than thirteen winters. Softening his gaze, Sebastian laid his hand on the boy's shoulder.

"Go on into the castle, lad. Tell the servants I ordered you a hot meal."

"Yes, sir!" The boy's face lit up as he began to trot away.

"Take his horse, Briand," Sebastian said, handing the reins to the young Wolverine.

Nodding, Briand led the gelding to the stables.

"What does it say?" Ethan looked over Sebastian's shoulder at the letter he held.

Crumpling the paper in his fist, Sebastian stalked away. "Ethan, go back to your post."

ಶಿಶಿಲ

Jewel opened the doors to the king's study, her heart pounding. She'd been found by a servant, laughing in the gardens with Meliena and Queen Arianna, telling happy stories of their husbands. The agitated servant practically dug his fingers into her arm to get her to follow. All she knew about the king's summons was that it was urgent.

Lifting her skirts, Jewel wasted no time, running the rest of the way, thinking in the back of her mind something horrible must have happened to Sebastian.

But as she threw open the doors, relief flooded through her. Sebastian immediately stood from his chair and ushered her into the room, making sure the doors were closed firmly behind her.

King Geoffrey paced back and forth, holding a badly wrinkled piece of paper in his hand.

"I think you should sit down, my lady Jewel," Sebastian said.

"Is something wrong, Bastian?"

"We have found Lord Merric," Geoffrey said, turning toward her.

At the sound of his name, a chill raced through her body. "Where?"

"He's returned to Evendria. Jewel..." the king began, unable to go on as he dropped his gaze back to the letter.

"What?" Jewel glanced from Geoffrey to her husband. "Bastian, what is going on?"

Sebastian knelt in front of her and took both of her hands in his. "Sweetheart, he has taken your father and your brother. He's threatening to kill them."

"But...my father? My brother? Why? Why would he do that?" Confusion clouded her mind. She didn't even remember her father or brother.

"He's offering a trade. He'll release your family unharmed and give us Malnan's Jewel for..."

"For what?"

"For you," he whispered.

An uncomfortable silence stretched between them as the realization of what Sebastian said finally sunk in.

"No. No, Bastian, I can't do that. Don't make me go." She sobbed, her body shaking violently.

Taking her into his arms, Sebastian stroked her hair as he held her tight. "I will never let that monster have you, Jewel. You know I will not."

She clutched Sebastian's neck as if she wanted to crawl inside him.

"What are we going to do?" she wailed into his shoulder.

Sebastian glanced at Geoffrey who crumpled the letter once more and tossed it into the fireplace.

"Do not be afraid, Lady Jewel," Geoffrey said, watching the flames consume the paper. "There isn't another man in the kingdom who is wanted more than Lord Merric. Mynos, King Kaas, and I have known for quite awhile that Merric returned to Evendria."

Sebastian gasped. "You *knew*?"

Geoffrey smiled. "Malnan's soul returned to the Jewel when she died, but she was able to contact Mynos through the power of his Crystal not too long after Merric fled the castle. She

225

cannot kill Merric in her state, but she has been working to twist his mind. The more he tries to use Malnan's Jewel, the more unstable he becomes." Jewel and Sebastian stared at King Geoffrey, their mouths wide open.

"And I must say," he said with a grin, "Malnan has been doing a fine job. A fine job indeed."

Chapter Thirty-Nine

Queen Arianna sat in her favorite pew near the front of the ornate, empty chapel. Sunlight poured in through the bright and colorful stained glass windows, giving the wondrous room a magical quality. It was quiet, almost unsettlingly so, as she sat and prayed, taking in the events that had happened to her over the past few days.

She'd been thrust into a world of courtiers and noblewomen, asked to bless babies and give advice about this or that. It was a noisy, busy world now, and Arianna often found peace in the quiet of the sanctuary.

She missed Geoffrey. His new duties kept him separated from her on most days. They frequently slept late in order to spend more time with each other, even if it was only in sleep. She could reach him at any time through their Remembrance bond, but she preferred not to disturb him when he was busy.

Rubbing her flat belly, Arianna's thoughts wandered. Lord Merric had been found once again in Evendria, and it seemed Malnan was driving him slowly insane. Sebastian and Jewel were preparing to confront him and she prayed for them too, for their safety. She also prayed Lord Merric wouldn't harm Jewel's family.

"I thought I might find you in here."

Arianna jumped at the sound of the quiet, yet booming, voice behind her. She sighed in relief to find King Kaas smiling behind her, his eyes sad. The chapel doors remained closed, and she wondered for a moment how he'd entered without her hearing them open. But then she realized he had probably used his magic to keep the chapel doors quiet. Or perhaps he'd opened a portal.

"Hello, Your Majesty." She bowed her head to him as her voice echoed loudly off the surrounding walls.

"Please, call me Kaas." He moved to sit next to her on the pew. Arianna scooped up her voluminous burgundy gown to make room.

"What brings you here?"

"We haven't talked much, you and I. Not since you married Sir...I mean *King* Geoffrey."

Arianna nodded, still trying to get used to the new title as well. Looking at King Kaas, she noticed a faint resemblance to her Uncle Seth. She hadn't thought much about it, but Kaas was part of her extended family. Her grandmother had been his sister, Princess Kendra of the elves, who'd defied years of tradition and circumstance to abdicate her throne to Kaas, her younger brother, for the love of a human Wolverine.

At the time, elves marrying humans was unheard of, and Kendra was disowned by her father and stripped of her royal title. But now, mixed marriages were becoming more and more common, and elves were being accepted into human society.

The fact that Prince Nicholas had wed Kaas's daughter, Princess Derekah, helped things along to that end. But now, Derekah was dead, killed by the hand of Lord Merric. Arianna's eyes filled with tears at the thought of their family destroyed by his hand—even their infant son. She hoped deep in her heart Sebastian would bring justice to Lord Merric soon and swiftly.

"Derekah was your cousin, you know," Kaas said as if reading her thoughts. "Albeit distantly." He stared up at one of the colorful windows and sat in silence for a few moments.

Arianna nodded. "Yes, I was just thinking about that." A few more moments of stillness passed before she whispered, "I'm sorry you lost her. I'm sorry you lost little Prince Ryon as well."

Kaas looked back down to Arianna. "I am sorry too at times, Arianna, but I cannot help but think it is all part of the Grand Maker's design."

Thinking about children dying brought her own thoughts back to her stillborn daughter. Arianna's gaze dropped to her hands as her eyes burned with unshed tears. She still mourned for her daughter and knew she would for the rest of her life. What kind of queen could she possibly be if she couldn't bear Geoffrey a child?

"You are sad." Kaas tucked a stray hair behind her ear.

Arianna nodded, sniffling.

"I am sorry to hear about your daughter as well, little niece," he said, reading her thoughts once again. He wrapped his arm around her shoulders. "It seems we both have much to mourn for."

Pulling out an intricately embroidered handkerchief, Arianna dabbed at her eyes and looked at her grand-uncle. "I think Mynos may have made a mistake choosing me as queen," she confessed.

"Why do you think so?"

She pressed her handkerchief against her face. "Geoffrey and I cannot have children, Kaas. How are we supposed to be the next royal house of Lyndaria when we cannot produce an heir? The people will not blame Geoffrey for it. They will look at me for the problem. I...I just don't know what to do."

229

Kaas smiled gently. "That is why I came to find you. I want to give you a gift." He took her hand. "Close your eyes."

Arianna hesitated for a moment, but did as he told her. "What gift?" she asked, only to be shushed by him as he closed his eyes.

After a few moments, a warmth spread throughout Arianna's body and she heard a slight ringing in her ears. She recognized it instantly as magic—and powerful magic at that. It coursed up her arms and flowed through her belly, making her sigh at the feeling. It washed over her like water, covering her body from head to toe. Before too long, Kaas squeezed her hand in his. "You can open your eyes now, little niece."

Arianna looked down at herself, as if she would spy something different. "What did you give me?"

"A most precious gift, Arianna," he answered. "I have opened your womb. You will bear Geoffrey a child."

Arianna stared at him in shock. Time seemed to stop as she gazed into the face of the elven king. She gasped, and her hands trembled when she brought them to her mouth. Without warning, she jumped into his arms. Incapable of actually voicing her immense gratitude, she merely sobbed into his shoulder, clutching his neck and feeling the burden lift from her shoulders.

"There is one other thing I want to give you," Kaas said, hugging her. Pulling back, Arianna once again dabbed at her eyes, her joy overwhelming as she smiled at him.

"Kaas, you have already given me all that I—" He stopped her with his raised hand.

"King Brennan and I came to an understanding when I gave my daughter to Nicholas. Their marriage was to be a uniting of our two kingdoms. Once they were king and queen of

Lyndaria, they would rule both men and elves. There would no longer be two separate kingdoms, but one united empire.

"Now that Nicholas and Derekah are gone I am faced with a dilemma. Our kingdoms are no longer united by marriage. However, we are still united by our treaty, a treaty that states the two kingdoms shall become one, that the king and queen of Lyndaria shall rule over them both."

"What are you saying, Kaas?" Arianna breathed, her eyes wide.

"I will be the last king of the elves, little niece. At the end of my reign, I will give my kingdom to you and Geoffrey."

Arianna could not have been more stupefied. Becoming the queen of Lyndaria had been quite a shock in itself, but now she was to be queen of the elves as well? "Are you...sure?" she said lamely, her mind refusing to work much beyond that.

Kaas nodded. "I also want to ask one more thing of you, Arianna."

"What?" she squawked, trembling.

"I want you to promise me that any children you and Geoffrey have will be regarded as my grandchildren."

Arianna's eyes filled with tears. She embraced him. "You have my word they will, Kaas. They will!" Arianna felt a bond growing between her and the elven king. He wasn't her true father, but at the moment, he was the next best thing. Sniffling, Arianna sat back and gazed at him with a gentle smile. "Will you answer one of my questions now, Kaas?"

"Anything you want to know, little niece." He returned her smile.

"What was my grandmother like?"

Kaas's smile widened.

Chapter Forty

Jewel stood on the battlements of the castle overlooking the ocean as a cool breeze ruffled her long, black hair. The water crashed on the rocks far below the cliffs and birds flew here and there, their mournful cries seeming to pierce her heart.

A chill settled inside her that had nothing to do with the coolness in the air. Ever since they'd returned to Castle Templestone, Jewel had not made love with Sebastian. He didn't pressure her in any way, yet she still felt guilty denying him. She knew he would never force her before she was ready, but when would that ever be?

Jewel had seen the looks the maids and servants gave her—looks of pity, and even some of contempt. She had heard their whispers, buzzing amongst themselves, wondering how long Jewel would deny Sebastian. It was never spoken of to her face, as the people would never think about shaming Sir Sebastian and Lady Jewel of Tabrinth, but they weren't blind. Everyone saw the looks of longing Sebastian gave Jewel and made their own conclusions.

Some of the gossip Jewel had overheard even alluded that if Jewel didn't satisfy her husband, he might go looking elsewhere. In some of the more crude whispers, a few servants even spoke of giving Sebastian what he wasn't getting in his own bed.

Tears collected in her eyes before she could stop them from falling. Sebastian would never seek solace in the arms of another woman...would he? Just the thought of it made her sick as she gazed out upon the crashing waves. Was she ruined forever? Had Lord Merric succeeded in ruining her for Sebastian? She had to believe it wasn't so, that her passion for her husband would return. But whenever Sebastian looked at her now, Jewel saw the hint of sadness in his eyes. She knew she'd denied him for far too long.

Taking a deep breath, Jewel tried to calm her rioting emotions as she stood. Sebastian was with King Geoffrey, going over a plan that would hopefully save her father and brother from the clutches of Lord Merric. She wished she didn't have to be a part of it, but she had to go. There would be no fooling Merric this time, and facing him was something she had to do, like it or not, even if she didn't remember her father and brother.

"Beautiful, isn't it?"

Whipping around, Jewel gasped at Mynos standing behind her, his human hands clasped behind his back as he gazed out upon the vast expanse of water. Jewel shivered as she looked at him, still not used to his slitted eyes and golden skin. Being in the presence of a dragon humbled her.

"Yes...yes it is," she stammered, not really knowing what to say to him.

"I come here sometimes to think. The ocean can be very calming if one is in turmoil."

Jewel nodded as he leaned against the wall right next to her, looking at the rocky beach far below. She trembled and wiped away more tears.

"Sebastian will never seek another, Jewel," the dragon said as if he read her thoughts. Perhaps he had. "He loves you more than he loves anyone else in this world. He will wait as long as it takes."

"But I don't want to make him wait, Mynos," Jewel finally said. She felt good talking about it with someone, even if it was with the ancient dragon. "He deserves better. I am ruined now."

"Do not say that. Never say that." Mynos turned those strange, slitted eyes to her. "What Lord Merric did to you is not something that cannot be healed. And I believe Sebastian is just the man to heal your heart. He is a good man, Jewel."

"I know." Jewel buried her face in her hands. "But I don't know how to overcome this. Every time I get close to him, I tense up—I remember *his* hands and *his* lips, not Bastian's..."

Mynos placed an understanding hand on her shoulder. "I've never told anyone else this, Jewel, but I think you of all people should hear it."

She brought her face up to gaze at the dragon. "What?"

"My sister was raped as you nearly were."

Jewel gasped. "Your sister?"

Mynos nodded and turned to look back out over the foaming water. "Her name was Estriel. She was a beautiful dragon, as silver as I am gold. She was in love with a human, and her love blinded her to the dangers of loving a mortal. We dragons live thousands of years, mortals only a scattered few. She was hardly ever seen as a dragon, however, preferring to live in her human form.

"She loved a magic user, a man who was fascinated by magic and fascinated by her. She gave him her heart, but he never returned her love. I tried to tell her, but she wouldn't listen, determined she could make him love her. She was a very skilled magic user, as all dragons are, and this mortal had it in his mind that if he copulated with a dragon, he would take on some draconic traits himself.

234

"Estriel rejoiced at first, thinking he finally loved her, seeing her for the woman she was. But that was not the case. The more her lover came to her, the more forceful he became until he ended up taking what she wasn't freely giving. Making love to my sister wasn't giving him any of the draconic traits he so desired. And he faulted Estriel for this.

"He waited until she was sleeping one night and stabbed her with a magical dagger, knowing only a magical weapon can fell a dragon."

Jewel gasped and covered her mouth to keep from crying out. Mynos's own sister? Raped by a mortal? New tears formed in her eyes as she leaned against him. "I'm so sorry, Mynos," she whispered, aghast.

Gazing at her again, Mynos gave her a sad smile. "That was many years ago, Daughter. But I remember vividly the moment I found her bleeding to death all over the ground, crying out in agony. She explained to me what had happened, and told me she didn't have the heart to fight back. She did love the mortal after all. But she pleaded with me to consecrate her body."

"Consecrate?" Jewel asked in confusion.

Mynos nodded. "It is the wish of every dragon upon their death that their bodies be consecrated and used as tools for learning and wielding magic." As he talked, Mynos pulled something from one of his pockets. "My Crystal is the result of Estriel's consecration."

Jewel's eyes widened as she stared at the sparkling talisman. "You mean it is the consecrated body of your sister?"

"Yes. But before she died, Estriel enchanted her own body so that my Crystal will always protect me. It can never do me any harm. She didn't want her Crystal to fall into the wrong hands and become so powerful as to never have a way to defeat it.

235

"She asked me to have mercy on her mortal love, but how could I when my sister was dead, almost before she had ever truly lived? I hunted that mortal down and... Well, I'm sure you don't want to hear exactly what I did with him."

Jewel shuddered, her own imagination racing. She tried not to think what a dragon out for revenge might do to a mortal man.

"Here, take this." Mynos held the Crystal out to her.

Jewel gasped, her eyes large. "I thought you told me never to touch it?"

"That was only because I didn't want it bonding to you, Daughter. It has since bonded to me. You will not be harmed. But you might find peace in holding my Crystal, in knowing you are not alone in your feelings."

Jewel held out her shaking hand and Mynos placed the gem in her upturned palm. Instantly, the Crystal's many voices tinkled through her head, and a soothing calm did indeed wash over her.

"Fear not, Daughter," the Crystal said in her mind. *"The man you love will never hurt you. Love him and cherish him, Jewel. You hold his heart in your hands."*

"Thank you," Jewel whispered as her breath caught. She gave Mynos a kiss on his golden cheek. "Thank you for telling me."

The dragon smiled as he gently took the Crystal from her hand. "I have something else for you, Daughter." He pulled out yet another gem, this one a winking emerald. "I made this talisman just recently when I consecrated Malnan's reborn body. In honor of my sister, I have named it the Emerald of Estriel. I want you and Sebastian to have it for your journey."

Jewel was unable to find a single word to say as the dragon placed it in her hand. Turning it in the light, Jewel watched as

236

the emerald caught the rays of the sun, twinkling its deep green brilliance.

"What does it do?" she said in awe.

"I have enchanted it as a portal stone."

"A portal stone?"

"Yes. It will open a magical portal and take you to anywhere you've been before. You do not need to have any magical ability to use it—you simply ask it to take you where you want to go. But it will not take you to a place you have never been." A few moments of silence passed between them. Mynos watched Jewel turn the emerald in her hands, marveling at its beauty.

"This gem also has the ability to communicate with both my Crystal and with Malnan's Jewel," he told her. "You will be able to talk to me or to Malnan whenever you like."

"Ah, you gave her the stone, I see." The voice of King Geoffrey boomed behind her. Turning, she saw his handsome smiling face and that of Sebastian not too far behind.

"Yes, Your Majesty," Mynos said.

"Then we should waste no more time in getting these two ready for..."

Jewel wasn't listening any longer. As she gazed at her husband, the words of the Crystal of Mynos echoed in her head. *"You hold his heart in your hands."* Gazing into Sebastian's beautiful blue eyes, she knew without a doubt the Crystal had spoken the truth.

She smiled at him and her heart skipped a beat as he flashed her a handsome grin of his own. She closed the gap between them and hugged him for all she was worth.

Chapter Forty-One

Jewel was nervous. She stared into the firelight and gazed once again at the sparkling emerald in her hand. Mynos had explained she should be the one to have it, as only she had been to Evendria. Even though she couldn't remember being there, the Emerald of Estriel would be able to open a portal to the city regardless. They were to leave in the morning—just her and Sebastian alone. The thought frightened her to her very core, but if anything, it strengthened her resolve to make things right between her and her husband.

Tonight.

She had told him she was retiring early due to an upset stomach, and he had let her go with a look of concern. She knew he suspected nothing, and it made her smile. She had ordered a hot bath for herself, as well as many large candles along with a few bottles of wine. Yes, tonight would be special.

The small fire she had lit was now a roaring flame, warming the chill from the room. Her hair was almost dry as she sat in front of it wearing nothing but her silk robe, combing her long black locks until they shone in the firelight. The room was aglow with candles and the bed turned down. Everything was ready.

Jewel's heart pounded as her anticipation grew, waiting for Sebastian to come to her from the dining hall. She felt like a virgin, and smiled at the thought. Sebastian had been her first and only lover. But tonight was another first as well, and Jewel knew she would never again let anything interfere with her love for her husband.

The door opened quietly when Sebastian entered, and Jewel's heart pounded in her throat. His eyes darted from the bed to the fireplace as he searched the room for her, closing the door behind him.

"What's all this?"

"For you. For us." Jewel took a deep breath.

He gave her a look full of longing. She knew what kind of picture she presented in front of the fire, her sheer robe hiding nothing from his eyes. The fact he'd lasted this long without confronting her was surprising. Sebastian truly was a good man.

Jewel arose, then walked slowly until she stood before him. He wore the familiar blue sash of the Wolverines and looked so handsome with his unruly hair. He pushed it out of his face. He closed his eyes, his jaw muscles twitching, and for the first time, Jewel knew the depth of his restraint. The scent of her rose soap had to be assaulting his senses, and yet he did not touch her.

"I've been waiting for you," she breathed.

He didn't open his eyes. Jewel could tell he was debating with himself whether or not to step away or pull her closer. With shaking hands, she began unbuckling his sword belt.

"Jewel, don't—"

"Shh." She placed her finger on his lips. When his sword thumped to the floor, she lifted his sash up and over his head. Finally, he opened his eyes.

"What are you doing?"

Jewel gave him a secret smile, pulling him closer to the fireplace. With one tug of her robe's belt, it fell open, revealing her skin. She thought her heart would beat out of her chest as she let the robe fall to the floor.

"Bastian," she whispered, trembling. "Make love to me."

If his sharp intake of breath was any indication, he was not expecting those to be her words. His eyes, however, were ablaze as they roamed her body.

"Are you sure, my lady Jewel?"

Jewel nodded and closed the gap between them. There was a moment's hesitation as she framed his face with her hands, but she gave him a loving smile and kissed him tenderly.

Sebastian was gentle, not wanting to scare her with the passion he was trying so hard to keep hidden. But he was lost when Jewel pulled him down to the floor in front of the fire without breaking their kiss.

When she darted her tongue into his mouth, Sebastian knew he couldn't hold back any longer. She was naked underneath him, and he wanted desperately to feel her bare skin with his own. But not before he kissed his wife and explored her mouth as he longed to do. He'd dreamt of this moment with Jewel, and nothing was going to stop him from giving her the loving experience she now wanted—and needed— from him.

Holding her head still with both his hands, Sebastian delved his tongue again and again into her mouth, playing with hers and tasting the soft flesh of her lips. Jewel matched his ardor, and wove her fingers into his hair, seeming to refuse to let go of his mouth, even for a moment.

When Sebastian finally did break the kiss, he slid his mouth down her neck. "I love you, Jewel. I love you so much!" He lifted his eyes back to hers only to see Jewel bite her lip as her eyes filled with unshed tears. Sebastian's own tears pooled as he traced her face with his fingers, his nose touching hers.

"I love you, too, Bastian." Jewel caressed his face. Kissing her again, Sebastian yanked his tunic free from his breeches. He stopped kissing her long enough to toss it over his head before his lips were on hers once more.

Jewel's hands flew all over him, trailing down his belly and tugging at the ties to his breeches as her mouth tasted his neck. It had been too long. Much too long.

"I've missed you," he whispered as she unlaced the ties.

Working her way back up his neck to his ear, Jewel suckled on his earlobe before she answered. "I've missed you too, my lord husband."

It didn't take long before Sebastian had kicked off his breeches, hovering above her, gazing down with a wicked grin. She felt him pressing against her and she gasped at the feeling, expecting to be frightened, but only feeling excitement.

Without a thought, she arched into him, asking him silently to enter her. But he shook his head and lowered his mouth to her breasts. She was disappointed only for a moment, clutching his hair at the first touch of his tongue on her nipples.

He did not deny her, but loved each of her breasts as if he had all the time in the world, igniting her passion until she was almost wild with it.

"Bastian, please!" She wanted so much to feel him inside her, to know that he and he alone possessed both her heart and her body.

"Not yet, baby." His hot breath teased her breasts, making her arch her body into his once again. "Not yet."

Jewel groaned her disappointment. "Bastian..."

"Shh. Just feel, my lady wife. Close your eyes and *feel*."

She did as he told her and felt him kiss her belly as he moved lower, kissing her thighs and kneading her breasts at the same time. She knew what he was going to do, but that didn't stop the whimper that escaped her at the first touch of his mouth between her legs. He took his time as he tasted her, bringing her closer and closer to the brink of ecstasy.

Jewel thought she would cry out in agony as he lifted her higher and higher, only to back away and start all over again. She scooted closer and dug her fingers into his shoulders, screaming loudly as her release finally came, holding his head down until the waves of pleasure receded to nothing more than tremors.

Sebastian lifted his large frame to cover her once again, kissing her sensitive skin the entire way. He stopped at her neck to give her a few playful nips before his mouth returned to hers.

They said nothing as they stared at each other. Jewel wrapped her legs around him in silent invitation and this time he did not hesitate.

"Does this hurt you?" He just barely pushed inside.

"No," she said with a gasp.

"I will never hurt you."

Pushing his hair from his face, Jewel smiled. "I know."

He kissed her, exploring her mouth once again as he slowly filled Jewel with his warmth, making her sigh with pleasure. Once he was fully inside, he made no move to continue, simply kissing her and waiting for her to adjust to the feel of him.

Jewel pushed her hips against his and urged his body with her hands. When he began to move, she would be ready to feel the heights with him all over again. He needed no more encouragement as he finally moved against her.

With Sebastian by her side, she could face Lord Merric and anything he threw at them. She could face anything. The dragon had been right. She was not ruined; she needed to be healed. And Sebastian was the only man who could heal her heart.

Those thoughts suddenly scattered as both she and her husband plummeted over the edge and rode out the waves of rapture together. It was a long time indeed before she had any coherent thought as they lay panting on the fur rug.

Jewel smiled. Her evening with Sebastian was only just beginning.

Chapter Forty-Two

The sky was pinkening with the dawn when Jewel awoke, a contented smile on her face. She sighed to herself, seeming to feel everything in stages—the comfort of the bed, the warmth of the blankets, and the feather-soft breath of her husband on her chest.

Sebastian had fallen asleep in her arms with his head between her breasts and his legs hopelessly tangled with hers. How silly she'd been for ever thinking he would dally with another woman. He had shown her many times during the night he wanted only her.

There wasn't a single inch of him that she didn't know intimately as she had taken her time in exploring his magnificent body. And he had returned the favor ten-fold. Jewel blushed at the memory of their lovemaking, remembering her shameless pleas to him, and Sebastian indulging every single one of them.

Threading her fingers through his clean hair, she kissed the top of his head without waking him. He had insisted in bathing in her cold bathwater after their interlude in front of the fireplace. Without warning, he'd pulled her into the small wooden tub with him. Jewel had shrieked with laughter at his playfulness, as well as at the cold water when it hit her heated skin. But Sebastian had smiled devilishly, despite the chill in the bathwater.

The look on his face had brought a blush to her cheeks, but when he brought his mouth down on hers all thoughts of the cold water were forgotten.

Somehow during the night, they had made it to the bed where Jewel remembered collapsing with him, exhausted beyond measure, but so very satisfied. Now their bodies lay tangled together amidst the blankets and Jewel silently wished to stay like this forever.

Gazing out the window, she watched as the sky continued to glow brighter. She shivered at the thought of having to travel to Evendria. Malnan's reports that she was slowly driving Lord Merric insane did nothing to quell the quaking in her heart at facing him again. He might be more dangerous now than he had ever been sane. Assuming the man had been sane in the first place.

But Jewel's thoughts were interrupted when Sebastian stirred, stretching on top of her and turning his face so his chin rested on her chest.

"Good morning, my lady." Sebastian grinned, his eyes hooded from sleep, making him so unbelievably sexy Jewel gasped at the sight. Grinning even more, Sebastian placed his hands on her pillow and drew his body flush with hers. Jewel felt his hard body pressing against her thigh and she couldn't help but smile herself.

"Again, my lord husband?" Her eyes widened in mock disbelief. "I thought I exhausted you last night."

"Ah, my lady," he whispered, pressing himself inside her ever so slowly. "I will always have strength enough to make love to you."

"I'll hold you to that, Bastian," she said in his ear as he began to love her anew.

It wasn't until much later when they had both once again drifted off into a contented sleep that the Emerald of Estriel suddenly flared to life, filling the room with its soft, ethereal glow. It had lain dormant on the bedside table the entire evening, and the abrupt appearance of life in the stone had both Jewel and Sebastian jumping out of the bed at the unexpectedness of it.

"Sebastian. Jewel!" The voice of Mynos filled the room.

"What is it, Mynos?" Sebastian took the gem off the table.

"I've just received disturbing news from Malnan that changes things in Evendria."

Jewel was almost too afraid to ask. "What news?"

"Malnan has learned Lord Merric isn't a mere lord from Westchester. He was once a Dark Knight of Darragh!"

At that admission, Sebastian's eyes widened and his mouth hung open in shock. *"What?"*

"There's more," the dragon continued. "He was Queen Darragh's Captain of the Guard on Shadow Mountain. I'm afraid he's using his knowledge of brainwashing to entice the entire city of Evendria against us as the Dark Knights once did to the city of Breckenwood. He's amassing an army."

Jewel and Sebastian looked at each other in disbelief.

"Are you telling us we'll have to fight more than Merric in Evendria?"

"Yes, Sir Sebastian."

Running his fingers through his hair, Sebastian sighed and handed the emerald to Jewel while he searched for his clothes.

"Malnan believes he will try and conquer the castle to take back the crown he lost. She's told me he is unstable enough to believe he can do just that. But we cannot send you and Jewel alone to the city. Come to King Geoffrey's study and we will discuss this further."

The light from the emerald went out and the weight of it pressed into Jewel's palm. She hadn't noticed it didn't weigh much of anything when it was sparkling with its inner fire.

Within moments, Jewel and Sebastian were dressed. Opening the door to their room, Sebastian ushered Jewel into the hall. But she stopped short.

Looking into the stone, she decided to test its power. "Take us to King Geoffrey's study."

Out of nowhere, a bright light appeared in front of them and stretched into a long, straight line before parting into two halves, ripping a hole in the fabric of reality. Jewel gasped in shock as Mynos glanced at them through the portal in the king's study.

"Well, are you going to step through, Daughter?" A knowing grin was on his ancient golden face.

Jewel's entire body trembled as she glanced at Sebastian and took his hand. He squeezed her fingers before he squared his shoulders and stepped through the portal.

Chapter Forty-Three

Jewel shivered when she walked through the magical doorway, feeling as if her body had been doused in ice water. As soon as she and Sebastian stepped into the study, the portal closed silently behind them. Jewel glanced at the faces that greeted her. They gazed at her calmly, as if magical doorways opening in Castle Templestone were an everyday occurrence.

Mynos sat in an overstuffed chair by the desk while King Geoffrey turned from the large window that looked out upon the ocean. Sir Cederick of Breckenwood stood leaning against the wall by the double doors.

"As you know, things have changed," Geoffrey began.

"I'm going with you, Seb," Cederick interrupted, peeling himself from the wall. Geoffrey looked at Cederick, bringing a blush to the big man's cheeks. "I'm sorry, Geoffrey," Cederick apologized, managing to look chagrined. "I'm just not used to... Well, *you know.*"

A tired smile played across Geoffrey's face. "It's all right, old friend," he said, rubbing the back of his neck. "I understand how you feel."

Jewel wondered if Geoffrey had gotten any sleep last night. But thoughts of last night had her own cheeks flushing with color, and she tried to concentrate on what the dragon had to say.

"Malnan contacted me during the night." Mynos dragged his hand through his hair. "I didn't disturb you, Sebastian, because I knew you were...occupied." That statement made Jewel's cheeks once again flare with heat. "That aside," he continued, "I believe I can quell the havoc Lord Merric is perpetrating."

"Are you sure?" King Geoffrey plopped into his chair behind the large mahogany desk.

Mynos nodded. "Yes, Your Majesty. I am bonded to my Crystal. Without it I am powerful, but with it, I can do many incredible things. I have no doubt I will be able to lift the spell he has placed over Evendria. He will not be striking the castle. You have my word."

"I don't want you hurting innocent people, Mynos." Geoffrey arched a brow. "Can you do this without any casualties?"

"I won't lie to you, Your Majesty. There may be some casualties, but lifting the enchantment will not cause any to be harmed. The people of the city will not remember what happened to them. I will make sure of it."

Geoffrey stared at the dragon with unblinking eyes for a few moments before he was satisfied. It looked to Jewel as if something unspoken had passed between them, but just what it was, she could not say.

"Regardless," the king said, "we will fortify the castle as a precaution. I will keep King Kaas and his mages here until I hear word from Mynos and Sebastian in Evendria."

"I am going too," Cederick piped up again. "I'm not letting Seb have all the fun."

Sebastian smiled. "It will be good to travel with you again, Cederick."

"And I can flirt with your wife while you beat some sense into this Lord Merric." Cederick gave Jewel a hearty wink. She laughed out loud.

Geoffrey grinned as well. "Cederick, you are incorrigible."

"I'm still going," he said, rubbing the hilt of his sword.

Geoffrey looked back at Sebastian. "Who do you appoint as Captain in your absence?"

Without the slightest pause, he answered. "Sir Ethan of Krey, Your Majesty."

Geoffrey nodded as if expecting nothing less. "Then we must let him know right away. I want you gone before midday."

"Yes, Your Majesty." Sebastian bowed slightly.

"Well, what are you waiting for?" Mynos asked pointedly, looking at Jewel.

She stared at him.

The dragon smiled. "Ask the stone to take you to the battlements, Daughter. Don't be afraid to use its power. Isn't that where Sir Ethan is patrolling right now?"

"Yes," Sebastian answered. "He should be patrolling near the gatehouse."

"Then give Sebastian the stone, Daughter, and let him use it."

Jewel slapped the Emerald of Estriel into Sebastian's open palm and looked on with astonishment. Her husband gazed down at the green gem in his hand and cleared his throat. "Take me to the battlements near the gatehouse."

Just as before, the portal opened before them, startling a few Wolverines on the other side. Jewel gasped as she looked through and saw Sir Ethan staring back in wide-eyed wonder just a few feet away.

"Sebastian?" Ethan glanced around the battlements as if expecting an ambush.

"Come through, Sir Ethan," King Geoffrey commanded.

Swallowing hard, Ethan composed his handsome features and took a tentative step through the doorway. As soon as he was through, the portal closed.

Mynos smiled widely. "Welcome, Sir Ethan!"

Ethan took in the king's study as if he had never seen it before. Grabbing a hold of Sebastian's shoulders, he pinned him with his gaze before breaking out in peals of laughter.

"I don't believe it," he exclaimed. "The men heard rumors about the new gem Mynos made, but I never thought I would see its effects first hand."

"It's a portal stone," Geoffrey explained. "It will take you wherever you've been before. Sebastian used it now to summon you."

"For what purpose?"

"I need you to act as Captain of the Guard when I leave for Evendria, Ethan," Sebastian said. "King Geoffrey is not going to leave the castle unfortified. I want you to prepare for a siege. Mynos thinks there will be no need, but after Castle Templestone was attacked by Queen Darragh's army, no one is going to take any chances."

Nodding, Ethan bowed slightly. "I would be honored to be your acting Captain, Sir Sebastian." Then he smiled wickedly. "And with you gone, I'll keep the lovely Jewel company."

Jewel smiled when Sebastian placed a possessive arm around her shoulders. "The Lady Jewel will be coming with me, Sir Ethan."

Ethan's look of disappointment was almost comical, but he grinned as he took her hand, kissing it lightly. "Ah, but what could have been, my lady." He sighed dramatically. Ethan winked at her when Sebastian growled. "Oh don't make such a fuss." Ethan straightened and slapped Sebastian on the shoulder. "It's no secret the Lady Jewel has room in her heart for only one man."

"Yes, and best you remember that man isn't *you*," Sebastian said dryly.

Without warning, Ethan laughed and hugged Sebastian. "You take care of my lady in Evendria."

"And you keep my castle safe."

They both looked at each other and smiled.

Chapter Forty-Four

The city of Evendria was a gleaming port city on the southern coast of Lyndaria. The white spires of a few buildings reached high into the sky overlooking the harbor, where tall merchant ships docked for trade. The ships came from far and wide, bringing their goods from the remote reaches of Lyndaria's four realms and beyond, to be loaded onto wagons only to start their journey anew along the rutted Merchant Road.

Evendria was the home of ten Wolverines in the king's service, as well as Lord Andrew of Evendria, Count of Wayhaven, the father of Lord Galen and Lady Isabella. Wayhaven was the name of the entire sloping valley Evendria was nestled in, and thus Lord Andrew oversaw most of the dealings at the port while his son took care of the minor dealings within the city. His manor stood on a small hill, looking out upon the harbor, the largest and most ornate building in the entire city.

The Count of Wayhaven was an honest and just man, well-liked among the locals for his generosity. Most had been shocked to learn of his daughter's betrothal to Lord Merric of Westchester, a rival port city on Lyndaria's eastern coast, but they had not questioned it. Such an odd match had to be a love match, or so they had thought.

All of these things slammed through Jewel's head as she stumbled on the Merchant Road outside the city gates only moments after stepping through the magical portal from King Geoffrey's study. Seeing the city again triggered memories that had been long since forgotten, memories she couldn't stop from clouding her mind. Sebastian clutched her before she fell face-down in the dirt, glancing back at the dragon for assistance.

"Are you all right?" he asked, steadying her.

Jewel nodded. "Yes, Bastian, I am fine. I just didn't expect to have my memories return to me so quickly."

"You remember?" He glanced excitedly over his shoulder at the white city gates.

"Yes. I remember everything now." With the memories of her home and family came the memories of the beating she'd received at the hands of Lord Merric. Jewel shuddered as they bombarded her, merciless in their invasion of her mind.

She had learned long ago that wearing the ornate necklace she now knew as Malnan's Jewel seemed to keep her safe from whatever magic Lord Merric was spinning. Somehow, he'd managed to entice her father to agree to their match. No matter how hard Isabella had tried, she had not been able to persuade her father that she did not want to marry him. It had been obvious Lord Merric was becoming impatient in his bid to have her.

When the day of their wedding finally arrived, Isabella refused to go through with it, and even looked for an avenue of escape, but her apartments were on the third floor of her father's manor, and Lord Merric had had the foresight to place a guard at her door. He entered her room unannounced that day and asked her one more time to come to him willingly. But how could she when the very sight of him made her blood run cold? She told him as much. Without warning, Isabella felt the first hard contact of his fist against her cheek. She felt as if she had been kicked by a horse as she reeled back, falling over her bedside table.

Lord Merric was like a wild man, beating her and kicking her until she could not fight him any longer. When he stopped his brutal assault and began unbuckling his belt, Isabella cried for help through her broken lips. She watched in horror as he untied his breeches, gazing at her with lust in his eyes, as if she were a gourmet feast awaiting his plunder. There was nothing her beaten body could do to stop him, let alone continue to breathe.

Yet moments before she lost consciousness, she could remember a flash of bright light. The smell of grass surrounded her, and Jewel hugged her belly. She remembered Malnan transporting her to the fields beyond the castle.

"Sweetheart, what's wrong?" Worry etched Sebastian's handsome features.

"I can remember everything, Bastian," she whispered, gripping the Emerald of Estriel with all her might. "*Everything.*"

Sebastian didn't ask her what she remembered. He knew. Drawing her into his arms, he stroked her hair and tried to calm her in his old familiar way.

Mynos and Cederick were silent for a few moments before the dragon spoke. "I must fly over the city to wield my magic. I have asked Malnan to keep Lord Merric occupied while I break his spell. He will not notice it. Once the spell has been lifted, the townsfolk will not remember a thing. It will then be safe to enter the city."

Cederick, Sebastian, and Jewel nodded at the dragon as he changed into his draconic form. Jewel still gasped at the sight of it—for a time she'd forgotten that Mynos was indeed a dragon, not a man.

255

"Now, Malnan!" He clutched his Crystal close to his body and launched into the sky. The wind from his wings blew dust and pebbles all around them on the Merchant Road as he gained altitude, forcing Jewel to turn once again into Sebastian's shoulder. Mynos truly was a magnificent being, and watching him in the sky was breathtaking as his golden scales reflected the sunlight.

Jewel shivered as she watched him fly across the city, knowing it wouldn't be long before they finally confronted the man who had wreaked such havoc in Lyndaria. She prayed for their safety and hoped against hope Malnan would be able to keep Merric's magic at bay.

Chapter Forty-Five

A flash of white light bathed the city of Evendria as Mynos flew low in the sky, his wings beating a staccato rhythm throughout the valley of Newhaven. Jewel watched with awe as the ancient dragon weaved his magic, lifting Merric's enchantment with ease. His Crystal flashed in his talons, absorbing Mynos's own magic and magnifying it hundreds of times stronger.

The power of a dragon was well known throughout the realms as the strongest of magics, and yet Jewel surmised that the power Mynos now wielded with his Crystal was inconceivable. If he wanted to, he could level the city, killing every soul present with barely a thought, and drown the entire valley of Newhaven with the waters of the Silver Sea. She shivered at the thought.

Jewel worried her bottom lip with her teeth. The time had now come for them to open a portal to her father's estate and confront Lord Merric. Her courage waned.

"My lady Jewel?" Sebastian rubbed the back of her neck. "Do not fret. Merric has no hope of defeating Mynos and Malnan."

"I'm worried about what he'll do to you, Bastian." She looked up at him with apprehensive eyes.

Sebastian gave her a cocky grin. "You should be more concerned for him, sweet wife." He patted his sword resting at his hip. "He has a deadly date with Fleetfire." The sword buzzed at the sound of its name and Jewel felt some of her unease lift from her shoulders. "Are you ready?"

Taking a deep breath, Jewel nodded and commanded the Emerald of Estriel to take them inside her father's sprawling manor on the hill.

☜☜⌘

The portal opened within her old bedchamber as Jewel, Sebastian and Cederick walked through. Taking in her surroundings, she shivered as she stared at the disarray. The bed was rumpled and unmade, and one of her dresses lay spread out upon it, hopelessly wrinkled. It looked as if it had been slept on. Clothing was strewn all about the room. Men's clothing. Was Lord Merric sleeping in her bedchamber? Thinking he had been lying on top of her dress made Jewel tremble and turn away with disgust.

"Where are we?" Cederick asked.

"This used to be my room," Jewel replied. "Now it looks like...it looks like..."

"It looks like that madman has been sleeping in here," Sebastian finished for her.

Jewel couldn't do much more than nod before she moved to the door. She couldn't stand to see any more. Sebastian's warm hand on her shoulder helped to steady her reeling emotions. Taking a deep breath, she turned the knob.

The hallway was quiet as they ventured out. Sunlight streamed in through high windows in the wall, illuminating the passage. Intricately woven carpets lined the floor, their colors deep and rich as the trio padded slowly down the corridor.

"Malnan," Jewel whispered into the Emerald, suddenly remembering she could talk to her through it. "Where are you?"

"Daughter!" Malnan's voice echoed eerily down the hall as the gem flashed to life. *"Merric and I are on the terrace."*

"And my father? My brother?"

"They are with us. Make haste! Mynos has lifted the enchantment on Evendria and I cannot hold Merric's mind for much longer."

"We must hurry," Jewel commanded, running to a large staircase. Without a thought, she bounded down one flight, and then another until they were on the first floor.

"This way!" She pointed toward the back of the manor. After navigating a few twisting corridors, they came to a large room with glass-paned doors open wide, revealing the beautiful day beyond.

The view from the terrace was breathtaking. It looked out over the harbor—the masts from the ships in port could be seen reaching high into the air. White clouds rolled lazily across the sky as the sun shone brightly, as if mocking the turmoil inside Jewel.

Looking at her father's face for the first time in weeks made her gasp in shock. How could she have forgotten this stoic, handsome man? Dark, thinning hair adorned his head and he sported a thick mustache on his upper lip. His nose sat crookedly on his face, proof it had been broken earlier in life. Laugh lines were etched in his face, yet he was not smiling.

Staring back at her, his eyes darted between Jewel and Lord Merric. She shook her head at him, trying to tell him not to alert Lord Merric to their presence. He appeared both happy and apprehensive at the same time, obviously conflicted in what he should do.

Her brother Galen sat in his chair and stared at the imposing visage of Lord Merric before him. Merric seemed to be explaining the intricacies of swordplay with the man, totally unaware of the threat of Jewel and the two Wolverines behind him. Galen did nothing but gaze up at him, a look of confusion on his face, almost as if he didn't know where he was. He resembled their father, except he was younger and even more handsome.

Sebastian gave Jewel a small kiss on her cheek. "Do not be afraid, my lady."

The hiss of his sword echoed all around them as Sebastian strode forth, sliding Fleetfire easily from its scabbard. Whipping around at the sound, Lord Merric found himself at the wrong end of the glowing weapon. Surprise showed on his face for a split second before he gazed down the blade. Jewel could see for herself the fire of hatred that ignited in Merric's eyes as he stared hard at her husband.

"Now where have I seen this scene before?" Sebastian taunted. "Hmm, let me think."

"Ah, Sebastian," Merric uttered with a cruel grin. "You did not disappoint me. You have brought my Isabella with you. Are you here to trade? Isabella for her family? Isabella for Malnan's Jewel?"

Sebastian's gaze flashed down to Merric's neck where the necklace holding the lavender gem was clasped. The talisman flickered wildly with its own inner light.

"No, I did not come here to trade," he said calmly. "I came to kill you, Merric."

The mad lord threw back his head and laughed. "You can try, Sebastian, my boy, surely you can try. I have amassed an

260

army in Evendria. I have but to summon the masses to defend me."

"Then summon them." Sebastian smiled slyly.

Merric closed his eyes with a smirk, yet after a few short moments, snapped his eyes open once again. "The weaves of magic. They are gone! What have you done with them, *Wolverine?*"

"What's wrong, Merric? Is your army not responding?"

Merric growled as he took hold of Malnan's Jewel, as if to channel his power through it. But the look of shock in his eyes told Sebastian all he needed to know. Malnan was blocking her magic from him.

Glancing toward the sky, Sebastian spotted Mynos approaching, his wings beating their familiar tempo across the bay. With a smile of triumph, Sebastian looked back at Merric, hooking the blade of his sword under the chain of the necklace.

"You won't be needing this any longer." He flung his sword upward, bringing Malnan's Jewel with it, up and over Merric's head. Sebastian grasped the hilt of his weapon with his other hand as the necklace slid down the length of the blade, dropping into his right palm. Without another thought, he tossed it into the air just as Mynos flew low over the grounds, catching the gem in his talons. The dragon's massive body blocked out the sun for a moment before he was gone.

"No!" Merric screamed. He took a step forward, not seeming to care that the point of Sebastian's blade dug into his chest. "You have broken the rules!"

Casting a glance at Jewel, Sebastian grinned, flinging his sword back into his right hand. "You are right, Lord Merric. I have broken all the rules." He turned back to the seething lord and a dark cloud passed in front of his eyes. "Now we finish this."

Chapter Forty-Six

"Isabella, is that you?" Jewel heard her brother's voice. "Who is that man with you?"

"He is no one of consequence," Merric snarled with a wave of his hand.

Galen's eyes clouded over. "No one of consequence."

Stepping forward, Jewel was livid at Merric's brainwashing magic. "This man is my *husband*, Sir Sebastian of Tabrinth, Captain of the Guard at Castle Templestone, and best friend to King Geoffrey himself!"

Merric's eyes flashed. "He won't be for long." With that, he grasped the hilt of his weapon and drew it out of its scabbard, every inch of the blade as black as night. Jewel felt a rough hand on her shoulder. Sir Cederick yanked her back. He stood in front of her and drew his sword as well.

"Yield, Lord Merric," Cederick demanded. "Yield and save your pathetic life."

Merric let out a guttural cry and lunged for Sebastian. Raising his sword high, he brought it down with all his might, only to clang loudly against the strong steel of Fleetfire. Sebastian's sword showered the terrace with sparks, seeming to protest the touch of Merric's foul blade.

Lord Andrew and his son scrambled from where they sat and raced inside the door of the manor, pushing Jewel against the wall, shielding her from the fight. Pulling away from them, she squealed, "Let me go. I need to see what happens!"

The sound of metal on metal reached her again and again as Lord Merric pounded on Sebastian. But her husband was smiling. He seemed to be deflecting the blows with ease, as if taunting the enraged lord. With every contact of the swords, a shower of sparks flew into the air.

As they continued to fight on the terrace, Jewel noticed a flash of gold out of the corner of her eye. Turning her head, she saw Mynos, in his human form, striding through the room with Malnan's Jewel around his neck and his Crystal in the palm of his hand. She shivered at the sight and at the malice he bore in his ancient, slitted eyes.

The dragon stopped at the threshold of the door and watched the spectacle on the terrace.

"Aren't you going to help him?" Jewel was frantic, worried for her husband.

Mynos didn't so much as glance her way. "Sir Sebastian needs no help, Daughter."

Glancing out the doorway, Jewel saw for herself that what Mynos said was true. Sebastian was finished toying with Merric. Instead of taking a beating, he gave it. Jewel gasped as she watched Sebastian in action, his sword flashing like a living being. She remembered the story he'd told her of facing eight Dark Knights on his own—earning his sword near Queen Darragh's fortress. It wasn't so hard to believe now. Her heart filled with pride just watching him.

Even though she knew nothing about swordplay, she knew Sebastian was the better man, parrying and thrusting with Fleetfire. He succeeded in drawing blood on both Merric's shoulder and thigh within a fraction of a second. Merric howled with rage. But as he lifted his black blade and brought it down brutally, Sebastian twisted his sword through the shower of sparks, deflecting the blow. Sebastian's deft block suddenly made Merric lose his grip on his sword.

With one heave of Fleetfire, Sebastian easily threw the tainted black weapon across the terrace with a loud clatter. Jewel watched in awe as Mynos lifted the Crystal toward the blade. Before her very eyes, Mynos's magic turned the sword into nothing more than a pile of black dust blowing away in the breeze.

Merric jumped back from the point of Sebastian's sword.

"You are beaten. *Yield.*" Sebastian growled.

"You do not want to fight me." Merric grinned, waving his hand as he had once before. For a split second, Sebastian lowered his sword, a confused look upon his face.

"No!" Jewel yelled.

Mynos flicked his hand and Fleetfire rose once again.

"Is that the best you can do, *my lord*?" Mynos scoffed.

Merric glared at the dragon. "You think to defeat me so easily?"

"You are already defeated!" Jewel called out, stepping next to her husband.

"Isabella," Merric said with a harsh grin, wincing from the wounds on his shoulder and his leg. "Come to me."

A sudden cloud fogged her brain, and Jewel had the uncanny urge to obey him. She took a hesitant step forward before Sebastian pushed her back, digging his sword into Merric's chest.

"You will never have her," he snarled, pushing his sword a little harder. Merric hissed in pain.

"You would not dare to kill an unarmed man." Merric's eyes blazed.

"Oh? You think I don't have it in me, Lord Merric? Do you think I have forgotten the beating you gave *my wife*? Or have I forgotten you almost *raped* her? Perhaps it slipped my mind that you *killed* the entire royal family for your own gain, not only the heir to Lyndaria, but the heir to the elven kingdom as well? Along with their little baby? Maybe I simply cannot recall you taking Malnan's life, or slamming Sir Duncan of Marynville against a stone wall, killing him instantly? Or perhaps I'm just too dense to consider that you enchanted the entire city of Evendria, not to mention holding my wife's family hostage, or stealing Malnan's Jewel? Do not fret, Lord Merric. I have a very *long* memory. I have it in me to kill you right here and now."

"Do it then, Wolverine." Merric laughed madly, ripping the front of his shirt, exposing his bloodstained chest. "Kill me!"

Mynos laid a restraining hand on Sebastian's shoulder. "Do not taint your fine sword with his blood, Son. Leave him to me."

Merric stared in horror at the dragon for only a moment before he turned and ran screaming down the steps of the terrace, racing across the yard.

Turning to Jewel, Mynos swiftly removed the lavender gem from around his neck. He handed it to her. "Bring Malnan back to me." He turned his sights on the man stumbling across the grass in his desperation to get away.

Jewel gaped in amazement as Mynos dashed down steps of the terrace himself, weaving his magic and shifting as he ran. With his draconic wings finally unfurled, Mynos leapt into the air, flying low.

Merric never had a chance.

With one fluid motion, Mynos swooped down and snatched the fleeing man in his powerful talons before beating his wings

265

and gaining altitude over the bay. All on the terrace watched in shocked disbelief as the dragon flew higher and higher in the sky until he could no longer be seen.

Jewel shuddered, remembering what Mynos had told her about the mortal who had slain his sister Estriel. He had refrained from telling her just what exactly he had done with that man. Jewel had a feeling Merric was going to get a taste of the same.

She felt a momentary pang of remorse for Lord Merric of Westchester.

Chapter Forty-Seven

"You have a wonderful family, my lady Jewel," Sebastian murmured, nuzzling his wife's ear. She smiled at him, pushing away his stray lock of hair as she always did. He leaned over her, his bare chest rubbing against her deliciously. Their makeshift bed on the dirt floor of the cave wasn't very comfortable, but Jewel wasn't about to complain.

Two days had passed since Sebastian had confronted Lord Merric, and both he and Jewel had been eager to fulfill Mynos's request to bring Malnan back despite Lord Andrew's complaints that they were leaving Evendria far too soon. Jewel had compromised and opened a portal to Castle Templestone, telling her father and brother to wait for her there. The Emerald of Estriel had then opened a portal for Jewel to the cave with the two remaining dragon's eggs, nestled somewhere in the foothills of the King's Mountains.

"I'm glad you like my family, Bastian," she said with a grin as she traced circles on his bare skin. "I believe my father approves of our match."

Sebastian made a face. "I'm not so sure."

"Why do you say that?"

"I do not believe any man is good enough for the Lady Isabella of Evendria, daughter of the Count of Wayhaven."

Jewel laughed heartily. "He is only making sure I am happy, Bastian. My father loves you."

Sebastian scoffed. "I think your brother would have challenged me to a duel if he hadn't seen me fight Lord Merric first."

Tears escaped Jewel's eyes, and she was unable to control her laughter. "You exaggerate!"

"I am serious." He grinned, trying hard not to chuckle. "You didn't hear what they said to me when they pulled me aside after you introduced me."

"And what did they say?" She stroked his cheek as he gazed down at her.

"They demanded we have a proper wedding."

Jewel nodded, expecting nothing less. "Well, Bastian, they weren't present for the first one."

"I think it is only due to the fact I am of high rank and regard with the Wolverines, not to mention good friends with the king himself, that they refrained from disemboweling me on the spot!"

"Would you do any less to our daughter's husband, should she marry without us present?"

That innocent comment brought a sudden fire to his eyes. Nudging her knees with his own, he moved his body to settle completely on top of her. "A daughter? Is that what you want, my lady wife? I'll be more than happy to try again and again until we get it right."

Jewel smiled at him, then looked away, wondering how much she should tell him. But he pulled her face back to him.

"Jewel?" he asked. "You aren't still apprehensive about making love to me, are you?" Looking into his eyes, Jewel saw fear creep into them. Her husband was afraid of nothing—except that.

Shaking her head, she opened her legs a little more, bringing his body closer to hers. He gasped in her ear. "What do you think, Bastian?" she whispered, kissing his neck.

"What then? What is wrong?"

A giggle escaped her. "Nothing is wrong. Everything is right."

Sebastian leaned back and regarded her with an arched brow. "What are you talking about?"

Grasping his face in her hands, she kissed his lips. "I'm pregnant."

He stared at her in shock. "Are you sure?"

"Well, I haven't had it confirmed by a physician, but I know what my body is telling me."

"How long? How long have you known?"

"I suspected it when Mynos told us to flee the castle after Merric first arrived, but I was too afraid of it, too afraid to tell you. Until now."

"Oh, sweetheart, a baby? We're going to have a baby!" Jewel cried with him as he hugged her close. "I love you." His voice was muffled against her shoulder.

"I love you too." She threaded her fingers through his hair.

Leaning up, Sebastian smiled through his sniffles. Jewel wiped away his tears with her fingertips. She was awed by her husband at that moment. He was so full of life, so full of love, and he would always protect her. She knew that now.

"I'm glad it was you who found me that day, Bastian," she told him, her own voice catching. "I'm so glad it was you."

He hugged her again, his strong arms crushing her to his chest. "I'm glad too, my lady Jewel. I'm so glad I found you."

Rebecca Goings

Without another word, he kissed her passionately, coaxing her tongue into his mouth. Jewel whimpered and wrapped her arms around him when he pressed inside her. She would never tire of making love with her husband, and the fervor of her response told him just that.

The pulsating light in the rear of the cave seemed to grow and diminish with each of their fevered heartbeats, but neither one of them noticed. Malnan's Jewel sat atop one of the two perfectly round, ancient dragon eggs that remained in the cave. It wouldn't be much longer before Malnan herself returned in the flesh.

Eventually Sebastian and Jewel would use the Emerald of Estriel to make a portal back to the castle, back to Mynos, back to reality. But not now. For now, they were content with the knowledge that no matter what tomorrow would bring, they would face it together.

Always.

270

About the Author

Rebecca Goings has enjoyed writing stories all her life. As a child, she frequently wrote romantic stories for her classmates, and still has most of them. Becoming an author has been her life's goal for as long as she can remember.

It wasn't until recently that Rebecca had the courage to query her work, but it has definitely paid off. Rebecca currently resides in the Pacific Northwest with her husband Jim and four beautiful children.

To learn more about Rebecca Goings, please visit www.RebeccaGoings.com. Send an email to Becka at rebeccagoings@gmail.com or join her Google group to join in the fun with other readers as well as Becka! http://groups.google.com/group/themagicofromance.

Look for these titles by
Rebecca Goings

Now Available:

Hearts Eternal
The Wolverine and the Rose
Leather and Lace: High Noon
Hearts Unbound
The Wolverine and the Flame

She's in danger from mysterious dark knights, she's discovering magic she never knew existed, and she's falling head over heels in love.

The Wolverine and the Rose
© 2007 Rebecca Goings

One night destroys Arianna's home, wipes out her family and flings her into a world turned upside down.

He's only kissed her once, but Arianna feels as if she's always known Sir Geoffrey, the Wolverine knight who saves her life. She can hear his thoughts, feel his memories. One kiss, and they're trapped in a bond they didn't choose and cannot break.

Their world's in terrible danger, their one hope the fabled crystal of the dragon, Mynos. But only a woman can touch the crystal and survive...

Book I of The Legends of Mynos series

Available now in ebook and print from Samhain Publishing.

Enjoy the following excerpt from

The Wolverine and the Rose...

Arianna awoke with a start. The moon had risen and it shone its pale light into her room. Was it her imagination or had she heard a faint tapping on her window? She didn't dare move, not even to breathe. Whatever was outside might hear her. She'd almost convinced herself she was hearing things when the sound came again, this time, even louder.

Glancing around the room, Arianna was looking for some sort of a weapon when a voice called to her.

"Rose? Rose, are you in there?" a voice whispered.

Her heart stilled. It was the man from the marketplace. He'd come for the scroll! Without another thought, Arianna bolted out of bed. She stopped herself before she reached the window, picking up a brush to run it a few times through her hair. When she opened the window, a cool night breeze caressed her shoulders. Unprepared for the chill, she shivered.

Bathed in moonlight, he stood before her window. He no longer wore the robe she'd seen him in at the marketplace. Instead, a long billowing cloak and dark, loose fitting clothes covered his muscular body. She sucked in her breath at the sight of him and stared, awestruck by his beauty. The current of the breeze played with his blond hair and the edges of his cloak. Neither of them spoke for what seemed an eternity as he stared right back at her with his amazing blue eyes. Finally he cleared his throat.

"Do you still have the scroll?"

"Yes," she answered. At that moment, she looked down and realized she wore nothing but her nightgown. He smiled as he must have realized it too. She blushed, the heat of it making her cheeks burn. "Please excuse me, sir," she said, dashing from the window and yanking the blanket from her bed.

"Oh that's quite all right," he said through his smile as he watched her.

Arianna couldn't stop gazing at him. He was so beautiful. She fought the urge to tell him so. She wanted to touch his face to make sure that he was real. She also wanted to kiss him again. The thought of it sent shivers up her spine.

"Please, milady, I haven't much time. Give me the scroll and I'll be gone."

With a sigh and a nod, Arianna walked to the loose floorboard and pulled it up, all the while trying to think of a way to keep this man here with her. She could think of no such reason. There lay the rose he had given her. Without water or sunlight, the flower that had once been so beautiful was now dead and wilted. She lifted it out of its hiding place and gazed at it for a few moments with a silent sadness. She laid it back underneath the floor, intending to leave it there for a keepsake.

Arianna pulled the scroll out of the niche, perhaps slower than she needed to. Defeated, sighing to herself, she rose from the floor, trying to hold the scroll and keep the blanket closed around her at the same time. Reaching out through the window, she handed it to him.

"I kept it safe for you," she told him.

"Thank you, Rose. You have done your king a great service." As he took the scroll from her, he also grasped her hand. "I regret that we have met each other under these circumstances. I am forever in your debt. If ever our paths cross again, I promise you it will be on different terms. Until then, sweet Rose..." He kissed her hand, pressing his lips to her skin and making Arianna tremble at the contact. He lingered for a moment, his warm breath caressing her wrist while his thumb stroked her beating pulse. He looked into her eyes and gave her a tender smile.

Without warning, a sharp scream shattered the still of the night. It came from somewhere within the farmhouse, only to stop short. In one fluid movement, the stranger leapt through Arianna's open window and drew his sword, pushing her out of the way. The hiss of his blade from his scabbard made every hair on her body stand on end.

"Stay behind me, milady," he said, pushing her back.

Arianna widened her eyes. The man's sword glowed a pale white, illuminating her room with a soft light. "What is happening?"

The man placed his fingers to his lips as he made his way to the door. The door flew open and Arianna's father stood in the hall holding his own rusty sword aloft. It glowed white—like the stranger's weapon.

Isaac stopped in amazement before entering, apparently shocked a man was in Arianna's room. But a look of recognition passed over his face as he stared at the stranger.

"It's *you!*" her father cried in frantic disbelief.

Arianna only had a moment to be confused before a Dark Knight came out of nowhere, raising his sword behind Isaac.

"Father!" she yelled, watching the black blade pierce her father's side. "*No!*"

"Take her and run. *Run!*" Isaac bellowed, as he turned to face his attacker.

The stranger wasted no time, seizing Arianna and pushing her through her open window. Like a shot, he was right behind her, sprinting across the yard toward the hill. Arianna stumbled, gasping in pain from her bare feet. The smell of smoke permeated the air before they even reached the top of the hill. By the time they reached the old oak, exhaustion weakened her limbs. She didn't remember the hill being so steep. Collapsing on the ground, she lay there for a few moments trying to catch her breath. Her heart pounded hard and she struggled for breath in the tall grass.

At that moment, Arianna noticed an eerie light fill the sky. Glancing over her shoulder, she saw the reason for it. "Oh God." Massive flames were consuming the farmouse.

"*No!*" she screamed as cold reality hit her. Meiri, her parents, everyone was in the burning house. "*No!*" she yelled again, starting to run back down the hill. The stranger pushed her down, landing on top of her.

"Rose, there is nothing you can do." his familiar voice yelled in her ear. "They are gone!"

She tossed her head from side to side in denial. He sat up and held her to him, attempting to comfort her in her grief. Arianna hugged him back fiercely, not knowing what else to do.

"They are gone," he said

"No! They can't be. No. I don't believe you! Mother! Father!" Arianna sobbed uncontrollably into his shoulder. "*Meiri!*"

"I'm sorry. I'm so sorry," the man repeated as he cried with her. "I brought this on you, Rose. I will not rest until I have made it right." Arianna barely heard him over her own wailing. The pain of reality was almost too much for her to bear. She cried so hard she couldn't breathe.

The stranger hooked his arms under her knees and carried her to his horse, whose reins were tied to the oak tree. Arianna was only vaguely aware that he'd lifted her into the saddle. As soon as she was astride, he jumped up to sit behind her.

"We must put miles between us and this place," he said in her ear. "Take one last look at your home, sweet lady. The only place you're safe now is with me."

Arianna stared at the gargantuan flames that licked the sky. She shuddered with grief and turned away, tears coursing down her cheeks.

"*Please...*" She couldn't bear to see anymore. With a squeeze, he took the reins and turned his horse to leave.

"Do you know how to ride?" he asked. She did not answer him. His grip around her waist tightened. "You just hold on."

Without another word, he kicked his horse into a gallop.

Fly Away

Discover the Talons Series

5 STEAMY NEW PARANORMAL ROMANCES
TO HOOK YOU IN

Kiss Me Deadly, by Shannon Stacey
King of Prey, by Mandy M. Roth
Firebird, by Jaycee Clark
Caged Desire, by Sydney Somers
Seize the Hunter, by Michelle M. Pillow

AVAILABLE IN EBOOK—COMING SOON IN PRINT:

Samhain
Publishing, ltd.

WWW.SAMHAINPUBLISHING.COM

GREAT CHEAP FUN

Discover eBooks!

THE FASTEST WAY TO GET THE HOTTEST NAMES

Get your favorite authors on your favorite reader, long before they're
out in print! Ebooks from Samhain go wherever you go, and work with
whatever you carry—Palm, PDF, Mobi, and more.

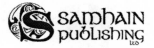

Samhain Publishing, Ltd.

Printed in the United States
122048LV00001B/175/A

9 781599 987538